# SMOKY MOUNTAIN SUMMER

## An Annie Mercer O'Dell Story

By
## Kenneth Lee McGee

To My Extended Family

I want to thank all those people who helped make this story come to life. A special thanks to Ryan Parker for the cover photo.

Chapter One

Annie Mercer O'Dell woke to the rays of the morning sun warming her face as it shone through her bedroom window. She looked at the clock and sighed. She peered over the edge of her bed to the floor where Matt Sullivan lay in his sleeping bag on top of an air mattress—still sound asleep.

"Matty, are you awake?" He didn't respond, so she tossed her stuffed bear at him. "Matty, are you awake?"

"Not really, Annie. Why did you hit me with your bear? What time is it?"

"Eight thirty. Are you ready to get up?"

"How about another half hour? We don't need to get up yet, do we?"

"We should if we are going to have breakfast at Grandpa Liam's house. He's probably been up for two hours already."

"How about if you take your shower first and that will give me more time to sleep."

"Okay, but you need to be getting up soon," Annie said.

She rolled out of bed and onto the air mattress. Matt was half-in and half-out of the sleeping bag. She leaned over and kissed him on his cheek. "You need a shave."

Annie tried to get up but Matt grabbed her shoulders and held her on top of the sleeping bag.

"Does that mean you won't kiss me until I shave?"

"That's right! You need to shave, shower and brush your teeth first. Then maybe I'll kiss you. Now let me go so I can get ready."

Matt relaxed his hold on her and she stood up. She grabbed some clothes from her dresser and headed to the bathroom. She was in the shower when her new cell phone rang. Matt grabbed it and checked the caller ID.

"Good morning, sir," Matt said to Detective O'Dell, Annie's father.

"Morning, Matty. Where is Annie?"

"She's in the shower. Should I give her the phone?"

Detective O'Dell laughed. "You would be risking your life

1

if you interrupt her shower. She might smack you where it would hurt. I just wanted to see if you guys are coming out for breakfast."

"Annie wants to as soon as we can get ready."

"How long do you think that will take?"

Matt looked at the clock on Annie's dresser. "We should be there in forty or forty-five minutes, I think."

"We'll wait for an hour, just to be safe. Annie sometimes takes a while to get ready."

Matt walked out into the hallway. "I think I just heard the water shut off. We should make it in forty minutes."

"See you when you get here," Detective O'Dell said and then hung up.

Matt knocked on the bathroom door and yelled, "Your father just called wanting to know when we are going to get there."

"What did you tell him?"

"Forty or forty-five minutes. Think we can make it by then?"

"As long as you don't take too long to get ready. Let me get dried off and dressed, then you can have the bathroom."

"Do you need any help?"

"Do you want to get punched out?"

"I guess that means you don't need any help."

"You are so smart, Matty Sullivan. Go get your clothes and I'll be done in a minute."

It took Annie three minutes to open the bathroom door. She was dressed but still needed to brush her teeth. Matt held his clothes in his hands as he waited.

"Do you still want me to shave?"

"You can wait till tomorrow. We need to hurry."

Five minutes later Matt was dressed and ready to go.

"That was quick."

"Doesn't take me long. Your hair is still wet," Matt said as he ran his hand through her short, curly brunette hair.

"It'll dry on the way. That's the advantage of this style. I don't need to do anything to it. Just wash it and let it dry."

"You look cute with your hair wet. Can I kiss you now?"

"One kiss, then we've got to go."

2

Matt held Annie in his arms and kissed her. "Do you remember what I told you last night, Annie?"

"I remember. Are you going to take it back now?"

"No, I meant what I said."

"I forgot what you said. Could you tell me one more time?" Annie grinned. She remembered exactly what Matt told her last night.

"I love you, Annie O'Dell. There! Should I say it again?"

Her eyes sparkled as she looked up at him. "You can say it as often as you want, Matty Sullivan. I'll never grow tired of hearing that."

"Do you still love me, Annie?"

She shook her head. "No way! You've got a scratchy face."

Matt playfully smacked her bottom.

"I suppose I love you, too," she said. "Come on. We've got to go. I'm starving."

Twenty minutes later Annie and Matt arrived at Grandpa Liam O'Dell's fifty acre farm outside of South Hampshire. Mace Franklin and his girlfriend, Erin Bezick, arrived seconds later and parked in the gravel driveway right behind Matt's car. They got out and waved at Annie.

"Hi, guys! I didn't know if you were going to make it this morning or not. I figured you would stay in bed all morning," Annie teased the friend she had known since second grade.

"I wanted to, but Erin made me get up. Did you and Matty just get here?"

"Just pulled in. I had to wake Matty up, or else he would still be sleeping."

Erin moved close to Annie, adjusted her red headband and whispered, "Did you guys?"

"No, of course not. Matty stayed in his sleeping bag all night. I know I don't have to ask what you and Mace did."

"Is Matt okay with waiting? He's not seeing other girls on the side is he?" Erin asked.

"No, he's not seeing other girls and he is all right with waiting for now," Annie said and then glanced over her shoulder at Matt and Mace. "But I'm not sure how much longer I can wait."

3

They walked into the house and Annie saw Keyshon Franklin in the living room. "Hey, how's my good buddy this morning?"

"Hi, Annie! About time you and Matthew Sullivan got here."

"Did I hear my name? How are you, Keyshon?"

"I'm fine, Matthew Sullivan. I'm hungry. Let's eat!"

Mace walked out of the kitchen munching on a stale donut. "Yeah, let's eat. I'm starving."

Matt laughed and said, "You're always hungry, Mace. I don't know why you don't weigh three hundred pounds the way you eat."

"I have a very high metabolism." Mace shrugged.

Annie walked over to the doorway and saw her father and his girlfriend Elisabeth Franklin in the kitchen helping Grandpa. "I'll be right back, Matty. I need to talk to Daddy for a minute," she said over her shoulder.

"Good morning, sweetheart. How was your night?"

"Oh, Daddy, it was so special! The best night ever!" Annie said as she twirled in a circle the way she did as a young girl who wanted to be a ballerina.

Keith and Elisabeth stopped moving and stared at Annie.

Dad finally asked, "Did you...?"

"No, not that! It was special because Matty told me he loves me and I told him I love him. It was wonderful!"

"I'm happy for you, sweetie," Dad said and then sighed.

He gave Annie a big hug, then so did Elisabeth.

"I'm happy for you, too, Annie," she said.

"Thanks, Mom." Annie only recently started calling Mrs. Franklin, Mom.

Mace walked into the kitchen. "Hey, enough of the mushy lovey dovey stuff. Let's eat already."

"Okay, Mace. We're ready," Elisabeth said.

Everyone went into the dining room except Mace and Annie. He grabbed her hand and held her back.

"I heard what you told your father, Annie. I'm happy for you, too. Matty seems to have changed and I think it's because of

4

you. He must love you if he's willing to wait."

"Thanks, Mace."

Annie hugged Mace, then saw Matt watching from the doorway.

"Are you guys hungry, or do I get to eat it all?" Matt asked.

Annie walked up to Matt and kissed him. "You better not eat my share if you know what's good for you."

Mace walked over to Matt and slapped him on the back. "Let's eat, Matt. We don't want to let Annie grab our food."

"She can eat quite a bit sometimes, can't she?"

"Annie! I want you to sit next to me," Keyshon said as he touched the chair next to him. "You can sit by Matthew Sullivan later. He can sit over there with Mace and Erin."

Annie grinned at Matt as she sat beside Keyshon. "Everything smells delicious."

Grandpa Liam sat at the head of the table, said a traditional Irish prayer and then everyone started filling their plates.

"The pan with the sausage and gravy is rather hot," Elisabeth said from the opposite end of the table from Liam. "I can fill everyone's plate if they pass it to me."

For the next few minutes everyone passed the plates of food around the table. Annie helped Keyshon and smiled at Matt several times.

"I want some ketchup on my scrambled eggs and potatoes," Keyshon said. He grabbed the plastic bottle, turned it upside down, shook it vigorously and squeezed.

"Be careful, Keyshon. That's an awful lot of ketchup," Annie said. "I can barely see your eggs and potatoes."

"I love ketchup! Do you want some, Annie?"

"Yes, thank you."

Mace and Matt loaded up their plates and checked each other's food to see who had the most.

"Do I need to buy bigger plates?" Grandpa asked as he paused to look at Matt and Mace.

"I can make do with this one," Mace said. "Of course I might have to fill it up two or three times. Could someone pass the maple syrup, please?"

5

Keith handed it across the table to Mace.

Elisabeth turned to her right. "What time is your train leaving, Erin? Is this the first time you've been home since school started?"

"I need to be at the station by eight tomorrow morning," she answered. "Annie was going to take me after we pick up Mace. He wants to go with."

Keith held a forkful of scrambled eggs halfway to his mouth as he looked at Mace. "To Nebraska?"

"I wish. Just to the station," Mace answered.

"How's my car running these days, Annie?" Grandpa asked about the Honda Prelude he gave her when she started working part-time to earn money for college.

"It's still running fine, Grandpa, and I haven't put a scratch on it."

Grandpa stared at Mace.

Mace noticed the look and shrugged. "I haven't either, not that I've driven it all that often. Someone is rather stingy about sharing her wheels."

"You never put any gas in it," Annie said.

"Hey! I'm just a poor student-athlete with barely enough money to buy the necessities. Food. Beverages. That stuff."

Soon the room was quiet except for the ting of utensils on plates.

Grandpa caught Annie and Matt sneaking glances at each other and grinning. He watched for a bit and then set down his fork with a thump. "All right! Will you two tell me what"s going on? You've been making eyes at each other instead of eating. Spill it!"

Everyone looked at either Matt or Annie and then at the other one.

"Nothing's going on, Grandpa," Annie said rather meekly.

Mace coughed and then grinned at Annie. She tried to kick him under the table but couldn't reach his legs.

"You are not leaving this table until you tell me what's going on," Grandpa said sternly.

Annie and Matt looked at each other and she twisted her hair around a finger. Matt knew that meant she was nervous, so he

6

cleared his throat. Everyone's attention turned to him.

"Principal O'Dell, last night I told Annie that I love her and I meant it. That's why we're acting a little different."

Grandpa looked at Annie for several seconds. "May I assume you said those words to him?"

Annie nodded and then grinned.

Grandpa looked at Keith. "Were you aware of this?"

"I've known for some time, but I guess it took them until last night to tell it to each other," he answered and then put an arm around Annie and squeezed her close. He smiled across the table at Matt.

No one said anything for several seconds until Keyshon asked, "Does that mean you and Matthew Sullivan are going to get married soon? It's all right with me if you do, but you still have to come over so we can play together." He looked around the table. "And can I have some more biscuits and gravy, please?"

Annie leaned over to Keyshon, kissed his cheek and said, "I'm not getting married anytime soon, but if I was, I wouldn't forget about spending time with my best bud."

Later, Matt and Annie helped Elisabeth clear the table. Elisabeth put the little bit of leftover food into Tupperware containers while Matt and Annie started doing the dishes.

Grandpa walked into the kitchen, saw what they were doing and said, "I do have a dishwasher. It's right there beside the sink. You don't have to do dishes by hand."

"I was just rinsing them off, Grandpa. We'll put them in the dishwasher," Annie said.

"I'm going to take Keyshon fishing in a little bit. You two are welcome to join us. I asked Mace, but he and Erin have better things to do," Grandpa said and winked at Annie.

She looked up at Matt.

"We can go fishing if you want. You might have to show me how though," Matt said.

"Haven't you ever been fishing, Matty?"

He shrugged. "Not that I can remember."

"I'm going to take a walk with your father," Elisabeth said and left the kitchen.

7

"I need to find some worms for Keyshon," Grandpa said.

Annie and Matt loaded the dishwasher and she leaned over and started it. She straightened up and caught Matt staring at the back of her jeans. "Were you looking at my butt?" she asked and then giggled.

"You have a nice looking bottom, Annie Mercer," he said and then wrapped his arms around her waist.

She put her hands behind his neck, brought his face down to hers and kissed him fiercely. He responded by moving his hands to her bottom and inserting his tongue in her mouth. Neither of them heard Keyshon enter the kitchen.

"I'm going fishing with Grandpa," he announced to get their attention. "Do you want to come with us, or are you going to kiss each other all day?"

Matt and Annie broke off the kiss.

She grinned at Keyshon and said, "If you promise not to tell anyone what we were doing, we will go fishing with you."

"I won't tell anyone except Grandpa and Mom," Keyshon said with a smile as he held out his hand. "Mace and Erin were kissing like that earlier and he had his hands on her butt, too. Mace gave me a dollar to keep quiet."

Matt laughed as he pulled out his wallet and handed Keyshon a five. "You're getting good at blackmail, Keyshon."

"I have expenses," Keyshon replied.

# Chapter Two

Annie punched her alarm clock and opened her eyes long enough to check the time. She poked Erin who was sound asleep beside her. "You need to wake up if you want to catch your train."

Erin groaned and the rolled onto her back. "If I have to get up then you have to get out of bed, too."

"Five more minutes," Annie said.

Dad walked into Annie's bedroom twenty minutes later. He coughed to get wake them up but that didn't work. "We need a pet dog. Then you'd have to get up to take him out." He stepped over and around Annie's clothes which were scattered all over the floor and knocked on her desk. "Trains do not wait for late passengers."

Annie opened her eyes. "What time is it?"

"Twenty after seven and Erin needs to be at the station by eight," Dad answered. "You better get a move on."

"Holy crap!" Annie swore and jumped out of bed. "Erin! Wake up! You're going to miss your train unless you get your butt out of bed right now."

"It's a good thing she packed last night," Dad said as he looked at Erin's suitcases. "I'll take these out to your car while you get dressed. Mace called. He's getting a ride over here."

One thing Annie and Erin learned during their first year of college was how to get ready for class in under ten minutes. They were ready to leave nine minutes later.

"Thank you for letting me crash here this week and for storing my stuff," Erin said to Annie's father.

"You're entirely welcome," he answered. "I don't know how you girls survive as roommates. You are total opposites."

"I'm used to her side of the room being a mess," Erin said.

Mace arrived and Annie started the car. "Let's go! See you later, Daddy," she hollered.

Dad waved as he watched her back out of the driveway.

"Do I look like crap?" Erin asked Mace. "We overslept and now I have to look like this all the way to Nebraska."

Annie checked the rearview mirror. "You look fine. Please tell me you aren't going to make out all the way to the station."

9

"We won't see each other for such a long time," Erin said.

"Just remember it's daylight, okay?" Annie said.

Mace and Erin kissed for a couple of minutes then stopped.

"Annie, has your father ever thought about buying a larger house? Maybe one with three bedrooms?" Erin asked.

"He did mention building a new house out at the farm after he retires," Annie said as she raced through a yellow light.

"Mom said he talked to her about that," Mace said. "I think if they get married, they will build a new house and live out there."

Annie made it to the station with ten minutes to spare. She lugged the suitcases out of the trunk while Mace and Erin said their goodbyes.

"Could you remove your tongue from Erin's throat long enough to carry these inside?" Annie asked with her hands on her hips.

"You can forget about a tip," Mace said.

Annie poked him in the arm. "I'm not a cab driver."

Erin checked in and Mace and Annie stayed until she boarded the train.

"I'll call you when I get home!" Erin yelled.

"I'll be waiting for the call," Mace said.

Annie poked him again. "She was talking to me."

Mace shook his head. "No way! She will call me."

"You are such a creep. She's going to call me."

Mace put an arm around Annie's shoulders. "Care to put your money on that, little sister?"

She frowned at him. "I'm not your sister yet and I just sent her a text to call me first so you'd lose your money, big spender."

"Me! A big spender? I'm not the one who gave Keyshon five bucks to keep his mouth shut about you and Matt making out in the kitchen out at the farm. What were you guys doing that Matt gave him a five, huh?"

Annie grinned and raced to her car. "I'll never tell," she hollered.

Mace chased after her and caught up to her before she could open the door. He turned her around and stood in front of her as she leaned against the driver's door.

"Why are you looking at me like that?" Annie asked.

"How am I looking at you?" Mace asked as he continued to stare into her eyes.

"I don't know, but you're creeping me out."

Mace broke off the stare when they spotted a SoHam squad car rolling slowly through the parking lot. It stopped when it came alongside Mace and Annie. The officer rolled down his window and looked at Mace and Annie. "Are you all right, Miss?"

"I'm fine, officer. I'm Annie O'Dell and this is my friend Mace Franklin. My father is Detective O'Dell. Robbery Division."

"It's nice to meet you. I know your father." The officer stared at Mace for a moment.

"Mace and I just dropped his girlfriend off. She's taking a train back home to Nebraska," Annie explained. She turned and unlocked the car door. Then she turned back to the officer and waved.

The squad car rolled slowly away and Mace walked around the car and got in. He buckled up and stared out the windshield.

Annie started the car and looked at Mace. "What was that all about?"

Mace frowned at her. "Do you really have to ask?"

Annie took several deep breaths to calm her still racing heart. "Why would a black officer stop and ask if I was all right just because I was with you?"

"How can you live in this city and be so naive?" Mace hollered. "Don't you realize there is still some racial inequality here? Do you ever wonder why African Americans still live mostly on the east side of the river?"

"I'm sorry, Mace. I guess I never think about stuff like that," Annie said as she blinked away a tear.

Mace shrugged and then held her hand. "I'm sorry I yelled at you. You don't think about that crap because you don't have a prejudiced bone in your body."

Annie grinned. "I don't like rutabagas even though I've never tried one. That's a prejudice."

"You're a goof sometimes, girl. Let's go home."

## Chapter Three

Early Monday morning Matt started his summer job working full-time for his father at The Hungry Lion. Matt was disappointed his normal work hours would be from three until midnight. Annie's summer job would once again be working a few hours a week for Mike Bushell, her father's attorney friend and taking care of Keyshon three days. She even signed up for a summer class at North Park College. She and Matt got together Monday evening at her house.

"It sucks, Matty!" Annie said as she put her bare feet on the coffee table. "It's summertime and you're going to be working till midnight. I'm working during the day. The only times we can see each other are Sundays and Wednesday evenings. I had such high hopes for this summer."

"I'm sorry, Annie, but it can't be helped. I need the money for college," Matt said as he sat next to her. "I'm glad I can live at home and commute."

"So do I! Need the money, I mean. At least my summer class is on Tuesday and Thursday nights."

"Maybe you can spend Wednesday nights at my house. Did you ask your father yet?" Matt asked.

"Yeah, I did," Annie said and then smacked her hand against the couch.

"Well, what did he say?"

Annie kicked the coffee table. "He said no. Actually it was 'no way in hell,' but he did suggest that you stay with me on the weekends."

"I can't say I blame him. My house is no place for a teenage girl to stay."

"I like your father, Matty."

"He's not the problem. It's his employees who are always around. He did say I could take two weeks off during the summer. Maybe we can go on vacation together. Do you think your father would allow that?"

"He might."

"You're eighteen now. You can make some decisions on

your own. You don't have to always do what he says."

Matt sounded upset and Annie thought he was upset with her.

"You know I can't disobey Daddy. As long as I'm living with him, I have rules to follow."

"Maybe we should get a place of our own."

"Oh yeah, right! That would go over great."

"I know that's not a possibility yet. We don't make enough money to pay rent."

"Matty."

"What, Annie?"

"Do you still love me?"

"You know I do. I guess I'm just a little frustrated that I won't be able to see you everyday the way I hoped."

"We will just have to make good use of the time we have together. Are you frustrated because I won't sleep with you?"

"That's not it, Annie. I hope you don't think I'm pressuring you for sex, because I'm not."

"I know you're not. Sometimes I wish you would though."

Matt turned to look into her eyes. "Why are you saying that, Annie? Do you want me to make love to you?"

"There are times when it's not easy to keep from attacking you. I mean that in a good way," she said and then leaned her head against his shoulder.

"I know what you mean. I feel the same way."

"Knock, knock. Can I come in?" Dad asked from the kitchen.

"Of course you can, Daddy. We were just talking about how many hours we are going to be working this summer. What would you say if Matty and I got a place of our own?"

"I've been thinking about that, Annie. I think you should go ahead and start living together. Get a place, start having all the sex you want. I'll even pay the rent and the utilities. It would be great to have this place all to myself," Dad said as he walked into the living room and sat in the recliner across from them.

Annie stuck out her tongue. "I know you're being sarcastic. I just wanted to see what you would say."

13

"You both know you aren't ready, right? How could you afford the rent and college?" Dad asked.

"We can't."

"Are you guys hungry enough for a pizza?"

"Sure," Annie answered.

"Good. I will order one and have it delivered. The usual all right?"

"Extra cheese, please."

"Right," Dad said.

The pizza arrived an hour later and they sat in the living room and watched a movie.

"I should be going, Annie. I know you have to get up early to watch Keyshon."

"Not tomorrow. Monday, Wednesday and Friday. Mace stays with him the other days. Tomorrow I have to work at the office but I don't start until ten. Why don't you stay here tonight?"

"Are you sure?"

"Daddy, do you mind if Matty stays over?"

"I don't mind. Do you need to let your father know?" he asked as he looked at Matt.

Matt stared at Annie's father with a blank expression.

"Sorry. I guess you're old enough to not have to check in. I'm just used to Annie's rules."

"I'll call him anyway. At least leave a message. He's probably busy tonight."

"I'll get the air mattress," Annie said as she got up. "It's in the garage. It's still inflated. I was too lazy to let the air out."

"You can always leave it in the basement, Annie," Dad said. "That way you won't have to blow it up every weekend."

"We could always share the bed, Daddy."

"Grab her, Matthew! I'm going to spank her bottom. I don't care if she's fifteen-years-old now."

Annie squealed as Matt grabbed her and held her on his lap.

"I'm eighteen now. I'm too old to be spanked."

Matt smiled as Mr. O'Dell teased his only daughter.

"Then you better behave."

"I'm behaving. It's not easy, but I'm being a good girl."

14

"I know you are, sweetie, and I know what you're going through."

"You guys aren't going to start talking about sex in front of me again, are you?" Matt asked. "You know it embarrasses me. No other kid I've ever known talks to their parents about sex like you and Annie."

"Will it embarrass you if I talk about..." Annie whispered in Matt's ear what she wanted to talk about. He turned red. It had never been easy to embarrass Matt Sullivan, but Annie managed it.

Dad looked at Matt and laughed. "I can't imagine what you said to Matthew to embarrass him so much, but whatever it was, stop it right now."

Annie looked at her father and grinned wickedly. She would never say out loud what she whispered in Matt's ear. Certainly not in front of her father. "I didn't say anything dirty to him," Annie answered with the look of an innocent angel.

"Yeah, right," Dad sighed. "Where is your mother when I need her? She would know how to handle you now. It's a good thing I don't have four daughters."

Annie ran out to the garage and returned with the air mattress. "I'm going to get ready for bed. Are you tired, Matty?"

"Not really."

Annie gave him a dirty look.

"I mean, I'm so sleepy. I need to hit the sack."

Annie grinned. "I have to take a shower first. You can stay out here with Daddy until I'm finished."

Annie got ready for bed and came out to kiss her father good night. She took Matt's hand and pulled him along to her bedroom.

"Leave the door open, Annie."

She rolled her eyes and answered. "I know the rules. Just don't look in the room if you don't want to see something you shouldn't. I might be naked. Is that against the rules?"

"Not as long as the door is open, sweetheart," Dad answered. He knew Annie was trying to get a reaction from him.

"Good night, sir. I'll see you in the morning."

"Night, Matthew. Is your car behind mine? I've got to leave

around seven. Seven fifteen at the latest."

"I parked on the street. I thought you might have to leave early."

"Thanks. Would you mind taking Annie's car to get an oil change in the morning? If you have time. It's past due and she always forgets."

"I'll take care of it. No problem."

"She's got the money for it. Don't let her tell you she's broke."

Matt laughed. "I don't fall for that anymore. I know her well enough now. She's got more money than either of us."

"Ain't that the truth!"

Matt joined Annie in her room. She was already in bed. Matt stripped down to his boxers and t-shirt. He kissed Annie good night.

"I'm going to read. Will it bother you if I do?" she asked.

"No, but I thought you were sleepy."

"I'm sleepy, but not ready to go to sleep," she said. "Does that make any sense?"

"It's as clear as three-day-old coffee. What are you reading?"

She turned on her side and held the book out. "It's *Grandpa, Lions and Kitty Cats*. It's a collection of short stories by a local author."

He looked up from his sleeping bag. "Cool cover. Remind me to bring my Discman with me the next time I crash here."

Annie's father sat on the couch and thought about his daughter. He realized she was almost a mature adult now, even though she sometimes acted like a child. He also knew it probably wouldn't be much longer before she decided the time was right for her and Matty to become lovers. He looked at the ceiling. *Amy Catherine, I sure wish you were here to see her now. You would be so proud. I hope you don't mind if I ask Elisabeth to talk to her to make sure she is prepared.*

# Chapter Four

"Do you miss Roosevelt High at all, Grandpa?" Annie asked as she walked with Keyshon and Grandpa to the lake on Tuesday morning.

Keyshon carried his fishing pole and a bucket for any fish they caught and decided to keep. He watched some birds overhead and nearly tripped. "I'm all right," he said to Annie, who had stopped walking.

"Annie dear, I don't miss the place a tenth of what I thought I would," Grandpa said. "I've been working on projects around the farm that I put off. I wouldn't have time to go back to work now. I planned to retire after this year anyway. I'm just a year ahead of schedule."

"Did you seriously let Keyshon drive your new riding mower?" Annie asked.

"I let him putter around the yard, but I didn't let him turn on the blades. I didn't show him how. He did all right. He didn't crash into anything."

"Do you think he will ever be able to drive a car?"

Grandpa shrugged. "I don't see why not. Other people with Down Syndrome do."

"Are you taking your medicine? You're not overdoing it, are you?" Annie asked. She turned around to check on Keyshon. "Are you coming?" she asked him.

"I saw a baby rabbit, but now I can't find it," Keyshon said.

"The rabbit is probably with its mother. Come on. The fish are waiting," Annie said.

Grandpa sighed and looked at Annie. "Your mother had the patience of a saint, bless her heart, and you are just like her in a lot of ways."

For two hours they sat on the edge of the dock with their poles in the water. Every time Keyshon hooked a fish, he would holler with glee.

"What kind is this one, Grandpa Liam?" Keyshon asked.

Grandpa helped Keyshon remove the small bluegill from the hook. "This is a bluegill. See this dark spot by the dorsal fin?"

17

"I see it," Keyshon said.

"See how the sides of its head and its chin are a dark blue?"

"I can see the blue." Keyshon held the fish in his hands as he inspected it. "Is this one big enough to keep?"

"I think we'll let this one grow a little bigger, buddy," Grandpa said.

Keyshon carefully placed the fish back in the water. "Have a good day, little fish. I might catch you again."

Annie whispered to Grandpa, "Do you have to tell him what kind of fish every time you catch one?"

"He forgets," Grandpa said. "They all kinda look alike to him. He caught a smallmouth bass last week."

Annie put a finger to her mouth for a moment. "I've caught catfish, crappies, bullheads and even a brown trout in your lake. Have you stocked any other species?"

"One year I stocked some yellow perch, but I don't think there are any left. I don't think there are any of those blasted carps in here. They would crowd out the good fish."

Eventually, Keyshon grew tired of fishing and they walked back to the house. Grandpa let him keep one bluegill.

"You seem to feel better now, Grandpa," Annie said as they walked through the grass.

"I thank the fresh air and exercise for that," he said. "That and a lack of stress. I never realized how much stress came with my job."

"Do you hear that?" Annie asked.

Grandpa stopped and listened. "That's Corey Hobbs' tractor. He took over for his father and farms my forty acres."

"Grandpa, do you ever worry about real estate taxes getting too high for you to keep the farm?" Annie asked.

"Not really." He pointed to the west. "There are forty acres back there that get farmed every year. That land is taxed differently than if it was woods or whatever. There's about ten acres around the house and barn and other outbuildings. Even some of that is grown for hay. Do you know the difference between hay and straw?" he asked.

"Yes, Grandpa," Annie sighed. "You've told me the

difference many times. Hay's for horses and straw is for hayrides," Annie teased.

Grandpa chuckled. "You know all this fresh air and exercise makes me feel ten years younger. Don't tell your father, but I've even thought about asking the widow Hobbs out for dinner."

"Really?" Annie asked. "Isn't she older than you?"

"No, she's about five years younger. Roy passed away about three years ago now, I guess. We see each other now and then."

"I don't think Grandma would mind if you have a lady friend," Annie said with a grin.

"Now don't start getting your hormones all riled up, child. At my age I think about companionship differently than you do. You and Matthew are just starting your lives."

"You always treated Matty better than his teachers," Annie said.

"I could see his potential and I didn't have to deal with him in a classroom. He knew what he was doing when he disrupted Vidmar's class." Grandpa chuckled and then said, "In a way I don't blame Matty. Vidmar can be rather boring."

"I had him for a teacher, too, but I didn't disrupt the class."

"That's because I would have come into the classroom and swatted your bottom," Grandpa said as he laughed.

"You wouldn't have done that. That would have embarrassed me to death," Annie said.

"I guess it worked. Now let's see what we can fix for lunch. All this fresh air and exercise makes me hungry."

## Chapter Five

The first week of work passed quickly for Annie and Matt. They ate dinner with her father on Wednesday and talked on the phone everyday. Saturday morning Matt drove to Annie's house. He parked in the street and walked up to the front door. Before he could even ring the bell, Annie opened the door.

"Good morning, young lady. My name is Matthew Sullivan and I was wondering if you would be interested in spending a few hours with me. I could show you some references if you'd like."

Annie put a finger to her mouth and looked him over from head to toe. "Oh, I'm sorry but I can't. My boyfriend is coming over today and I'm going to spend time with him. I haven't seen him since Wednesday and I can hardly remember what he looks like." She moved a hand to her hip, stared at him for a moment, then said, "Tell you what. You can hang around until he gets here then I'll take whichever of you is better looking. Would that work for you?"

Matt shook his head. "That's all right. I have a girlfriend and I was hoping to see her today."

Annie's father was in the living room and heard their conversation. He walked over to the front door.

"Are you going to let Matty in the house or not? Breakfast is almost ready."

"Is that who this guy is?" Annie asked in a high-pitched voice. "I didn't even recognize him. Why don't you come on in the house?"

Matty grinned as he stepped inside and picked Annie up in his arms. He kissed her as she put her arms around his neck. "So you didn't recognize me, huh? Do you remember me now?"

"Kiss me again. I seem to recall a guy who kissed me like that."

Matt kissed Annie again.

"Nope! That didn't ring a bell."

"Maybe I should just toss you on the floor then." Matt moved over to the couch and dropped Annie there.

She got up on her knees and held her arms out. "Maybe I'm

starting to remember you now."

Matt held her in his arms as they kissed again.

"Are you two going to eat or just keep kissing each other?"

"I'm hungry. Let's eat, Matty. Daddy made corned beef hash skillets for breakfast. They smell so good."

"Can we go back to kissing after we eat?" Matt asked.

"Oooh! I like that idea. Come on. I have to tell you about what happened Thursday morning."

Annie and Matt joined her father at the kitchen island to eat. Annie explained what happened Thursday at the office.

"Mr. Bushell had this client who was wanted for missing a court date. There was an arrest warrant out for him."

"I kinda know how that works, Annie."

"So you do, huh? Anyway, this guy showed up and the police came to take him in. He decided he didn't want to go so he took off running. He wasn't watching where he was going because he was looking behind him. He turned and splat!" Annie clapped her hands together. "He ran right into Officer Markevich. He's this mountain of a dude."

"I've met him, Annie."

"Isn't he just huge? This client just crumbled to the floor like he ran into a brick wall. That was the most exciting thing that happened to me this week. I guess it doesn't sound too exciting now that I think about it."

"I'm glad you don't have to deal with anything more exciting than that, Annie. If you had to work with Matthew, I would worry. How has your week been, Matty?"

"Just the usual stuff at the bar—a few fights. Nothing too serious. The bouncers took care of everything. Tonight will be busy, but I get out of there at midnight."

"Are you coming over after that?" Annie asked. "Can I have more ketchup, please?"

Matt handed Annie the ketchup bottle and watched as she poured it over the remains of her skillet. "As long as your father doesn't mind."

"You don't mind do you, Daddy?"

"Of course not. Just try not to stay up all night. I need some sleep. What are you guys going to do tomorrow? Any plans yet?" Dad asked.

Annie added more ketchup to her plate and looked at Matt. "We haven't talked about it yet. We will probably go see Grandpa for a little bit."

"Would you like a skillet to go with your ketchup?" Matt asked.

"You know I like ketchup," she answered then wrinkled her nose at him.

"He would like that. Elisabeth and I are taking Keyshon to a ballgame. The Cubs are playing the Cardinals and Keyshon is excited about going."

"Is he excited about the game or just the hot dogs?"

"Probably the hot dogs," Dad said and then laughed. "I need to get ready."

After breakfast Matt helped Annie with the dishes.

"What time do you have to leave for work?"

"Two thirty or so. I need to be there a few minutes before three. I can change here."

"Before I forget, did you ask your father for the thirteenth off?" Annie asked. "That's the day of Kristen Keasling's graduation party."

"I mentioned it and he said it was all right, but I have to work a half day on Sunday."

"At least we can go to the party together. It will be fun."

"More fun than Derrick's party?" Matt asked.

"Yes! Because now we are a real couple. Back then we were just... I don't know what we were."

"Friends. We were friends and now we're..."

"Friends with benefits!" Annie grinned.

Matt raised his eyebrows. "I haven't gotten any of those benefits yet."

Annie waved a finger at him. "You get to kiss me. Isn't that a benefit?"

"It's a very good benefit."

Matt kissed Annie and placed his hands on her bottom as her father walked into the kitchen.

Dad noticed Matt's hands. "That's a penalty for illegal use of hands."

Matt jerked his hands away.

"That's better," Dad said. "I'm going to take off. Not sure what time we'll get back, sweetie. I'll see you guys later tonight."

"Bye, Daddy. Have fun at the game and say hi to Keyshon for me."

"Will do."

Matt and Annie finished cleaning up the kitchen. They sat on the couch and Matt moved close to kiss her.

"Matty, I think we should go somewhere just to get out of the house. If we stay here, we will just end up kissing and making out."

"Is that a bad thing?"

"No, but it might lead to something more. What would you say to running out to see Grandpa and having lunch with him?" Annie asked.

"That sounds okay to me. I can see if he needs help with anything."

"That would be so sweet of you. He's too proud to ask for help, but if you tell him you can help he will be more willing."

"I'm ready to go if you are."

"I just need to grab some stuff and I'll be ready."

A half hour later they pulled into the driveway at Grandpa Liam's farm. He was in the front yard mowing. He waved, stopped the mower and headed over to where Matt parked. Annie ran to greet him.

"Hi, Grandpa! We thought we would come and see how you're doing. I haven't seen you since Tuesday." Annie hugged him. "When did you get that?"

"I bought it Thursday and had it delivered." He kissed her cheek. "How's my favorite granddaughter doing today? Hello, Matt. It's good to see you, too."

"We're both doing fine. We came to see if we could help you with some chores. Matty has to be at work at three, but we can work for a few hours. What do you need done?" Annie asked.

Grandpa wiped his brow with his handkerchief and looked

23

around. "Well, I suppose Matt could do the trimming if he would like."

Matt nodded. "I can do that."

Liam set Matt up with his gas powered trimmer while Annie weeded the flower beds in the front yard. Liam watched Annie for a few minutes and recalled how his late wife used to love to work with her flowers. Annie was beginning to look more and more like her mother and grandmother. Liam looked at Matthew Sullivan and thought about how much he had changed and matured. He realized how much Annie and Matt loved each other. "Aw, my sweet Elsie, I remember what it felt like to be young and so in love."

"What did you say, Grandpa?" Annie asked as she wiped some sweat from her face.

"Nothing, sweetie," he said with a smile.

An hour later Grandpa and Matt put the mower and trimmer back in the machine shed.

"There! I think the flowerbeds are finished," Annie said.

"They look much better. Thank you, Annie. Let's take a break."

Grandpa and Matt sat on the front porch glider and tried to wish a cool breeze into existence. Annie sat on the wooden railing.

"I think we need some liquid refreshment. What would you like, Matt?" Grandpa asked.

"I could go for a beer, but I'll settle for water since I have to work later."

"What would you like, Annie?"

"What are you having, Grandpa?" Annie stood up, put her hands behind her back and used her innocent little girl look on him.

"Okay, you can have a beer if you want. Just one though."

"I'll get the drinks. You and Matty can sit out here and talk."

Annie ran in the house and returned with water for Matt, a beer for Grandpa and a Coke for herself.

Grandpa looked at her Coke. "I thought you wanted a beer."

"I just wanted to see what you would say if I asked for one."

"I think you are old enough to have a beer if you want, Annie. I drank my first beer when I was ten."

"I might have one later."

They talked about the need for rain and the high cost of Chinese tea for several minutes in the hot, still air.

"Do you want another water, Matty?" Annie asked as the sweat dripped from her forehead into her eyes.

"Sure. I can get it, Annie. Do you want another beer, Mr. O'Dell?"

"I'm good, thanks. Matt, you can call me Liam or Grandpa if you want. I'm not Principal O'Dell anymore."

Matt opened the wooden screen door and said, "Okay. I'll call you Grandpa. I can't call you Liam. It would feel too weird."

"Have you got your schedule for next semester, Annie?" Grandpa asked.

"My classes are all set. Pretty much the same schedule as last year. No classes before nine and nothing after two. Tuesdays and Thursdays I only have two classes."

"What's your schedule like, Matt?" Grandpa asked as Matt handed him another beer.

"Pretty close to Annie's. We planned it that way so we could have more time together. I will have to work part time, but we will still see each other more than last year."

"Grandpa, what would you say if I told you Matty and I wanted to get a place together?"

"First I would paddle your bottom, then I would shoot Matthew where it counts."

"Grandpa!"

"If you have to ask permission, then you are too young. What did your father say after he told you to go ahead?"

"He was against the idea. How did you know what he would say?"

"Because I told him the same thing when he wanted to have your sainted mother move in with him. He wasn't serious. He just wanted to hear my reaction. I take it you two are thinking about it

25

for later on down the road."

Annie looked at Matt. "We have thought about it. We couldn't afford to do it now. Maybe in a couple years."

"You could always get married, Annie. I hear kids still do that. What are your thoughts about this, Matt?"

"I love Annie very much, but I think we are too young to get married or live together. We still have three years of college left. After that, who knows?"

Matt smiled at Annie and blew a kiss in her direction.

"There's more to being together than sex," Grandpa said.

"Grandpa! How can you say that?"

"What? Sex? I was young once, too. I remember what it was like. Of course your great grandfather would have shot me for real if I misbehaved with your grandmother."

"How old were you when you got married?" Matt asked.

"I was nineteen and Elsie was seventeen. She had just graduated from high school and I was in college. I worked a full-time job as well. Elsie worked until your father came along. After he was born, we were going to have another but she miscarried. The doctors advised us that it would not be safe for her to have another baby."

"So you wanted more kids."

"Yes, I wanted more, but it was not meant to be."

"Did Mommy and Daddy want more kids?" Annie asked.

"They did. They tried, but then she got sick so they couldn't." Grandpa tried in vain to keep the emotion out of his voice.

Liam looked at Annie and she jumped down from the railing, moved in between Grandpa and Matt as Grandpa held out his arms. He hugged her tightly. Matt watched and sensed the love between Annie and Grandpa Liam. He was her only living grandparent. Liam was the last living sibling from the family of four boys. Annie's mother's older sister was still alive but lived in England. Annie had never met her.

"What would you kids like for lunch? I was just going to have a sandwich."

"We could just make sandwiches, Grandpa. We don't need

much. Matt will have dinner at work and I was going to meet up with Mace for dinner. He's lonely without Erin around. We are going to eat at the Lion so I can see Matty. Do you want to join us?"

"Thanks, but I'll pass, Annie. I've got some leftover lasagna that Elisabeth brought over and I thought I would make a salad. Thanks for asking though."

"Is there anything else you need done today?"

"Well, I was going to change the bed sheets in all the bedrooms."

"I can help with that," Annie said as she jumped up from the glider.

Annie helped Grandpa in the bedrooms while Matt worked outside in the yard. Matt noticed a few things that needed to be done, so he took the initiative to do them. It didn't take long to finish and Annie made sandwiches for the three of them. After lunch, Annie and Matt needed to get home so Matt could get ready for work.

Grandpa walked over to Matt's car with an arm around Annie's waist. "Thanks for coming out to see me. I appreciate the help, too."

"You're welcome, Grandpa." Annie hugged him. "Maybe we can see you again next Sunday. I love you!"

"I love you, too, sweetie. Take care, Matt. Thanks for the help."

Matt waved. "No problem. I like to work outside more than at the Lion."

"Go figure. Now there's a breeze," Grandpa muttered. He watched as they drove away. *What is the widow Hobbs' phone number? I just might call her up and see if she would like to have dinner in the city.*

## Chapter Six

When they got back into SoHam, Matt stopped by his house to get a clean shirt for work. He grabbed a few extra shirts to leave at the O'Dell house. He took Annie home and showered and shaved there.

"Are you and Mace still coming for dinner tonight?" Matt asked.

"I think so. I need to call him to make sure. Should I make a reservation?"

"I think maybe we can find a table for you and Mace somewhere. Maybe in the alley," Matt teased.

Annie smacked his arm. "I was going to kiss you before you left for work, but I don't think I will now."

"All right. I'll find you a table inside."

Matt left for work and Annie called Mace.

"Are we still on for tonight?"

"Sure. Are you going to pick me up?"

"I will if you buy dinner."

"No problem! I'll buy," Mace said.

"You're only saying that because you know dinner will be on the house. Mr. Sullivan never lets me pay for anything now."

"The best reason to eat at the Lion."

"You are so cheap!" Annie exclaimed. "Do you ever take Erin anywhere nice?"

"Is Darby's considered nice?"

"You're impossible. I'm glad we're not dating."

Mace laughed. "You couldn't handle me."

"Why would I want to?" Annie asked. "What time do you want me to pick you up?"

"Seven too late?"

"That should be fine. Matty can take a break around then. I hope."

Annie picked Mace up just before seven. They arrived at The Hungry Lion a few minutes later. Matt found a table for them near the back in the corner.

"I'll join you soon if it doesn't get too busy."

28

"Hurry back," Annie said.

She and Mace ordered an appetizer and pop. Matt managed to get away a few minutes later. He sat next to Annie and kissed her.

"Did you guys order yet?"

"Just some loaded tater skins so far. How long is your break?" Annie asked as she held his hand.

"Maybe thirty minutes at the most. Can you order a Lion burger for me with fries."

"You want pepperjack cheese?"

"Yes, please. I'll be back in a few minutes."

Annie ordered for her and Matt. Mace ordered the largest burger on the menu. He would have no trouble finishing that along with his fries. Matt came back just as the food was ready.

"I've got twenty minutes to eat. Could you pass the steak sauce please?" Matt asked.

Annie handed Matt the sauce. "What time will you get off tonight?"

"I should get out of here at midnight. I'm not closing up. I should be at your place soon after."

Annie felt stuffed after finishing half of her burger and most of her fries. She got a box to take the rest home.

"Are you gonna finish those fries, Annie?" Mace asked. "They won't be that good later."

"No, you can have them, Mace." Annie pushed her plate across the table to Mace. "How can you still have any room? You've eaten enough for a whole family. I'll take my burger home. You will probably be hungry later."

Mace shrugged. "It's my high metabolism."

"What are you and Mace going to do tonight?" Matt asked.

"We might just hang out at his house until Daddy gets home. I want to see Keyshon. I want to see how many hot dogs he ate."

"I should get back to work, Annie. You know Dad won't let you pay right."

"Is it all right if we leave a tip?"

"Sure, that's all right. Not more than ten bucks though."

"Okay, I'll see you later."

"Have fun. Should I bring anything home with me?"

"If you're hungry. Otherwise, I don't need anything."

Matt kissed Annie and went back to work. Annie and Mace scrounged up twelve dollars for the tip and headed out a few minutes later.

Mace rubbed his jaw as they walked out to Annie's car. "Man! Who would have ever thought a couple years ago that Matthew Sullivan would be in love and give up sex? Totally unbelievable."

"He hasn't given it up..."

Mace grabbed Annie's arm. "Oh, really. Are you holding out on me, girl? I thought we told each other everything."

"I meant he has just put it on hold for now."

"I'm just messin' with you, Annie. You don't have to tell me if you guys go ahead," he said but then added, "Of course you can if you want."

She shook her head. "We're not kids anymore. I might want to have a few secrets."

They arrived at the Franklin home and after sitting on the living room couch for twenty minutes, Mace rubbed his stomach.

"What's wrong with you?" Annie asked. "Does your belly hurt from all the food you scarfed down?"

"I could eat some ice cream about now."

"You're hungry already?" Annie asked. "That's impossible. There are countries in Africa that don't eat as much as you."

"Yeah. You want any?"

"No way. I'm still full. Maybe later though. Save me a scoop, okay?"

"There's a couple new movies by the TV. We could watch one of those if you want."

Annie looked at the choices. "I've seen both of these. Can we just go out to see a movie?"

Mace shrugged. "I suppose so."

"I'll buy the tickets, but you gotta buy the popcorn and pop."

"Fine. We can split a large popcorn."

30

"Oh, my God!" Annie rolled her eyes. "You're so cheap."

"Maybe I wouldn't be if there was going to be something in it for me afterward," Mace said as he touched Annie's leg.

Annie smacked his arm hard enough to hurt her hand.

"Ow!" Mace hollered. "That hurt, girl."

"You deserve that." She flexed her fingers to ease the pain. "Just because we made out once doesn't mean it will ever happen again."

"I was just kidding, Annie. Jeez! I know you're in love with Matty."

"You just miss Erin. Maybe you should go out to Nebraska to see her."

"I don't even know where Nebraska is." Mace held out his hands. "It could be in Canada for all I know."

"You know where it is. Don't play dumb with me."

"You could go with. Erin would like to see you, too."

"Yeah, right. I would be the third wheel or whatever. You wouldn't want me around. Have you ever met her parents?"

"No, I didn't have a chance to see them when Erin got to school. I didn't know her then, remember?"

"I forgot. Maybe you'll meet them this year sometime. They do know you're half black, don't they?"

"That's half African American," Mace said.

"Excuse me! I forgot I have to be politically correct."

"Are we going out or not?"

"Are you finished eating the ice cream?"

"Yeah, I'm done. Let's go."

Annie drove over to the mall and they argued about which movie to see. Annie wanted to see *Hope Floats* and Mace wanted to see *Godzilla*.

"*Hope Floats* is a chick flick. I might see that with Erin because I would get to make out afterward."

"*Godzilla* is a stupid monster movie," Annie said.

"Wouldn't you rather see the 'hope sinks' movie with Matty?" Mace asked while making a kissing motion.

"Yes, but it will be gone before we have a chance to see it."

"Coin toss?"

31

"Fine! I get to toss it and you have to call it in the air, otherwise I win by default."

"Deal," Mace said as he bumped fists with her.

"Give me some change." Annie held out a hand.

Mace shook his head but dug in his pocket for a coin.

Annie flipped the quarter and Mace called heads. He won.

"Crap! I hope Godzilla tears down the theater."

"Don't be a poor loser and give me back my quarter, girl."

"Extra butter on the popcorn, please. I'll grab a couple seats on the left side of the middle section."

Mace bought the popcorn and pop and found Annie.

"I brought extra napkins so you don't wipe your hands on my shirt like last time."

"Did you bring two straws?" Annie asked.

"No, why?"

"I have to share a straw with you? That's gross."

Mace frowned at her. "You've never had a problem with that before. Why now?"

"Just kidding. At least I don't have to kiss you."

"You wish you could."

"Been there. Done that. I'll stick to kissing Matty."

"Anything else?"

Annie shook her head. "Not yet. We're supposed to go see Jennifer Wednesday after I get off work."

"Has he seen her lately?" Mace grabbed a handful of popcorn.

"No, not since she came home from the hospital."

"Maybe you guys can have a kid soon."

"Yeah, and you and Erin can have twins."

"I think the movie's starting."

They sat quietly through the movie until Annie got cold.

"I'm cold" she whispered. "Would you put your arm around me?"

"Sure, Annie."

Mace rubbed her arms for her and put an arm around her until she warmed up.

"Thanks, Mace."

"Anytime, Annie Mercer. We're still best friends."

Even though Mace brought extra napkins, Annie forgot and wiped her hands on Mace's shirt. He didn't mind. When the movie ended, Annie carried the empty popcorn and pop containers. Mace put his hands on her shoulders and arms to warm her up again. As they left the theater they ran into Victoria Madison and Christopher Braun.

"Hey, guys! We didn't see you in the theater," Annie said as she looked up at Christopher. *With your California surfer dude looks you could do a lot better than Victoria.*

"Hi, Annie. Hey, Mace. Where's Matt? Did you guys break up?" Victoria asked a little too cheerfully.

"No, Matty was working so I came with Mace. How are you doing?"

"All right. It was good to see you, but we gotta run." Victoria pulled on Christopher's arm and dragged him away.

"See you guys," Annie said as she waved.

"What was up with her?" Mace asked.

"Got me," Annie answered and then shrugged. "I haven't talked to her since school ended. Did you hear how she asked about me and Matty?"

"I caught that. Does it bother you that she and Matt... you know"

"I try not to think about that. Thanks for bringing it to my attention," she said and then poked Mace in the ribs.

"Sorry, Annie."

"It's all right," she said then sighed. "It's just part of Matt's history. I have to accept that as part of who he is or was."

Annie took Mace home and waited for her father, Elisabeth and Keyshon. They finally got home and Keyshon sat next to Annie on the couch.

"Did you have a good time at the game?" Annie asked.

"It was okay, but there were too many people." He covered his ears and added, "It was too loud, but the hot dogs were good."

"How many did you eat?"

Keyshon tilted his head and used his fingers to count. "Three and a pretzel and some nachos."

"I hope you don't get sick. You eat almost as mush as Mace," Annie said then kissed his cheek.

"I saw these real tall buildings, too," Keyshon said. He stood up and put his hands over his head. "Some of them were taller than this."

"I'm glad you had fun. I need to get home. I'll talk to you later."

"Good night, Annie. Say hi to Matthew Sullivan for me."

It was eleven before Annie got home. She changed into some summer pajamas. Dad came home a few minutes later.

"I thought you were spending the night with Mom," Annie said.

"I'm going back. I just needed to grab a few things that I should have brought with me. You and Matty will have the house to yourself."

"We aren't going to do anything, Daddy. Nothing that we need to hide."

"Speaking of hiding," Dad said as he pointed at her pajama top. "That doesn't hide much."

"I'm not going to wear a bra to bed and he can't see through this. I'll try not to lean over too far if you're worried about that."

Dad sighed. "Sorry, but I'm a dad. It's my job to worry about that stuff. Good night, sweetie. I'll see you tomorrow. I want to grill out if it's not raining."

"Night, Daddy. Sleep well."

Annie picked up some clothes from her bedroom floor and fixed the air mattress for Matt. He arrived just before twelve thirty with some loaded tater skins. He and Annie sat at the kitchen island as he ate.

"How was the rest of the night?" Annie asked as she put her elbows on the island and propped her chin in the palm of her hands.

"Not too bad. It was busy, but we scheduled enough help to handle it."

"I fixed your bed already."

"Thanks, Annie. I want to shower before we go to bed."

"Daddy was here for a little bit. Keyshon was happy to see

me. He told me all about the game and how many hot dogs he ate."

"Did they stop here?"

"No, just Daddy. He needed to get some clothes. Mace and I went to see *Godzilla* then I went back to wait for Daddy. I wanted to see *Hope Floats,* but I lost the coin toss."

"How was *Godzilla*?" Matt asked as he finished the tater skins.

"It was all right. I got cold and made Mace put his arm around me. Oh! After the movie we ran into Victoria and Christopher."

"How are they doing?"

"Okay, I guess. She asked if we broke up since I was there with Mace. I think she was hoping we did."

"I'm sorry you saw her, Annie."

"It's okay. You are a different person now."

Matt needed to wind down from work, so he and Annie stayed up until two. Matt took a shower and they headed to bed. Even though they were alone and tempted to share her bed, Matt knew Annie would let him know when she was ready.

They slept until eleven. Matt woke up first and used the bathroom. When he came back, Annie was starting to wake up.

"What time is it?" Annie asked as she stretched her arms over her head.

"It's just after eleven. Are you hungry?"

"I will be after I wake up all the way."

"I'll make some coffee if you want."

"I don't need any. I think we have some apple juice. I'll drink that. If you want coffee though, go ahead and make some. I've gotta pee."

Annie came out to the kitchen after she took care of business. Matt placed two glasses of juice on the counter along with two chocolate pop tarts.

"Oh, a gourmet breakfast. Thank you, Matty. What do you want to do today?" she asked while biting into the pop tart.

"I thought your father said something about grilling out this afternoon."

"Here, or at Grandpa's? Or at Mom's house?" Annie asked.

"I think it was here. Do you mind if I use the bathroom first?"

"I don't mind. Go ahead."

Matt showered, shaved and did what he needed to be ready for the day. Annie finished her juice and pop tart and found clothes to wear. She was in the shower when her father called.

Matt answered her cell phone. "Hi, Mr. O'Dell."

"Hi, Matt. Is Annie close? I need to talk to her. It's important."

Matt looked at the phone and then at the bathroom door. "She's in the shower. Should I take the phone to her?"

"You could just tell her, I guess. Just be careful. She might throw something at you for interrupting her shower."

"I'll be careful and I won't peek at her."

"That's wise. She would be pissed if you did." *I might be pissed if you did. Annie might not care.*

"What do I have to tell her?" Matt asked.

"It's about Keyshon. He's sick. On second thought, I should tell her myself. Could you give her the phone without making her mad?"

"I'll risk it. I'll take her the phone now. Hang on," Matt said.

He knocked on the door and opened it. He couldn't see through the white-with-blue-flowers shower curtain, but was careful to warn Annie he was coming in. "Annie! Your dad needs to talk to you. It's important."

Annie stuck her head out of the shower. "Why are you always interrupting my shower? Are you trying to see me naked?"

"No, but your father's on the phone. It's important."

"What's wrong? Is it Grandpa?"

"You'll have to talk to him. He just said it was important."

"Hand me the phone and don't peek."

Annie turned off the shower as Matt handed her the phone without looking at her. He stuck out the phone and she grabbed it.

"Daddy, what's wrong? Is Grandpa all right?"

"Grandpa is fine, but Keyshon is sick. We're at the

36

emergency room now. Don't get too upset. He's going to be fine, but I think all the food he ate yesterday at the game was too much for him to handle. I just wanted to let you know in case you tried calling here. There. You know what I mean."

"Thanks, Daddy. Should we come over to St. Bart's?"

"I don't think you need to. I'll call you back if they are going to keep him here."

"Okay, Daddy. Thanks for calling."

"I'll talk to you later, sweetie."

Annie ended the call. "Matty, will you hand me my towel and take the phone."

Matt took the phone and handed Annie her towel. "Should I leave?"

"Just give me a minute to dry off a little and wrap up in the towel."

Matt sat on the toilet and waited without looking at the shower curtain. Annie dried off and wrapped the towel around her. She opened the shower curtain and stepped out.

"Did you hear?"

"Yeah, Keyshon is sick. Do we need to go to St. Bart's?"

"Daddy said not yet. If they're going to admit him, he'll call back."

"I'm sorry I interrupted your shower."

"It's okay. I was almost done anyway," she said as she held up her towel. "Did Daddy warn you about looking at me?"

"Yeah, he told me to be careful. I think he was more worried you might throw something at me than he was worried about me seeing you naked."

"Maybe he thinks you have already seen me naked," Annie said. "Should I loosen the towel and let it fall?"

Matt took a deep breath. "As much as I'd like that, maybe you shouldn't."

Annie got dressed and an hour later Dad called again.

"Is Keyshon doing better?" Annie asked.

"They're going to keep him overnight just to keep an eye on him. He's in room 323 if you want to come and see him."

"Thanks, Daddy. We'll be there shortly. Is Mace there?"

"Yeah. Keyshon wants to see you, too."

"We'll be there as quick as we can."

Annie hung up and she and Matt left right away. They parked and ran inside. They took the elevator up to the third floor and looked for room 323.

"It's over here, Annie," Matt said.

They quietly walked into the room.

Keyshon saw them right away. "Hi, Annie! Hi, Matthew Sullivan! I'm all better now, but I have to stay here tonight. Did you come to see me?"

"I heard you were here so I wanted to see you." Annie sat on the side of the bed and kissed Keyshon on the cheek.

"I guess I ate too many hot dogs because I threw up a few times and hurt my belly right here." He pointed to the spot that hurt. "Did you marry Annie yet, Matthew Sullivan?"

"Not yet, Keyshon. Do you think I should?"

"If you don't, I will!" he said with a big grin.

Everyone laughed and Annie kissed Keyshon again. "I might have to take you up on that, little buddy," she said and then grinned at Matt. "Matty hasn't said he loves me all morning."

Keyshon shook his head. "Annie O'Dell, you can't call me little buddy anymore because I'm taller than you."

Keyshon was released the next morning with instructions to take it easy for a few days. By the end of the week he was back to normal.

# Chapter Seven

Kristen Keasling's graduation party was on Saturday the thirteenth. Matt and Annie decided to take Mace along so he didn't have to borrow his mother's car.

"There's a spot just in front of that red car, Matty."

"I see it, Annie," Matt said. "I was afraid we would have to park in the next county. There might be more people here today than last year's party for Derrick."

Matt maneuvered his car into the empty spot.

Annie jumped out. "I know Lainey and Cindy are coming but Adrien and Bryce are stuck working."

"I hope there's enough food," Mace said.

Annie shook her head. "All you think about is food."

Mace grinned. "That's not all I think about."

Annie rolled her eyes. "You are such a creep. Why does Erin like you?"

"What's not to like?" He struck up a pose like the Heisman Trophy.

"Don't ever do that again if you want to be my friend."

Mace straightened up and pointed at her legs. "Make sure you don't sit on the deck railing like last year."

"Did you have to bring that up?"

"What are you talking about, Mace?" Matt asked.

"Last year Annie was sitting on the deck railing."

"Yeah, I remember that now. So what happened?"

Annie poked Mace's arm. "Mace is reminding me to be a lady and keep my legs together."

"I was just trying to protect your modesty, Annie."

Annie smacked both guys. "Let's find Kristen. I want to say hi to her and catch up on the latest news."

Annie and Matt looked for Kristen while Mace headed right for the food.

"Hey, there's Lainey and Cindy by the pool. Come on, Matty. Let's talk to them." Annie waved and got Elaine's attention. "Hi, guys! Have you been here long?"

"We got here about a half hour ago. You?"

"We just got here. There are so many people here. Have you seen Kristen?"

Cindy glanced around looking for Kristen. "She is mingling with relatives right now. Did Mace come with you?"

"Yeah, he headed right for the food. Go figure."

"I bet he misses Erin."

"Yeah, he does. I told him to go to Nebraska to see her, but he thinks it's in Canada somewhere. I don't think he's ever been west of the Mississippi River except to play ball."

"He is clueless sometimes," Elaine said.

"Are you guys hungry? Should we grab something to eat?" Cindy asked.

"Yeah, maybe we can get some food before Mace eats it all."

Annie, Elaine, Cindy and Matt headed to the deck where all the food was being served. They saw some other friends along the way and stopped to talk.

Annie grabbed Matt's arm. "There's Emmy Colasanti and she's not with Tony Bertucci. Did they break up? Have you guys heard anything?"

"I haven't heard anything, Annie. Is she with that older guy?" Cindy asked.

"It looks like it. He looks like he's ten years older than Emmy. I'll ask Kristen when I see her. She'll know the scoop."

A few minutes later they saw Kristen and Annie asked about Emmy.

"Tony is in South Bend. That guy is just a friend."

"He looks so much older than Emmy," Cindy said.

"Yeah, I know. I think she knows him from church."

"Does Tony know about him?" Annie asked.

"She told me that he does. He wasn't real happy about her coming with him. His name is Scott Simmons."

They climbed the stairs to the large wooden deck and got in line to grab some food.

"Hey, Mace, is there anything left for us?" Annie asked.

"Come on, guys. You know I wouldn't let you starve. I left a couple small pieces of chicken for you."

40

They hung out at the deck for a while. Annie was tempted to sit on the deck railing, but Mace gave her a hard look so she didn't.

"Do I hear music playing somewhere?" Elaine asked.

"I think so. Do you wanna dance, Mace?" Cindy asked.

Mace swallowed the last bite of a chicken strip. "Sure! Come on. Let's dance for a while. Keyshon showed me some new moves."

"Come with us, Matty," Annie said as she grabbed his arm. "You can watch if you don't want to dance."

Even Matt got into the dancing. He danced with Annie, Elaine and Cindy. Mace danced with everyone in his area. Annie saw Emmy dancing with Derrick Keasling. She remembered how Derrick kissed her when she was in junior high. Later, Annie danced with Derrick.

"How do you like Arizona?" Annie asked.

"I'm enjoying my time there. I've adjusted to the heat." He twirled her around.

"Wow, I didn't expect that," she said. "Are you playing tennis?"

"I have a scholarship to play and I will probably go to law school there. Are you going to leave North Park since Kristen will be there?"

Annie grinned and said, "I'll see how it goes for one semester."

She saw Emmy with Barry Newton and watched as he chased her with a bottle of water in his hand. *Emmy and Barry are old friends, kinda like me and Mace, but I doubt Emmy ever kissed Barry Newton like I kissed Mace.*

Matt put an arm around Annie's shoulder and leaned close to her ear. "Are you having fun, Annie?"

"Yes I am, Matty. Are you?" she asked as she smiled.

"I'm happy as long as I can be with you."

"That's so sweet. Do you really mean it?"

"You know I do. Do you want to take a walk?" Matt asked.

"Are you going to try to kiss me if we do?"

Matt smiled. "Absolutely!"

41

"Then let's go!"

Annie took Matt's hand and they knew just where they wanted to go—to the lake along the trail behind the house. It didn't take too long to reach the lake.

"Matty, look. These might be the same ducks and geese from last year."

"Well, they certainly look familiar," Matty said.

"Oh, hush. You're teasing me," Annie said.

Matt took Annie in his arms and kissed her passionately for a few minutes before they noticed Derrick and his girlfriend.

"Hi, guys. Sorry if we interrupted. This is Amber Quinlan. Amber, this is Annie O'Dell and Matt Sullivan. They are friends from Roosevelt High and they attend North Park College now."

"Hello, Annie," Amber said. "I believe we met at the Barclay party."

"We did. It's good to see you again," Annie said. "This is Matty."

"It's nice to meet you, Amber. How is Arizona treating you, Derrick?" Matt asked.

"I love it. I'm just home for a few days, then I'll be heading back. My folks rented a place in Aspen for July and a bunch of us are going out there."

"That sounds like fun."

"We should let Annie and Matt have their privacy, Derrick," Amber said.

"That's okay." Matt waved. "We were heading back to the house. It was nice to meet you, Amber."

Annie and Matt headed back to the house and looked for Mace.

"He's probably by the food if I have to guess."

"You're right, Annie. There he is with Lainey and Cindy."

By seven Annie and Matt were ready to leave. They dragged Mace away from Elaine and Cindy.

"Mace, Matty and I are ready to leave. Are you coming with us? You could always walk home."

"Can I grab another plate for the road?" he asked.

"No!" Annie yelled. "How can you be such a pig?"

"I was kidding, Annie. Chill already."

"Sorry, I didn't realize you were kidding."

Mace grabbed another deviled egg from the bed of ice. "I danced with Emmy Colasanti while you guys were off making out somewhere."

"Did you ask her about the guy she was with?"

"Yeah. He split to go to work, but Emmy wanted to stay. She and Tony are still together. She's a sweet girl—kinda quiet and shy, but she has amazing eyes."

"Tony is a pretty big guy, Mace."

Mace stuffed the egg in his mouth and held up a hand. "I wasn't making a move on her. I'm not stupid, you know. She's in love with Tony."

"Come on. We have to get you home."

"Why? So you guys can go make out some more?"

"Maybe," Annie said. "Do you miss Erin?"

"Who?"

"I'll call her when I get home and tell her what you said."

"I thought you were my friend, girl."

"Do you remember Erin now?" Annie asked.

"You know I miss her."

"Nebraska is only a few hours away by plane."

"Do they have airports now? Do I need a passport?"

"They even have electric lights and automobiles. Most of the Indians are tame and hardly ever scalp white folks anymore. Don't know about black guys though," Annie teased.

"That's African Americans."

"I don't think the Native Americans care one way or another," Annie said and then giggled.

They dropped Mace off at his house and he called Erin right away. He did not want to give Annie a chance to tell her something to get Mace in trouble.

# Chapter Eight

Annie was watching Keyshon just like she usually did on Monday when Mrs. Franklin came home from work a few minutes early.

"Keyshon, would go to your room and listen to some music for me? I need to talk to Annie for a minute."

"Sure, Mom. I'll see you on Wednesday, Annie O'Dell," he said and then headed to his room.

Elisabeth waited until Keyshon was out of the room and she could hear some music playing. She turned to face Annie. "Let's sit on the couch."

"Okay," Annie said and then sat down.

Elisabeth took a deep breath and then smiled nervously at Annie. "Please don't be upset, but your father asked me to talk to you."

"Why would I get upset? What did Daddy want you to talk to me about?"

"Sex."

"Sex! Why?"

"He's worried about you, Annie."

Annie shrugged. "He shouldn't be worried. We had the 'talk' when I was younger. I know about sex. Why is he so worried now. Is it because of Matty's reputation? Matty hasn't been pressuring me or anything. We haven't even been making out much. We're always working."

"Maybe worried is not the proper word. He's concerned you might have questions he can't answer."

"I do have questions." Annie twisted her hair around a finger. "The only friend I feel comfortable asking is Erin and she's in Nebraska. Does it bother you that Mace and Erin are doing it?"

"No, of course, I'd rather they weren't, but as long as they are careful. They are old enough to make that decision. What questions do you have?"

"Should I go on the pill even though I'm not having sex yet?" Annie asked softly.

Elisabeth tugged at the earring in her right ear. "I would

suggest you go on the pill if it's a possibility you and Matthew might become sexually active in the near future."

"Should I make him use a condom even if I'm on the pill?" Annie asked more comfortably.

"You should always make your partner use protection," Elisabeth said and then paused. "Your father does."

"Ooh, too much information." Annie shuddered. "What about the cramps I get before my period?"

Elisabeth smiled. She and Annie talked for a half hour about sex and female issues.

"Thanks, Mom. Tell Daddy I'm glad he wanted us to talk. I feel better now."

"You should tell him. He will appreciate it," Elisabeth said. "If you ever have any questions or just need to talk, I'm here for you. There are times when a girl needs an older woman around."

After dinner that night Annie sat on the couch with her father. "I talked to Elisabeth today," Annie said.

He set his beer on the coffee table. "Oh, what did you talk about?"

"Daddy! I know you asked her to talk to me about sex. It's all right. We had a good talk and I feel better now. I had some questions you wouldn't be able to answer because you're a guy."

Dad put an arm around her and pulled her close. "I'm glad. I've always tried to answer anything you asked but... well... you know."

"You've done a great job, Daddy."

"So, are you... you know?"

She elbowed him in the side. "No, but I do need to see my doctor."

He looked into her eyes. "You don't look sick."

"I'm not sick, but I kinda need a prescription."

He stared for a moment. "Oh, I get it now."

# Chapter Nine

"How do I get to Nebraska? Can I fly there from SoHam?" Mace asked.

"No, you have to go to Florida and use the space shuttle," Annie said with a straight face.

Mace sighed. "Aw, come on, girl. Can I take the train?"

"How dense are you? Did you already forget how Erin got home?"

"I'm not sure I could handle a train ride. The team traveled by bus or by plane if it was too far away to take a bus," Mace said. "I'm used to that. I would rather fly since it would be quicker."

"Are you seriously thinking about going?" Annie asked.

"Yeah! I need to see Erin just to make sure she isn't missing me too much."

"Oh, it's not because you miss her at all," Annie teased.

Keyshon came into the room after hearing Mace and Annie talking. "Can I go with you, Mace? Erin probably wants to see me more than you."

"Aren't you the funny guy," Mace said. "You think she misses you, huh?"

"I know she does. Can I go?"

Annie stepped in to rescue Mace from being the bad guy. "I need you to stay here with me, buddy. Nebraska is far away and I would miss you too much."

"Okay, I'll stay here with you and Matthew Sullivan. Is Matthew Sullivan coming over today?"

"Not today, Keyshon. He's at work. He's filling in for someone who called in sick."

"Are you going to marry him soon, Annie?" Keyshon asked. "Then you can kiss him all day long."

"We're too young to get married. Maybe in a few years."

"Can I marry you until he gets old enough?" Keyshon asked. "You don't have to kiss me. We can just play together. I could teach you all my dance moves."

"I think I will just wait for Matty, little buddy. I only want to get married once."

46

"Okay, I'm going to my room. I wanna watch TV."

"See you later, Keyshon." Keyshon went to his room and Annie asked Mace, "Do you even know where in Nebraska Erin lives? It's a pretty big state."

"I know the name of the town is Kearney, but I don't have a clue where it might be. You know where she's from. Where is it?"

"Do you have a map?"

"Oh sure. I always keep a map of Nebraska in my pocket just in case I might need one," he said as he pretended to be searching his pockets.

"You don't have to be sarcastic with me. Does your mom have a road atlas in the house?"

"Yeah! There's an old one in the desk in the kitchen. It's pretty old."

"I think the town will be in the same place," Annie said.

"Now who's being sarcastic."

They walked into the kitchen and Mace found the atlas. He opened it on the kitchen table and they looked for Kearney.

"Here it is! It's kinda right in the middle of the state. It's on Interstate 80. Do you know Erin's address?" Annie asked.

"Yeah, she sent me a letter and her address was on the envelope."

"Did you save the envelope?"

"I'm going to smack you. I'm not totally stupid."

"I think the best way for you to get there is by train like Erin did. You could fly into Omaha, but then you'd have to take another flight from there. Let's call the travel agent Daddy uses and see how much it would cost," Annie suggested.

She called and talked to someone stuck working on a Sunday. Fifteen minutes later she thanked the person and hung up.

"Flying on such short notice would be too expensive. If you want to wait a month..."

"No way. I want to go as soon as possible," Mace said. "Maybe tomorrow."

Annie grinned. "You must be really horny."

He frowned at her then asked, "Wanna go with me? We could drive."

"I can't go anywhere until August. Matty and I are going on vacation then."

"Just the two of you?"

"Yes! Just the two of us."

"Does your father know about this? Is it gonna be your honeymoon?"

"Daddy doesn't know yet and it's not a honeymoon."

"Yeah, I bet," Mace said with a grin.

Annie smacked Mace and he noticed she was blushing. He decided not to tease her about it anymore. They placed a phone call and Mace purchased his ticket. He would take the train from South Hampshire into Chicago, then on to Kearney. The train would leave Chicago at 10:30 P.M. and arrive in Kearney just after noon on Tuesday the 23rd.

"That's a long trip," Annie said.

"Yeah, but once I get on the train in Chicago, I can sleep until we get to Kearney."

"Just make sure you don't sleep too long and forget to get off," Annie said.

"You're so funny, girl."

"Actually, the train doesn't go to Kearney. It goes to Holdrege. Erin will have to meet you there."

"That's fine with me," Mace said.


Annie arrived at the Franklin home early Monday morning.

"Annie, Mom said I could go with you to the train station as long as you don't mind," Keyshon said.

"I was hoping you would come with me, so I don't get lost," Annie told Keyshon, then walked into Mace's room. "Have you got everything packed? Do you have..."

"Yes, Annie! I've got everything. I double checked."

"What about your ticket? Where is it?"

"Do you think I'll need it?" Mace asked with a straight face.

"All right. I'll be quiet. Keyshon!" Annie hollered. "We're ready to go to the train station."

"I'm ready to go, Annie."

"Did you call Erin? Does she know you'll get there in the middle of the night?" Annie asked.

"Yes to both questions. She said she would pick me up sometime in the morning. I'll hang out at the station."

Annie and Keyshon drove Mace to the station. His connection to Chicago didn't leave for a half hour.

"Are you going to wait or do you have to get back?" Mace asked.

"We can wait. Is that okay with you, Keyshon?"

"Sure. I want to see his train." Keyshon looked in both directions along the tracks.

Annie and Keyshon waited with Mace until he could board the train.

"You be good for Mom and Annie, okay. I'll see you in a week," Mace told Keyshon.

"I'll be good. Have a good time. Say hi to Erin for me."

Mace hugged Keyshon, then turned to Annie.

"You better call Mom when you get there. She will worry about you."

"I will. See you in about a week." Mace started to board the train with all the other travelers.

"Hey! Don't I get a hug or anything?"

"Sorry. I forgot."

Mace hugged Annie and boarded the train. Annie and Keyshon watched until it left.

"Let's go. Would you like some chocolate chip cookies?"

"That sounds good," Keyshon said and then rubbed his belly.

"We'll make some this afternoon after lunch."

"I want to add the chocolate chips," Keyshon said.

Mace settled in for his long trip. He made his connection in Chicago without any problem. He tried to sleep, but was too keyed up. It would be thirteen hours to Holdrege, Nebraska. He talked to Erin again before leaving Chicago. She would pick him up at the station. He listened to the radio through his headphones to pass the time and, eventually, was able to grab a little sleep.

Mace arrived in Holdrege, collected his bag and looked around for Erin. He spotted her with a young man who he assumed was her brother. "Erin, I made it." He waved to get their attention.

Erin ran over to Mace and he hugged her.

"I'm so happy to see you. How was the trip?" Erin asked.

"Boring. The last hundred miles seemed to take forever but maybe that was partly because I was so anxious to see you and the battery died on my player. Do you know how hard it is to find a radio station out here that doesn't play country music?"

"Are you hungry? Did you eat on the train?" Erin asked.

"I ate a little, but a sandwich was five bucks. I could use some food."

"Oh, Mace, this is my brother Eddie. Eddie, this is Mace Franklin. Dad made Eddie come with me since it's rather early, or late depending on how you look at it."

They guys shook hands and Eddie offered to carry Mace's bag.

"Thanks, Eddie, but I got it."

"Erin told me you play basketball and won the state championship in high school."

"Yeah, we had a bunch of good players," Mace said.

Eddie added, "Erin told me her roommate said you were the best player."

"That would be my friend, Annie O'Dell. She's a little biased," Mace explained.

"I played ball for Kearney Senior. We had a decent year."

Mace grinned. "Maybe we can play some hoops while I'm here."

"Are you guys coming or should I let you walk home?" Erin asked. "I'm kinda in a hurry to get home."

It took thirty minutes to drive the thirty-some miles to Kearney and the Bezick home.

"Are you ready to meet my parents?" Erin asked. "They'll still be asleep, but they get up early."

"I'm a little nervous," Mace admitted. "They do know I'm African American, right?"

"They are aware of that, but I haven't told them everything

50

about our relationship."

Mace nodded and then sighed. *So they don't know we've been sleeping together. Great!*

Eddie opened the door and Erin and Mace walked inside.

"We could sit on the couch if you want," Erin said. "I'm too awake to go back to bed."

"I'll take Mace's bag to my room. I'm going back to bed," Eddie said.

"Thanks for going with me," Erin said.

"You owe me big time," Eddie said with a grin.

Erin and Mace sat on the couch and fell asleep within five minutes. They didn't wake up until shortly before seven. Erin woke up because of the aroma of coffee brewing in the kitchen. She nudged Mace. He woke up and looked at Erin.

"It's time to meet the parents," she said. They walked into the kitchen. "Mom and Dad, this is Mace Franklin."

Erin's father set his coffee cup down, stood up from the table, walked up to Mace and offered a hand. "Welcome to our home, Mace. Erin has been acting like a cat with ten tails in a room full of rocking chairs."

Erin rolled her eyes. "Oh, Dad! I have not."

Mom Bezick walked into the room wearing an apron. "She has, Mace. Take my word for it. You're probably tired. I hope you don't mind sharing Eddie's room. We've only got three bedrooms and Erin and Franny share one."

Mace smiled. "I can sleep anywhere, Mrs. Bezick. The couch is all right. Erin and I crashed there when we got here."

*I noticed. At least you were at opposite ends of the couch.* Mom thought. "Don't be silly. Eddie will sleep on the couch. He's used to that when we have company."

"Mom, is Franny still asleep?" Erin asked. "I thought she would have gotten up to meet Mace."

"I sent her to the store. I needed more bacon and eggs. She should be back soon."

Erin grinned at Mace. "Franny is anxious to meet you. I showed her a picture of us together and I think she's got a crush on you. Don't tell her I said so."

51

"You must be hungry after that long ride," Mom said. "I'll get some breakfast ready. Erin told me you have a strong appetite. I hope you like ham and potatoes"

"Sounds good to me," Mace said. "Erin, where's the bathroom?"

Eddie walked into the kitchen and heard Mace's question. "I'll show you. Follow me." Eddie showed Mace his bedroom and the hall bathroom. "We have to share the bathroom with my sisters. They can be in there for hours sometimes so be prepared. Dad's lucky. He and Mom have their own."

Franny got back from the store. "Where's Mace? I can't wait to meet him."

" I think he's in the bathroom. Just be patient, Franny. He'll be here for a week," Mom said.

Mace came back to the kitchen.

"Mace, this is my littler sister Francine."

"Please call me Franny and I'm only three years younger than Erin. She makes it seem like I'm still a baby. I'm only two years behind her in school though."

"It's good to meet you, Franny, and you don't look like a baby to me," Mace said with a grin. "You look a lot like Erin."

Mace told them about his family during breakfast. "Mom works at a bank. She's a vice-president in the loan department. I've got one brother."

"I told them about Keyshon already," Erin said. "I showed them a picture."

Dad Bezick coughed and then said, "Erin mentioned something about your father."

"He split after Keyshon was born with Down Syndrome. Haven't seen him since. Usually its the black fathers who leave their families, but it was the other way around for us. Did Erin mention my father was white?"

"She told us and I'm sorry he deserted you and your mother and brother," Mom said as she passed the platter of bacon and eggs to Mace. "You can eat all you want."

Mace filled his plate again. "Mom and Mr. O'Dell are in a relationship now."

"That's Annie's father. She's my roommate," Erin explained.

Mace inherited enough of his father's genes to make it obvious he was from a mixed family. After breakfast Erin offered to take Mace on a tour of Kearney.

"Can I go with you guys, please?" Franny asked.

"Franny, I think Erin would like to have Mace to herself for awhile," Mom said.

"It's all right, Mrs. Bezick. I don't mind if Franny joins us."

"Are you sure, Mace?"

"Yeah, it's all right. Erin and I will have time together later."

Erin and Franny showed him all around Kearney. It was not nearly as large as South Hampshire. Erin showed Mace both high schools and a house where they used to live. They drove past the grocery store where all three kids worked part-time.

"Well, that's about all there is to Kearney. Not much is it?"

"It seems like a nice little town. Kinda out in the middle of nowhere. Is that why you came to North Park?" Mace asked. "I don't remember you ever telling me how you ended up there."

"Dad knew about it. He lived in West Aurora a few years as a kid."

"Have you always lived in South Hampshire, Mace? Is that your real name?" Franny asked smiling at him.

"I've always lived there and it is my real name. Mom just liked it for some reason," he explained.

They returned to the house.

"What do you want to do until lunch?" Erin asked.

"Doesn't matter. What do you usually do?"

"We would usually be working, but we both got most of the week off. We have to work on Friday and Franny has to work Saturday evening. Eddie has to work his regular shifts though," Erin said.

Mace and Erin decided to go for a walk around the neighborhood to kill time. Eddie was asked by his mother to accompany them.

"Looks like you're stuck with me," Eddie said.

"Is it always this deserted?" Mace asked.

"Most people are at work and it's too hot and humid for kids to be outside," Erin said. "Have you called your mother?"

"Shoot! I forgot. I'll call her now." He called his mother's cell phone and they talked for a few minutes. "What do your parents do all summer? Don't they get bored staying at home?"

"Dad likes to go to auctions and estate sales. He doesn't buy much, but he likes to look. Mom keeps busy with her lady friends. They meet for lunch a couple of times a week and they visit people in the hospital. Stuff like that."

"Sounds like fun," Mace teased.

When they got back to the house, lunch was ready. Mace loaded up on ham and beans. After lunch he asked Erin, "Does your mother always cook this much? If she does, I'll gain twenty pounds before I leave."

Erin shook her head. "She's cooking for you. Normally, we would have a light lunch if Franny and I were even here."

Mom suggested everyone play a board game. Eddie and Franny instantly remembered they needed to visit friends, so Mace and Erin were stuck playing Scrabble for a couple of hours.

Eddie was scheduled to work that evening, so he ate an early supper before leaving. Mace listened to the two sisters talking to their mother while they helped in the kitchen. Mr. Bezick watched Mace's reaction.

"What are your plans for after college, Mace?" Dad Bezick asked as he sat in his chair and read the daily newspaper.

"I would like to coach basketball. Probably start at the high school level and maybe move up to college if I get an opportunity. I want to have a family and a nice home."

"White picket fence and all—the American dream, huh?"

"I suppose so. If I thought I had a chance to play pro ball, I would give it a shot, but that's not likely to happen."

Dad set down his paper. "Are you being modest or realistic?"

"Realistic. I'm pretty good for the level of competition we play against. There are a couple guys on the team who will play pro ball unless something happens."

"Like an injury?"

"That, or maybe they don't work hard enough. Anything can happen. That's why I want to make sure I get a good education. Basketball is my ticket for that."

"You won't get rich teaching at the high school level. We know that for a fact," Dad said and then chuckled.

"You seem to be satisfied. There are things more important than money—like food! That smells good whatever it is."

Dad Bezick smiled and said, "I'm content. I have a wonderful family, a decent job and home, and I love my wife more than ever."

Erin heard Mace and her father and came out to see them. She kissed Mace in front of her father. Mace looked for a reaction, but her father didn't react one way or another.

"We are having fried chicken, mashed potatoes, corn on the cob and homemade gravy. I know you like that," Erin told Mace.

"If you are as good a cook as your mother, I'm going to propose tonight," Mace said to tease Erin.

"Mom is a much better cook."

Franny came out of the kitchen and walked up to Mace. "I'm a better cook than Erin. You can propose to me if you want."

"You girls go back and help your mother," Dad ordered. "Mace isn't going to propose to anyone tonight."

Mace and Erin used an opportunity after supper to get away and be alone at last. Erin drove the family's second car.

"Do your parents know anything about our relationship?" he asked.

Erin shook her head. "They don't know we have slept together. I'm not like Annie. I don't tell my parents everything."

"What about Franny?"

"She knows. I couldn't keep it from her. Eddie suspects, but he's too shy to ask. I don't think it would bother him if he knew the truth. He has a girlfriend and I know they have made out and maybe even more."

"He seems like a good brother."

"Yeah, he's always been good to us. We tease him sometimes, but he's goodhearted about it."

"Where should we go?" Mace asked as he checked out Kearney at night. "Wanna see a movie? What is there to do in this town at night?"

"Not a whole lot. Most people are in bed early. There is a restaurant that stays open all night."

"I'm not hungry right now. Maybe we should just go back to the house. I don't want to lose your parents' trust the first night I'm here."

Erin took Mace back to the house where they wound up playing board games with the whole family until eleven. Mace had fun even if he and Erin didn't have a chance to get romantic.

"Okay, that's all for us tonight. We usually go to bed right after the news," Mom said. "Do you need anything before we turn in, Mace?"

"Thanks, Mrs. Bezick, but I'm good."

"Eddie should be home soon. He'll sleep on the couch. Sleep well."

Erin's parents went to their room and closed the door.

"Do you want to see our room?" Franny asked. She pulled Mace down the hallway without waiting for an answer. "This is it. Dad bought us a new king-sized bed and a new dresser last year. It gives us more room than the old bed."

Mace glanced around the room. He could feel the breeze that moved the lacy white curtains and touched the light pink paint. "I don't see any dolls or stuffed animals."

Erin walked into the bedroom carrying her nightgown. "We aren't like Annie. We put our childish toys away years ago." Erin kissed Mace's cheek. "You need to leave so Franny and I can get ready for bed."

"I'll see you in the morning."

"I know you called your mother, but did you call Annie?" Erin asked.

"Crap! I forget. I'll call her now. She'll still be up."

Mace went to Eddie's room.

Franny closed the bedroom door, got in bed, turned to Erin and asked, "Did you and Mace have a chance to do anything while you were out?"

56

Erin shook her head. "No, we kissed a few times but that was all."

"Are you going to make love while he's here? I know you want to because you've been so cranky at times."

"I'm sorry if I've been a witch."

"It's all right. I understand you've missed him," Franny whispered. "So are you?"

"If we get a chance. You better not say anything to Eddie. I know you won't say anything to Mom or Dad."

"I would never do that. If I did then I could never tell you anything about my boyfriends."

"Do you have a new boyfriend, Franny?"

"You know I have been going out with Reed Wittemore for six months now. I know you think he's too old for me."

"Franny, he's twenty! He's older than Mace for crying out loud."

"I'll be seventeen soon. I'm not a baby and besides you dated Mike Zimmerman and he's older than Reed."

"That's different. Have you and Reed done anything?"

"Nothing more than I told you about before. Certainly not as much as you and Mace," Franny said, then tilted her head. "Why did you ask if Mace had called your roommate?"

"Didn't I ever tell you about Mace and Annie?"

"If you did, I forgot."

"They've been friends since they were kids. They're almost like brother and sister now that Mace's mother and Annie's father are in a serious relationship."

"Oooh! You'll have to tell me more about that sometime," Franny said and then giggled.

"Hush! Mace might hear you."

"Do you want to double with us this week?" Franny asked.

"Sure. We could do that."

"How about tomorrow night?"

"I think that will work."

Franny turned over on her side. "I'll call Reed to check."

# Chapter Ten

Detective O'Dell came home from work Tuesday just in time for dinner. Annie arrived home earlier and made spaghetti because it was quick and easy. She put together a salad and placed garlic bread in the oven.

"That smells good, Annie. How was work today?"

"Boring! I spent the whole afternoon filing and typing. How was your day? Catch any wanted criminals?" Annie asked as she dumped the spaghetti into a large bowl.

"No one important. Did you hear from Mace?" he asked while loosening his tie.

"Not yet. He said he would call, but he's probably busy with Erin," Annie said and then grinned. "I might not hear from him all week. I'm sure he and Erin are making the best of their time together. Any other SoHam news I should know about?"

"Oh, Howard Lombardi passed away."

Annie opened the oven and pulled out the garlic bread. "What did you say?"

"Howard Lombardi died."

"When?" Annie tossed the oven mitts on the counter.

"Sunday night or Monday morning. I'm not sure which."

"Lombardi, huh? Should I know that name? I think I've heard it somewhere." Annie checked the fridge for salad dressing. She pulled out a bottle of Kraft Italian and one jar of Marie's Thousand Island.

"How can you call yourself a sleuth and not know that name?" Dad asked.

"I haven't had much time for sleuthing lately, Daddy."

"You know the Keasling kids and Tony Bertucci, right?"

Annie opened the fridge again and grabbed a beer for her father. "Yeah."

"He was their grandfather. Carmen Lombardi is his son."

Annie shrugged because she didn't recognize the name.

"Matt will know Howard and Carmen Lombardi. Howard's daughters, Maria and Karla, are Tony's and Derrick and Kristen's mothers."

58

"Duh! I guess I never knew their mother's names," Annie said as she slapped her forehead. "How did he die?"

"Cancer, I think. He had been sick for a while. He was kind of a recluse in his last years. He was always protective of his privacy."

"When are the wake and funeral? Are you going?"

"Yes, the wake will be on Thursday the 25th and the funeral is the next day. I will pay my respects to the family. The chief and mayor and everyone on the city council will be there. Every politician in the city will show up. It will be a circus." Dad sighed and took a drink of his beer. "Howard Lombardi was an important man in the city. I'm sure Cormac and Matt will want to pay their respects, too."

"Should I go with you?"

"I think it would be nice. Your friends will be there. Howard lost his wife just about a year ago."

"I think I remember you telling me about that now. You went to the wake but I didn't go."

"Grandpa went to school with Carmen Lombardi. They were good friends for a time. You might have heard rumors that Carmen is connected—like the rumors about Cormac Sullivan. They're just rumors. Not true at all, but they both take advantage of the rumor when it suits them." Dad took another swig of his beer, then set it on the island. "I'm going to change clothes, then we can eat. I want to hear more about your day, sweetie."

Dad changed into jeans and a clean shirt. They sat at the island to eat.

"Why was Howard Lombardi so important?" Annie asked.

"He was a businessman and wielded a ton of political clout. If you wanted to run for office in SoHam, or the county, you would need the support of Mr. Lombardi if you wanted any chance of winning." Dad drained his beer and added, "Have you ever heard of Bertucci and Keasling Construction?"

"I've come across that name at Mr. Bushell's office."

"It was started by Mr. Lombardi's daughters' husbands."

"Oh, I get it," Annie said then grinned.

"Have you been pulling my leg the whole time?"

59

Annie shrugged. "I'd like to say yes, but that would be a lie. I didn't remember the name at first."

They finished eating and Dad put the dishes in the dishwasher as Annie put away the leftovers.

"Would you like to watch a ballgame with me since Matty's working?" Dad asked.

"Who's playing?"

"Cubs and Reds. I'll probably fall asleep. Baseball is so slow compared to other sports."

Annie laughed. "It's better than watching golf or bowling. Not as exciting as watching chess."

Dad fell asleep around ten. Annie woke him up so he could go to bed. She got ready for bed and started reading *A Collection of Bones* by Geoffrey Deacon from where she left off the night before. She was dozing off when her cell phone rang just before midnight.

"I knew you'd still be awake," Mace said. "I made it to Nebraska all right."

"Thanks a lot, doofus. I was asleep. Do you know what time it is?"

"It's almost midnight," he said as he looked at the clock on Eddie's dresser.

"For real? I thought Nebraska might be in a different time zone. It's halfway around the world."

"Eddie's clock says midnight."

"Whatever. What did you do today? Did you have time to... you know?"

Mace told Annie about his day and how much food Mrs. Bezick cooked.

"So you stuffed yourself and played Scrabble and Monopoly all day, huh? I told Daddy you and Erin would be making out."

"I kissed her a couple times, but that was it. Her parents are teachers which means they don't work in the summer. They'll be here all the time."

"Poor baby," Annie teased. "Where are you now?"

"The brother's bedroom. He's snoozing on the couch and

60

before you even suggest it, Erin and Franny share a bedroom and a bed."

"Your prospects for any romance sound pretty thin."

"Are you smiling about that?"

Annie giggled and then shook her head. "You have my sympathies."

"You'll understand one of these days, Annie."

"Is there anything to do out there?" Annie asked.

"Not unless you like going to auctions and watching beans grow."

"Beans?"

"Whatever the farmers grow. It doesn't look like corn. Erin gave me a tour of Kearney. Lasted three minutes."

Annie laughed. "I think you might be exaggerating."

"Not by much. The town closes when the sun goes down."

"Do you want to come home?"

He snorted. "I'm not giving up that easily. I've got a few days to make a move. Oh, her sister's cute and Erin said she kinda has a crush on me."

"Poor child," Annie said. "She must be mental."

"You're such a riot. I'm hanging up. I might call you again."

"I might pick you up at the train station," she teased. "Night, Mace."

# Chapter Eleven

Erin and Franny chose Wednesday night for their double date. In the meantime, Mace and Erin hung out around the house. Someone was always around so they didn't have any opportunities to be alone. Strangely enough and in spite of what he told Annie, Mace didn't seem to mind. Just being with Erin made him happy.

"So, where are we going tonight?" Mace asked in the afternoon.

"I thought we could go to El Potrero. It's probably the best Mexican restaurant in town. After that we could go to a movie."

"That sounds all right to me. Maybe we can make out in the theater," Mace said as he kissed Erin's forehead.

"What makes you think I want to make out with you, Mace Franklin?" Erin asked with a straight face.

"Just wishful thinking."

"If it's not too crowded we might be able to kiss a little."

"Are there any places to go parking in this town?"

"Mr. Franklin! How would an innocent girl like me know anything about that? We'll ask Franny," Erin said.

"You're joking right?"

"Sorta, Franny probably knows some better places to go than I do. She's had more boyfriends than me."

"Really? She doesn't seem like the type."

"She likes boys. It doesn't mean she's a 'bad girl' or anything. She just likes to go out with different guys. The guy she's dating now is twenty years old."

"Did you ever go out with him?"

"He asked me out a few times, but the only time I was with him was on a group date. He tried to kiss me, but I didn't let him."

"Who's driving tonight?" Mace asked.

"Reed will drive since he has to pick us up. He's got a nice car. I think it's a '97 Ford Escort. Kinda small backseat though."

"And you know that because?"

She smacked his arm. "Because he took Franny and me to the store and I sat in the back. Are you jealous?"

"Should I be?" Mace shrugged.

"You are absolutely hopeless sometimes, Mace."

Later, Franny asked, "What are you wearing tonight, Erin? Do you like this top? It's new."

Erin pulled a clean pair of jeans from her dresser and looked at the top. "It's pretty red."

"It will match my lipstick. You should wear something sexy for Mace." Franny checked the closet, pulled out a flannel shirt and handed it to Erin. "Like this."

Erin threw the shirt on the bed. "You are so funny."

"How about this one?" Franny pulled a white top out of the closet. "It has buttons down the front."

"So?"

Franny rolled her eyes. "Go ahead and wear a t-shirt for all I care."

Reed stopped by the house at six. He complimented his black jeans and black dress shirt with dusty brown boots and a well-broken-in tan cowboy hat.

"Reed, this is Mace Franklin from South Hampshire. He's Erin's boyfriend," Franny said. "I told you about him, remember?"

"Hello, Mace. It's nice to meet you. You're a basketball player, right?"

"Yes, I play at school." Mace compared his jeans and t-shirt to Reed's attire and resisted the impulse to call him podner.

"He's on scholarship to play ball," Erin said proudly.

Mace got the impression Reed was checking him out.

Reed stared at Mace for a few seconds, then asked, "Are you girls ready to go?"

"Just give me a second to let Mom know we're leaving."

Erin walked into the kitchen and informed her mother they were ready to leave.

Mom set her rolling pin on the counter, wiped some flour from her arms and said, "Have a good time, Erin. Make sure Franny behaves. I'm not sure I totally trust Reed with her. He's too slick, if you know what I mean."

"I'll keep an eye on her, Mom. Don't wait up. We might be late getting home."

"Try to be home by midnight at least."

They were seated right away at El Potrero. Reed held the chair for Franny as she sat down. Mace noticed and got the feeling Reed was trying too hard to impress Franny. He thought she needed to be careful with that guy. For some reason Reed reminded Mace a little of the 'old' Matt Sullivan. Mace looked over the menu and asked Erin for advice.

"Everything is pretty good," Erin said.

"What do you usually order?"

"I like the enchilada combo platter. I usually order the one with two enchiladas, but you will want the one with three."

"I am kinda hungry."

The waitress brought chips and salsa and took their drink orders.

"So, Reed, what do you do? Are you in college?" Mace asked.

"Yes. There is a campus of the University of Nebraska here in Kearney and I take classes there. I commute from home and work part-time on my grandfather's ranch. I take care of the cattle and the horses."

"Sorry if I sounded like I was grilling you or something."

"It's okay," Reed said then chuckled. "Mr. Bezick was much tougher on me. I still don't think he likes me much."

"He doesn't like any boy I go out with, Reed," Franny said.

"He thinks you are too old to be dating Franny," Erin said.

"Boys my age are so immature. I don't like to waste my time with them."

The waitress brought their soft drinks and took their food orders. Mace ate most of the chips before their food appeared. Everyone was quiet when the food did arrive. Reed talked to Franny as they ate but didn't say much to Erin or Mace. They hung out at the restaurant for a little over an hour. Reed and Mace split the check and left a generous tip. Mace and Erin climbed in the backseat and Franny sat in front with Reed.

"Are we still going to a show or is there something else to do?" Mace asked.

Franny giggled and Erin gave her a hard look. "What are you laughing about, Franny? Is there something you want to do?"

"Oh come on, Erin. You know you want to go somewhere and make out with Mace."

"Is that what you want to do? Go somewhere and make out with Reed?" Erin asked as she frowned at her sister.

"Yes! At least for a little while. I know a place we can go."

Erin listened as Franny told her about the new place where kids went to have some privacy.

"Okay, we can go there, but we can't stay too long and remember Mace and I are with you."

"Maybe you should remember that I am here with you, Erin. You are in the backseat after all."

Mace sensed some tension between Erin and Franny and spoke up, "Maybe we should just go to the movies like we planned. I don't think I would be comfortable making out with another couple in the car with us."

Mace convinced Erin and Franny to go to the show instead. They were able to hold hands as they enjoyed the comedy Mace had seen in SoHam several months prior. After the show they went back to the Bezick home. Mom and Dad were still awake, but were about ready to go to their bedroom.

"We didn't expect to see you kids home so early. Did you have a good time?" Mom asked.

Erin nodded. "Yes, we did. We went to El Potrero, then saw a movie."

"We are going to bed. I'll see you in the morning. Oh, tell Eddie there is a plate of food for him in the fridge if you see him."

"I will. See you in the morning, Mom. We'll be quiet."

"Good night, dear."

The kids gathered in the kitchen to talk.

"Are you hungry again, Mace?"

"Sorta. Is there anything to make a sandwich with?"

"Probably some leftover ham."

Erin looked in the fridge and found some ham and roast beef. She showed them to Mace and he chose the roast beef. Erin made a sandwich for him.

"Anyone else want one?"

"No thanks, Erin. I should get back home."

"Do you have to leave already, Reed?" Franny asked.

"Sorry, Franny, but I should. I've got to work in the morning."

"Will you call me tomorrow?"

"Of course," he promised.

Reed looked at Mace. "It was nice to meet you, Mace. Good luck on the court next year."

Mace stood and shook Reed's hand. "It was good to meet you, too. Maybe we will see each other again soon."

Reed left for home and Mace and the girls waited up for Eddie. They stayed in the kitchen, which was at the other end of the house from the bedrooms. This way they could talk without disturbing the parents. Eddie arrived home just after eleven.

"Hey, Eddie, how was work?" Erin asked. "Oh, there is a plate for you in the fridge unless Mace ate it already."

"I didn't eat it. It's still there."

"Thanks. Man! Work was a killer today. I unloaded the grocery truck by myself. I'm wiped out. How was your double date? Where'd you go?"

"We went to El Potrero and a movie."

"And?"

"That's all! We didn't go anywhere else."

"Too bad, Mace," Eddie said with a grin.

"He talked us out of going parking. Franny and I were willing to go, but Mace got cold feet."

Eddie looked at Mace with surprise.

"It just felt strange with Franny and Reed in the car."

"It wouldn't have bothered me," Franny claimed. "I'm going to bed. Are you going to stay up, Erin?"

"For a while, Franny. I'll be there soon."

Franny headed off to bed while the others talked. Eddie finished his late supper and went to the basement. Mace and Erin moved to the couch in the living room and kissed for a few minutes before Erin decided to stop.

"See you in the morning, Mace."

"Night, Erin. Sleep well."

66

# Chapter Twelve

Annie rushed home after working a few hours at Mike Bushell's office because she decided to attend Howard Lombardi's wake with her father.

"Give me a few minutes and I'll go with you," she said as she raced to her bedroom.

"Take your time, sweetie," Dad said, which meant hurry up in Dad-speak.

She showered and decided to wear the only black dress she owned. She got dressed and brushed her hair. She glanced in her mirror, decided her hair was hopeless and walked to the living room where her father waited on the couch wearing one of his nicer black suits.

"Do I look all right, Daddy? My hair is such a mess."

"You look perfect, sweetie. Thank you for wearing a dress. You look so pretty when you dress up."

When Annie and her father arrived there was a long line of people waiting to pay their respects. Matt went earlier with his father, but they didn't stay too long. Annie missed Matt by a few minutes.

"You don't need to wait in line with me, Annie," Dad said. "Why don't you see if you can find your friends? They are probably around here somewhere."

"Thanks, Daddy. I'll see you later."

Annie looked around and saw Tony Bertucci.

"I'm going to go talk to Tony. He's over there and Emmy is with him."

Dad sighed and said,. "Well, you know where to find me if you need me."

"Don't leave without me, okay?"

"I wouldn't think of it," he answered.

Annie walked over to join Tony Bertucci. Emmy Colasanti was with him. She was holding his hand. Annie gave them both a hug. Their eyes were red from crying.

"I'm sorry for your loss, Tony. I know how much I cried when Grandma died and when Grandpa suffered his heart attack."

"Thanks, Annie. It's nice of you to come. Your grandfather's doing okay now, isn't he? He stopped by earlier before the crowd got here and he seemed okay. Just between you and me, I was always a little afraid of Principal O'Dell."

"Grandpa can be a little intimidating at school, but he's really sweet. And yes, he's fine. He is retired and keeping busy on the farm. You look very handsome in your suit, Tony."

"Thanks, Annie. You look nice, too."

"I like that dress, Annie. It fits you better than this one fits me. I borrowed it from Diane," Emmy told Annie.

"It looks all right, Emmy." Annie adjusted the shoulders a bit and smiled. "It might be a little big on you."

"At least it's not too short," Emmy said.

They were quiet for a moment until Annie mentioned, "Grandpa Liam is the only grandparent I have left. How about you, Emmy? Do you have any grandparents left."

"I still have one grandmother alive—Grandma Sandusky. She's ancient. I don't think Mom even knows how old she is and Grandma won't tell. She insists she's going to live to be a hundred."

"Grandpa Howard was my last one. The rest are all gone now. Grandma and Grandpa Bertucci have been gone for years. I don't remember them at all."

Annie looked up at Tony, smiled and said, "Daddy told me that Grandpa and your uncle Carmen went to school together. Daddy said they used to be good friends."

Tony nodded, looked at Emmy then back at Annie. "Uncle Carmen, your grandfather and Emmy's father were all in the same grade in school. That's kinda different. Your grandfather and Emmy's father are the same age."

"Mom and Dad were much older when they had me," Emmy said. "They've never said, but I was probably a surprise."

Derrick and Kristen Keasling joined them.

"Hi, Annie. Thanks for coming. Is your father here?" Kristen asked. "Mom said Uncle Carmen talked to your grandpa earlier."

"Daddy's waiting in line," Annie said as she pointed. "I

guess we'll be here for awhile."

Derrick smiled at Emmy. "I didn't realize there would be so many people here. The mayor was here and someone from the Governor's office."

"Daddy said all the local politicians and big shots would be here. I didn't realize your grandfather was so important," Annie said.

Derrick replied, "He was just Grandpa to us."

"Will you guys be all right if I take Emmy with me?" Kristen asked. "I want to get something to drink."

"We will manage somehow," Derrick answered teasingly.

"You should come with us, Annie. There's a room in back with some refreshments for the family."

"Maybe I shouldn't, Kristen. I'm not family," Annie said.

"Don't be silly. That's just what Emmy said. No one will care if I bring my friends with me."

Kristen took Emmy and Annie to the room with the refreshments. They got some water and a few cookies and sat at a table in the corner.

"Did you know Grandpa Lombardi well, Emmy?" Annie asked.

"I met him a couple times, but I didn't know him."

"I didn't remember, but I met him a few times, too, when I was with Daddy. I was just a kid."

Emmy took a sip of water, then sighed. "I didn't even know he was blind for all practical purposes. I feel so stupid that I didn't know."

"What? He was blind. Get out! I met him and he didn't seem handicapped at all. When did he lose his sight? Did the cancer cause it?"

"No, it was another disease and it happened about two years ago," Kristen told Annie. "Up until a few days ago, he could see a little bit of light. He couldn't see enough to recognize anyone, but his hearing was okay."

"Well then, I feel stupid, too. I never realized he was blind. Of course, he was just sitting in a chair when I saw him."

"Grandpa Howard fooled a lot of people. He was too proud

and stubborn to become dependent on other people," Kristen said with pride. "He would tell me about President Roosevelt and how he was crippled but didn't complain."

"I didn't know Teddy Roosevelt was crippled," Emmy said.

"No, the other one," Kristen said. "Teddy Roosevelt is who our high school was named for. Grandpa knew Franklin Delano Roosevelt."

"See! I'm stupid." Emmy decided to tell Annie another story that might embarrass her. "I didn't realize Kristen and Tony were cousins for the longest time. I thought they were friends because of the business their fathers started."

"I'm sure there are lots of kids at school who never knew that, Emmy. Didn't they ever tell you?"

"I thought I told her, but I guess I either didn't or Emmy didn't hear me," Kristen said. "Everyone just assumed she knew, so no one actually thought it was necessary to mention it."

"That's kinda funny. You guys are so close."

"Emmy is like my sister and best friend all in one." Kristen smiled at Emmy.

"I grew up with Lainey and Cindy and we were always close, but we don't see each other much anymore. We live in the same dorm, but they are roommates and are always together. Plus, they're both in serious relationships now. I probably won't see them much this summer."

"Are things okay with you and Matt?" Kristen asked.

Annie smiled and Emmy grabbed her hand. "I know you guys are in love. I know a little about how Matt was before, but he seems to have changed. He reminds me of Rory Porter in some ways."

"If you don't want to talk about that we understand," Kristen said.

"It's okay, Kristen. I know he was pretty wild. Everyone assumes he slept with every girl he dated, but that's not the case. He wasn't an angel—don't get me wrong," Annie said. "But he didn't bother to refute most of the rumors about him."

"He is charming, Annie," Emmy said.

"Are you seeing anyone special, Kristen?" Annie asked.

70

Kristen shook her head. "I don't want to get involved in anything serious yet. I have been dating some guys from North Park, but haven't met anyone that I would want to spent the rest of my life with."

Emmy looked around as more people entered the room. "Should we go see if Tony and Derrick are okay?"

"You just don't want to be apart from Tony for very long, Em," Kristen teased.

"I just want to be there if he needs anything," Emmy whispered.

Kristen and Annie smiled at each other. They understood how much Tony meant to Emmy. They headed back and found Tony and Derrick sitting on a couch in the hallway. Tony held out his hands and Emmy took them in hers. Kristen plopped down on the couch between the guys. Annie stood next to Emmy. Soon Annie felt hands on her shoulders. She didn't need to look to know it was her father.

"I'm ready to go anytime you are, sweetie."

"Okay. Please give me a minute, Daddy."

"Take your time. I'll be waiting over there by the door."

Annie waited until her father was out of hearing range. "I guess I should go. I'm sorry again about your grandfather."

The guys got up and hugged Annie. She could feel Tony's strength even though he hugged her gently.

Derrick told her, "We appreciate you coming, Annie. Tell Matthew thanks and I'm sorry I missed him."

"We should get together more often. Maybe we can double date sometime," Tony said.

Annie nodded. "I think I would like that, Tony. It would have to be on a Sunday because of our work schedules. Matty is so busy. I'll call you and we can plan something."

Tony stood behind Emmy with his hands on her shoulders. Annie realized how tiny she was compared to Tony. Annie hugged Emmy one more time before she rejoined her father and they left.

# Chapter Thirteen

On Thursday, Erin and Franny took Mace to some of the nearby tourist attractions. They spent the morning in Kearney and after lunch decided to go to North Platte, about a hundred miles away.

"What is there in North Platte worth seeing?" Mace asked while driving along I-80.

"I want to take you to the Fort Cody Trading Post," Erin replied. "It's mostly a tourist trap, but I like to check out the Native American jewelry."

"Would you buy me a cowboy hat to take back to SoHam?"

"Do you really want a cowboy hat?" Erin asked.

"Reed wears one and he pulls off the look."

Erin shook her head and laughed.

"What?" Mace asked.

"I was picturing you in a cowboy hat with a big Afro."

Mace drove while Erin sat in the front seat. Franny stayed in the backseat and tried to sleep during the boring trip along I-80.

"We need to take the next exit," Erin said while pointing to a sign. "It's just off the Interstate."

Mace slowed down and took the exit.

"Turn here and it's that building over there that looks like a fort," Erin said.

Mace pulled into the parking lot, they got out and Mace grinned. "Do I need to be afraid of getting attacked by Indians?"

Erin looked at Franny and rolled her eyes. "We can only hope."

Erin showed Mace some of the jewelry she liked. They wound their way around the crowded store for an hour.

"Let's go outside and check out the giant Indian," Franny suggested.

"What?" Mace asked.

Franny grabbed his arm and pulled him outside into the large backyard. "See over there?"

"Ah, I get it. It's a statue."

"Duh!" Franny teased.

Since they were away from home and parents, they were free to talk about anything and everything. Franny asked both Erin and Mace many questions about their sex life as they walked around checking out the covered wagons and other pieces of the Old West..

"Are you turning red, Mace?" Franny asked. "Is it possible for you to blush?"

"Guys are always accused of talking about sex all the time, but girls are worse," Mace said. "How can you ask how long we take to make love?"

"When I have sex, I want to make sure I don't get cheated out of my time," Franny said and then giggled.

"Are you going to sleep with Reed?" Erin asked.

"Not yet. I might when we have been together for a year or more. I'm not ready to do that yet. It just makes relationships more complicated. I might even wait until I'm in college."

"Do you know where you want to go to college, Franny?" Erin asked.

"I've been thinking about North Park," Franny answered. "Would it bother you if I came to SoHam for college?"

"I would love it. We could be together for two years at school."

"We wouldn't have to be roommates. It might even be better if we aren't."

"I can't imagine having a better roommate than Annie O'Dell—except maybe Mace," Erin said.

"I don't think the college is that liberal," Mace replied. He glanced around to make sure no one could hear their conversation.

"Have you seen enough, Mace?" Erin asked.

He nodded and they headed back inside.

"You should come to SoHam, and visit me this year. I've got an idea," Erin said. "I'm going back two weeks before classes start. You could come with me then and see the campus. I'm going to stay with Annie and her grandfather out at the farm. I'm sure there is an extra bedroom."

"That would be fun. School doesn't start until late this year," Franny said. Then she grinned at Mace. "Maybe you could set me up with a friend so I could have a meaningless sexual relationship."

Erin knew Franny was teasing Mace so she played along. "That's a great idea, Franny. It would be better to gain some sexual experience with someone you might never see again."

Mace shifted his attention from one sister to the other.

"There are plenty of guys to choose from, Franny. Do you have a particular type in mind?" Erin asked and kept a straight face.

"He would have to be handsome and taller than me. It would be nice if his thing was bigger than average," Franny said while looking at Mace.

"That's it! I'm out of here. I'm not setting you up with someone just to get laid, Franny," Mace said as he walked out of the Fort Cody Trading Post.

Erin and Franny giggled and then ran after him.

"Mace, I'm sorry. We were only teasing you," Erin said.

Franny grinned and then shook her head. "I was dead serious. I want to lose my virginity to a college hunk like you, Mace."


"What time do you have to be at work, Erin?" Mace asked as he finished his biscuits and gravy on Friday morning.

"I start at nine and have to work eight hours," she answered. "I will get a half hour for lunch if you want to meet me somewhere."

Franny walked into the kitchen and sat down. "I don't have to work until this afternoon. Mace and I could do something."

Mace smiled at Franny, then turned to look at Erin. "What? Why are you frowning at me?"

"I'm frowning at both of you."

"Why me?" Franny asked. "I'm trying to make sure Mace doesn't get bored."

"You could get dressed before you come out to the kitchen," Erin said.

Franny looked at her pajamas. "I'm covered. Mace can't see anything."

Mace glanced at Franny's pajamas.

"Mace!" Erin hollered.

He shrugged. "She's right. I can't see anything."

Erin rolled her eyes. "Go ahead and do whatever you guys want. I need to get going. Mom! I'm ready to go."

Mrs. Bezick walked into the kitchen and held out a sales paper. "Erin's father and I are going grocery shopping. Would you and Franny like to join us?" she asked Mace.

Franny shook her head. "Mom! Why on earth would I want to spend anymore time in that place than I have to? I'm sure Mace would rather do something else than buy groceries."

"Do you have any requests for dinner tonight, Mace?" Mrs. Bezick asked.

"I'm always good for fried chicken and mashed potatoes," Mace answered.

"That's what we'll have. We will eat when the girls get home from work. Eddie will probably hang out with his friends. He might eat with us, or he might not. There's usually a ballgame somewhere around Kearney."

Mr. and Mrs. Bezick took Erin with them to the store. Eddie disappeared after grabbing a quick breakfast.

Franny got dressed and came back out to the kitchen. Mace looked at her shorts and t-shirt.

"What would you like to do? We could see if the pool's open. Did you bring trunks?"

He shook his head as he checked out Franny's legs. "I didn't think to bring any."

"Too bad. I bought a new bikini last week and I haven't had a chance to wear it yet," Franny said. "I could model it for you if you want."

"Maybe you better not, " Mace said. "We could go for a walk."

"Are you afraid to spend time in the house alone with me?" Franny asked.

"I'm not afraid, but you are pretty cute and I don't want to give Erin any reason not to trust me," he said.

"Erin told me you had sex before you guys did it."

75

Mace lifted his eyebrows. "Yes, but I didn't know her then."

"Would you have gone out with that girl if you knew Erin back then?"

Mace shook his head. He and Franny went for a walk and killed a couple of hours. Mace ate lunch with Franny and the parents. Then Franny left for work and Mace wondered what he would do all afternoon.

Eddie came home grabbed a bite to eat and saw Mace in the backyard. "Hey! You want to go with me? One of my friends bought a hot rod and he's trying to get it in shape for the drag races."

Mace shrugged. "Sure, why not? I don't know much about cars, but I can watch."

By the time Mace and Eddie returned to the house the girls were home from work and dinner was about ready. After dinner, Mace helped Erin clear the table and do the dishes.

"Reed called and wants to take me to a movie. You guys want to come with?" Franny asked Mace and Erin.

"Your call, Erin."

"Might as well. If we stay here, we'll end up playing Monopoly again."

Saturday was Mace's last day with Erin and her family. He needed to catch the train in Holdrege at one o'clock in the morning on Sunday. The family ate breakfast together and then Erin's parents left to spend most of the day at several auctions and estate sales. Erin helped him get his laundry done, then Mace packed for the return trip.

Franny walked into Eddie's room and saw Mace packing. "Now's your chance. Mom and Dad are gone. Eddie's working and I'm going over to Viola's to spend the afternoon. I have to work three hours later tonight."

Franny meant her friend Viola Okwara.

"Just remember to change the sheets if you do anything," Franny said and then grinned. "Have fun."

For the first time since arriving in Nebraska, Mace found

76

himself alone in the house with Erin. He closed his suitcase, grinned at Erin and kissed her. "Your place or mine?" he asked.

"My place. I would feel too weird if we used Eddie's bed."

Mace kissed her again.

The moment was spoiled when Grandma and Grandpa Bezick walked through the front door. "Harold! Lois! Are we too late to catch a ride?"

"Who's that?" Mace asked as he broke off the kiss.

"Shoot! That's Grandma and Grandpa. They must have wanted to go to the auction."

"Or else your mother told them to come over and check up on us," Mace said.

Erin ran out to the living room. "Hi, Grandma. They left already. Do you know where they were going?"

Grandpa shook his head and held out his arms to hug Erin. "No idea. Where's this boyfriend of yours? I hear he's half black."

"Grandpa!" Erin exclaimed.

"I'm right here, sir," Mace said as he walked into the room.

"I hear you've been treating my granddaughter well. I appreciate that. Tell me about yourself." Grandpa motioned to the couch.

Mace sighed and spent the next hour talking to Grandpa and Grandma. Any thought of even kissing Erin had been blown to smithereens.

Grandma and Grandpa stayed for dinner and ended up playing bridge with their son and daughter-in-law. They insisted Erin and Mace watch and learn how to play the game. Mace surrendered any hope of ever kissing Erin again.

"Mom, it's time I took Mace to Holdrege. He has to catch his train," Erin said around eleven o'clock.

Dad checked the time. "Franny, since Eddie isn't here you have to go with your sister. I don't want her driving home by herself this late at night. I would go with you, but I'm sure Erin will want to have some time to say goodbye without me or her mother around."

"I don't mind," Franny said, then turned away from her father and rolled her eyes. *Ya think.*

"Thank you for your hospitality, Mr. and Mrs. Bezick. It was nice to meet you and everything," Mace said.

"You're welcome to come and see us anytime, Mace," Mrs. Bezick said.

Mace got a hug from Erin's mom and a handshake from her father. Franny and Erin drove Mace to the station. They arrived early with an hour to wait. They sat on a bench and talked until the train was almost there.

"It was nice to meet you, Franny. I hope you come back with Erin later. We might be able to find a sexy guy for you to... meet."

"That sounds like fun," Franny hugged Mace and kissed his cheek.

Mace held her close and whispered in her ear, "You deserve better than Reed whatever his name was. Don't settle for him."

"I won't. I hope I can find a guy like you, Mace."

Mace released Franny, then kissed her cheek. He turned to Erin and held her. Franny moved a few feet away to allow her sister some privacy.

"I'm sorry we didn't get to do what I know you wanted, Mace."

"It's all right, Erin. I would feel guilty if we had. Your parents and Franny and Eddie are special. I'm so glad I got to meet them. I can't wait until you get back to SoHam though."

Mace kissed Erin and held her in his arms until he needed to board the train. He waved goodbye from his seat as the train left the station.

Franny put her arm around Erin's waist as the train departed and asked, "Did you guys ever... you know?"

Erin shook her head. "Something always interrupted us and when we did have a chance, it didn't feel right."

"Do you love Mace?" Franny asked.

Erin smiled.

# Chapter Fourteen

"What time are you supposed to pick up Mace, honey?" Dad asked Annie from the doorway of her bedroom on Saturday morning.

"I think he's supposed to get in around four. He told me he would call me when he's here," Annie answered as she picked up some of her dirty clothes from the floor.

"Are you hungry? Do you want some breakfast?"

She shook her head. "Not really. My stomach feels kinda queasy."

"Are you all right? You're not coming down with something are you?" Dad asked as he put a hand to her forehead. "You don't feel warm."

"I don't think so. It might just be nerves."

"Is there something bothering you that you want to talk about?" Dad asked as he sat on the edge of her bed.

Annie sat next to him and he put an arm around her shoulders. "It might be the pills I'm taking. Mom said that sometimes they affect different girls differently. I might need to go back to the doctor and try a different one."

"If you need to go, do you want Elisabeth to take you?" Dad asked.

Annie looked up at her father. "I would feel better if she did, Daddy."

"That's all right. I'm not upset by that at all. I think it's great that you and Elisabeth are becoming even closer than before."

"I know you'd rather I wasn't on the pill at all but..."

"I'm just glad that you aren't rushing into anything, sweetie." He kissed Annie on the top of her head. "And I'm glad Matty isn't pressuring you either."

"I'm going to pick up Matty after I get Mace. He's only working until four. We're going out to the farm to help Grandpa for a couple hours."

"Tell him I said hi. Do you have plans for this morning?"

"I told Lainey and Cindy I would go shopping with them. Why? Do you need me to do anything?" she asked while setting her laundry basket on the floor in front of her closet.

"No, have a fun day. It might be pretty late before I get home, but I will come home tonight."

Annie parked in the street at the Mackens home. She got out and before she could get to the front door Maddy Mackens ran out to greet her.

"Hi, Annie. Can I go with you guys? I want to go shopping, too, but Cindy says I'm too young."

"I don't think you are too young, Maddy, but it's not my decision to make."

"I'm fourteen now. I just had my birthday and Cindy doesn't want me to go because she and Lainey are going to talk about their boyfriends. I know what they've been doing. I'm not a child."

"You can go if your mother agrees, but you have to stay with me," Annie said.

"Good! I'll ask Mom."

Maddy ran back in the house to find her mother. She ran past Cindy and Elaine. Annie followed close behind.

Cindy looked at Annie. "Tell me you didn't say she could come with us."

"I told her she needed to ask your mother. That's all."

"Mom will give in to her. She always does," Cindy said then sighed.

"So what?" Annie shrugged. "I told Maddy she would have to stay with me if she went. She thinks you and Lainey just want to talk about sex."

"That's not true," Cindy insisted.

"Come on. I know you guys are going to talk about it. Maddy is just curious."

"She's too young..."

"Have you forgotten what it was like to be her age already. You were just like her when you were that age, Cindy."

Maddy came running out of the kitchen with her mother trailing behind. "Mom said I could go and you have to be nice to me."

Cindy put her hands on her hips. "Mom! Does she have to

80

go? Why do you always give in to her?"

"Would you please take her along? She needs to buy some new clothes for school and I haven't had time to take her."

"All right, but if she gives me any grief, I'm going to leave her at the mall," Cindy said as she frowned at Maddy.

Cindy and Elaine got in the backseat and Maddy sat up front with Annie. The new mall where they wanted to go was fifteen minutes away. Maddy talked to Annie about how excited she was to be in high school.

"I can't wait for school to start, Annie. It will be so exciting to be at Roosevelt."

"It's a big place, Maddy. It might take a while to find your way around."

"I've been there enough times to know where everything is. I won't get lost."

"Just remember it takes several minutes to get through the hall between classes. It's even more crowded than when we were there."

In the back seat Cindy and Elaine talked about their boyfriends, Adrien Coyle and Bryce Harper. Elaine and Adrien were officially engaged now, but they hadn't set a date for the wedding. Elaine was thinking they would wait until she graduated, but Adrien didn't want to wait that long.

Cindy asked Elaine, "When is Adrien leaving for Kansas City?"

"He has to be there by the beginning of August, the third, I think, so he's going to leave on Saturday the first. We still have a little time to be together yet. Did Bryce ever find another guy to share the apartment?"

"No, they decided it wouldn't work because there are only three bedrooms."

"Why did they even need a fourth guy?" Elaine asked. "They knew there were only three bedrooms."

"Just to cut down the expenses. Christopher and Randy were going to share one of the rooms, but Bryce decided they could manage all right with just the three of them."

"That makes it easier for you and Bryce to be together. You

81

can get all lovey dovey."

"I heard that, Lainey!" Maddy shouted from the front seat.

"You just mind your own business, Maddy Mackens!" Cindy shouted. "Do you want me to tell Mom that you kissed Paul Rooney the other day."

"Go ahead! I'll just deny it. Mom will believe me."

Cindy said, "I'm not going to be spending any time in Bryce's apartment anyway."

"I won't tell if you do, Cindy. I like Bryce. He's funny and he likes to tease me," Maddy said then turned back around to talk with Annie again and let her sister talk to Elaine.

"Do you know what your schedule is going to be yet?" Annie asked.

"Not yet. Registration isn't until the tenth and eleventh. Will I find out where my locker is then?"

"You should. If you want I could get you into school and show you just where it is," Annie said as she waited at a red light.

"I hope it's in a good spot so I can make it to my classes on time."

"Most of your classes should be on the first and second floor."

When they got to the mall, Annie helped Maddy pick out some new clothes. Annie didn't try on anything but did see a dress that she thought Matty would like.

Matty called her on his break. "Hey, Annie. How has your day been?"

"All right. I went shopping with Lainey and Cindy. Maddy came with us. She is growing up so fast. Do you know she is taller than me already?"

"She's starting high school, right?"

"Hard to believe, but yeah. She picked out some new clothes for school. Lainey and Cindy found a couple things to buy."

"Did you buy anything?" Matt asked.

"No, I saw this dress in Lane Stuart's that I thought you would like, but I didn't buy it."

"Why not? You can buy new clothes, too."

82

"I would have, but it was too expensive. It was over a hundred dollars," Annie said.

"Maybe tomorrow I will take you back there and buy it for you."

"You don't have to do that, Matty."

"I like buying you new things, Annie."

"You should spend your money on Jennifer."

"Oh, I got a call from Joni today at work. Both she and Beverly got jobs in the same school district in Peoria. They will be moving soon."

"Are you sad about that?"

"I'm happy for them, but I won't be able to see Jennifer very often. That's probably for the best though."

"You will always be her father, Matty."

"Her biological father, yeah, but not a real father to her. Ya know, Annie, I would feel worse if Jennifer had been a boy. I think a boy needs a father around. Maybe a daughter can get by without a father easier than a son could.

"I grew up all right without a mother around," Annie said. "Doesn't mean I didn't miss her."

"Yes, you did. You are so lucky that you have the best father in the world."

"I'll tell him you said so, Matty," Annie said then chuckled.

"Maybe you shouldn't. He might think I was just trying to flatter him for some reason. I should get back to work now."

"Okay, I'll pick you up after I get Mace."

"Just be careful at the train station, Annie. Your father told me someone's been stealing purses down there."

"I will be all right."

"See you later. I love you."

"Love you, too."

## Chapter Fifteen

Mace arrived at the SoHam train station just after four and called Annie. It took her twenty minutes to get to the station. She picked him up and Mace seemed a little too quiet.

"Well! Are you gonna tell me how it was, or do I have to torture you?" She poked his side as he buckled his seat belt.

"I had a great time. Erin's family is super nice. Her parents are..."

"That's not what I want to hear and you know it. Did you and Erin... you know."

"No, it just wouldn't have felt right to do it at her home with her parents around."

"So they don't know?"

"Only her sister Franny knows for sure. Eddie has his suspicions, but her parents don't know yet."

"What is Franny like? Erin talks about her quite often. I think Erin misses her when she's here."

"Franny looks a lot like Erin. Same green or gray eyes. I can never tell what color they are for sure. Same brown hair."

"Does Franny wear a headband like Erin used to?"

"I never saw her wearing one, but Erin was wearing one again. Franny wants to go to school here and I think she might come with Erin at the end of summer."

"That would be terrific. Does Franny have a boyfriend? How tall is she, by the way?" Annie asked.

"She's going out with an older guy, but I don't think it's too serious. I told her not to settle for him because I think he's kind of a jerk. I think he just wants to get in her pants."

"So she's like me then."

"Whadda you mean, like you?"

"She's a virgin, silly!"

"Are you still..."

Annie smacked Mace's arm. "You didn't answer my question."

"What was it again?"

"How tall is she?"

84

"Oh, that one. She's a couple inches shorter than Erin so she would be two or three inches taller than you. She is heavier."

"And you know this because?"

"I picked her up and gave her a hug when I left. That's why. She is a lot like Erin except maybe a little more interested in boys than what Erin was. That's what her mother told me anyway."

"I hope she comes with Erin. I want to meet her."

"Why are we going to Matt's house? Isn't he working today?"

"Yes and no. He worked the early morning shift and got off at two," Annie answered.

Annie stopped at the Sullivan house and picked up Matt.

"Hey, Mace. How was your trip?"

"It was all right, but I couldn't ever live there. Kearney is out in the middle of nowhere. I would go nuts."

"Did her parents like you?" Matt asked.

"I got along great with them. Her mom is nice. Erin has a younger sister named Francine who looks a lot like her."

"Everyone called her Franny," Annie told Matt.

"Don't get mad at me for asking but did they seem all right with your... color?"

"I never sensed any hint of prejudice from her family at all. There were a few people I met that thought Erin shouldn't be with me."

"Some people are just ignorant, Mace. I certainly don't know how that must feel but I've never... well... I guess I've never thought much about your ethnic background. I don't mean that in a bad way. I guess I have always thought of you as Mace Franklin and as a friend," Matt said.

"Hey, let's not get all mushy or something. I know you're my friend. I don't hold it against you that you're Irish," Mace replied.

"Will you two knock it off before I throw up."

"Is your stomach bothering you again, Annie?"

"Just a little bit in the mornings."

Mace looked at Annie, then at Matthew. "Annie Mercer is there something you're not telling me?" Mace asked as he put a

85

hand on her shoulder.

"I've just been feeling queasy in the mornings lately." Annie realized what Mace was thinking. She smacked his arm again. Harder this time though. "Mace Franklin, I am not pregnant! I'm just having a reaction to some medication I'm taking."

"You mean the 'pill' you're on."

Annie looked at him. "How did you know?"

"I told him, Annie. I didn't think it would matter if Mace knew," Matt admitted."

"I guess it doesn't. Anyway, that's why my stomach's been feeling funny. I am going to see if Mom will go with me to the doctor sometime if this keeps up."

Annie dropped Mace off at his house. She and Matt spent a few minutes talking to Keyshon.

"Grandpa told me we could go fishing. Are you going out to the farm to see him?"

"Yes, we are. Do you want to come with us?"

"I need to pack my clothes first. I'll be ready in a couple minutes."

Mom walked up to them holding his backpack. "I have your bag ready, Keyshon. You have a good time with Grandpa."

"I will, Mom. We're going fishing in the lake. Do you want me to bring a fish home to eat for dinner?"

"Maybe you should just catch the fish, then put them back in the lake so they can swim around," Mom suggested.

"Okay, I'll do that."

Elisabeth watched as Keyshon walked out to the car with Matt and Annie.

Keyshon looked at Matt and Annie. "Are you married to my Annie now, Matthew Sullivan?"

"No, Keyshon. We haven't gotten married yet, but I do love her a lot."

"Good! I love her a lot, too. You can go ahead and marry her. I will find someone else to get married to someday."

"Thank you, Keyshon. I appreciate that."

Matt hugged Keyshon, then Annie did, too. She whispered in his ear. "Any girl would be lucky to have you for a boyfriend,

Keyshon. You are the sweetest young man in the world."

"And the best looking, too!" Keyshon boasted.

"Yes, you are the best looking, too, little buddy."

"I'm not so little anymore Annie. I'm taller than you now."

"You don't have to rub it in. Come on. We have to get to the farm so I can put you to work before it gets dark."

"Not me!" Keyshon shook his head. "I'm going fishing with Grandpa. You and Matthew Sullivan have to do the chores."

"Grandpa might make you do some chores, too, Keyshon. You need to help around the house," Annie said.

"I will, Annie. If Grandpa asks me to."

"I know you will," Annie said as she smiled at him.

"Hi, Grandpa! Where are you?" Annie asked as she and Matt walked into the house.

"In the kitchen, Annie. I was just finishing my supper. I have some leftovers in the fridge in case you get hungry later."

"I know it's late, but Matty and I are here to help with the chores and we brought Keyshon with us. That way you don't have to go into town to get him."

"Where is my fishing buddy?" Grandpa asked.

Matt pointed outside. "He's digging up worms."

"Maybe you should tell him that I already have enough bait for us to use."

"I'll go tell him, Grandpa."

"Thanks, Matty."

Grandpa hugged Annie and she kissed his cheek. "How are you feeling today?"

"I feel good. I feel ten years younger. How are you, Annie? Your father told me you have been a little under the weather lately."

"I'm all right. It's just this new medication I'm taking."

"You don't have to hide it from me, child. I know you are on the pill."

"Grandpa!"

"I may be old, but I'm not totally ignorant. I must say I wish you would wait until you are older and married, but it is your decision to make."

"I haven't done anything yet. I just wanted to be prepared in case I do. I'm still your sweet and innocent granddaughter."

"You will always be sweet and innocent to me." Grandpa hugged her. "Even when you are a mother yourself."

"I love you, Grandpa. Have fun with Keyshon. Matty and I will be here for awhile, but we will have to take Keyshon home at some point."

"There is a list on the fridge. You can do whatever you like as far as the chores go."

Grandpa and Keyshon spent an hour and a half fishing until Grandpa took him home.

Matt and Annie completed many of the chores before it got too dark. They returned the list to the fridge.

"Do you want to see what Grandpa has here for dinner or would you rather get something at home or the Lion?" Annie asked Matt.

"Can we eat at your house? Do you have any leftovers?"

"I made some stuffed green peppers last night. There's some of that left."

"Sounds good," Matt said.

It took about a half hour to get home from the farm. Annie heated up the leftover stuffed green peppers and put together a salad while Matt showered. Annie was letting him use a drawer of her dresser for some of his clothes. He hung a couple of shirts in her closet. Matt was in the shower when Annie walked into the bathroom.

"Dinner is ready, Matty. I made a salad and heated up the leftovers. Why aren't you out of the shower yet? And why was the bathroom door open?"

"I guess I just forgot to close it. I'll be done in a minute."

Annie looked around the bathroom. "Where's your towel? Were you going to air dry or something?"

"Shoot! I forgot to grab one. Will you get a clean towel for me, sweetie?"

"Maybe I should make you get it yourself."

"Annie! Come on. Be nice. I'd get you a towel if you needed one."

"I wouldn't forget my towel," Annie said.

"Please! Would you grab me a towel?"

"Okay, just give me a minute. Are you gonna stay in the shower or are you gonna get out?"

"I'm gonna stay in here until I have a towel."

"Fine! Be that way," Annie teased Matt. She got a towel from the linen closet and set it on the toilet. "Here's your towel, Matty. Hurry while the food is warm."

He stuck his head out. "Be there as soon as I can."

Matt got ready and joined Annie in the kitchen. She had a plate ready for him and was sitting at the island eating.

"This smells good. I didn't know you knew how to make this."

"I never made it before. I just used a recipe. How does it taste?"

"Let you know in a second." Matt tried a couple of bites and smiled at Annie. "Not bad for your first try."

Annie glared at him. "Now that you've tried the salad, how about the stuffed peppers?"

"Oh, you wanted me to try the peppers."

"Smart-ass!" She stuck out her tongue at him.

Matt tried the stuffed peppers and smiled. "They're good Annie. Just as good as the ones at the Lion."

"Thanks, it's the same recipe. I just wanted to know if I could do as good a job as the chefs at the restaurant."

Matt's cell phone rang and he saw it was his father calling. "What's up?"

"I hate to ruin your evening, but Charlie called in. He was in a minor accident. Could you cover for a few hours?"

"Sure, Dad. I'll be there as soon as Annie can get me there."

Matt finished his dinner and changed his shirt. Annie drove him to The Hungry Lion and went inside to say hi to his father.

"Hi, Mr. Sullivan. How's business?"

"Hi, Annie. Not too bad today, but it's been a slow week. How are your father and grandfather doing?"

"They're both doing all right. Grandpa spends most of his time fishing. He took Keyshon Franklin with him today."

"I know Keyshon. Nice kid."

"See you later, Mr. Sullivan. I'm gonna pick Matty up later. Oh, the stuffed peppers turned out rather nicely. Matty liked them. He actually thought I made them."

"I knew you got them from here," Matt said.

"Yeah, sure you did. You thought I made them from scratch and don't try to convince me otherwise. Call me when you're ready to come home," Annie said and then blushed as she looked up at Mr. Sullivan. "I mean to my house."

Annie gave Matt a kiss and took off.

Cormac Sullivan looked at his son.

"What?" Matt asked.

"She's in love with you."

Matt smiled. "And I'm in love with her, Dad."

"Good. She's a keeper," Cormac Sullivan said as he slapped Matt on the back.

Annie left the house at eleven thirty to pick up Matt at The Hungry Lion. She pulled into the parking lot and parked several rows away but under a light at least. She got out and locked her car. *Judging by how many cars are here, I would say the place is still pretty busy.* Annie thought as she walked inside. She heard music and loud conversations coming from the bar side of the place. She looked around for Matt and waved when she saw him coming out of the kitchen.

He spotted her, waved back and hurried up to the front.

"Hi, Matty. I'll wait here for you."

Matt gave Annie a kiss on the cheek. "I won't be too long, Annie. I just need to talk to my father before I leave."

Matt spent a few minutes talking to his father, then joined Annie.

"Are you hungry, Matty?"

"Not really. I ate a sandwich earlier. Let's go home. I'm tired. It's been a long week."

Annie smiled because Matt referred to her house as home.

Twenty minutes later Annie pulled into the driveway and saw her father's new Honda minivan parked in front of the garage. She and Matt walked in through the back door.

Dad looked up when he heard them. "Where have you been?"

Matt explained about having to go back to work.

"Hi, Daddy! How was your day? Catch any hardened criminals?"

"No, but I did arrest this old lady for jaywalking."

"I hope you threw the book at her. You can't let them get away with jaywalking. The next thing you know she will be having illegal garage sales." Annie pointed a finger at Matt and shook it as she joked with her father.

Matt shrugged. "I never jaywalk."

"I booked her and tossed her in the tank with a bunch of other old lady murderers and other creeps.

"Good for you, Daddy."

"I'm just doing my part to keep SoHam safe for the drug dealers and other fine upstanding young citizens of our fair city."

Matt shook his head. "I'm starting to get used to your sense of humor, Annie. You and your father should be comedians."

"Are you hungry or did you eat already?" Annie asked her father.

"I ate dinner with Elisabeth and Grandpa. Keyshon wore my ears off talking about fishing. I'm going to bed. It's been a long week."

"That's the second time I've heard that from the so called 'men' in my life," Annie said as she put her hands on her hips. "What's up? I'm not ready to go to bed yet."

"You can stay up, Annie, but I'm going to bed," Matt said.

"Fine! The air mattress is already in my room. I'll be up for a while longer."

Both Matt and her father kissed Annie good night on the cheek and headed to bed. They were both asleep within ten minutes. Annie checked on them later and changed into her pajamas. She stayed up to read for another thirty minutes before going to bed herself. She kissed Matt but he didn't wake up.

# Chapter Sixteen

"Daddy, are you going to sleep all day? It's already nine."

Her father opened his eyes and looked at Annie. "I suppose I should get out of bed. Is that breakfast I smell?"

"Yes, and it's about done. Now get out of bed and get dressed. We have a full day ahead of us."

Annie kissed her father on the forehead and returned to the kitchen. Her father got up, used the bathroom, showered and got dressed. Annie walked into her bedroom where Matty was still asleep on the air mattress. She knelt and kissed his cheek.

"Are you going to sleep all day, too. Breakfast is about ready so get up."

Matt grabbed her wrist and held onto her. He sat up and kissed her on the mouth.

"Stop that! You haven't brushed your teeth yet."

"I still want to kiss you." Matt grabbed her around her waist and pulled her on top of him. He was kissing her when her father walked into the room. Annie was still in her pajamas.

"Annie, will you leave Matthew alone and take care of breakfast before it burns."

Annie squealed as Matt tickled her side. "He's the one who was holding me and not letting me go."

"Annie, how can you say that? I was just sleeping and not doing anything wrong when you came in here and jumped on me. You were trying to make me kiss you and who knows what else."

"Annie! How could you do that to Matt," Daddy teased.

Annie managed to get away from Matthew and stood up. "You men are insufferable. I don't know why I'm even cooking for you." Annie stormed off to the kitchen to finish breakfast.

Matt and Mr. O'Dell looked at each other and laughed.

"She woke me up a few minutes ago. Do you know what she has planned for today?" Dad asked. "She said something about 'a full day ahead of us,' but I'm not sure what she meant."

"I don't know either. I suppose I better find out."

Matt got up and went into the kitchen. Annie was busy by the stove so Matt came up behind her and held her shoulders. He kissed the top of her head.

"Good morning, sweetheart. Did you sleep well?"

"Yes, I did but not nearly as long as you or Daddy. I had to get up and start cooking."

"It smells delicious, Annie."

Annie turned to face Matt. She looked down at his boxers. "Will you put some clothes on, Matthew Sullivan? What if Daddy came in here and saw you like that."

Matt smiled deviously and pressed against Annie.

"Stop that or you won't be getting any breakfast."

"Maybe I want something else..."

Annie's father walked in the room and cleared his throat. Annie looked around Matt at her father.

"Hi, Daddy. Matty was just going to get dressed. Breakfast will be done in a couple minutes. There is coffee."

Matt walked around the kitchen island in the opposite direction so Det. O'Dell didn't see him from the front.

"What are these big plans of yours for today, sweetie?"

"Okay, since you are off today and Elisabeth isn't working and Mace and Keyshon aren't doing anything, I want us all to go to the zoo. How about it?" Annie asked.

"That would be all right with me. What did Matt say?"

"I haven't asked him yet, but I'm sure he will agree to go."

"If he wants to spend the day with you that is," Dad said then grinned.

"Yeah, well, I guess so."

"What time do you want to leave?"

"I thought if we got there by eleven that would give us enough time to see everything, then come back here and make dinner. Can we grill out tonight?"

He shrugged. "Don't see why not. What do you want for dinner?"

"Burgers and dogs. Maybe a chicken breast for Mom. We could pick up some potato salad from the store and I could make baked beans."

"Sounds okay to me, Annie. Should I call Elisabeth and inform her of 'her' plans?"

93

"We can eat first. I'll tell Matty. Just help yourself to however much you want. It might have to last you until dinner."

Annie headed down the hallway to the bathroom. She knocked on the door and opened it. Matt wore a towel around his waist as he brushed his teeth. Annie moved behind him and put her hands on the towel.

"Should I take this towel away from you?"

"Go ahead. I have my underwear on."

"Party pooper!" Annie sighed in resignation. "I want to go to the zoo today with everyone."

"Even Grandpa?" Matt asked.

"Everyone except Grandpa. He told me no because it was too much walking for him."

"Sounds all right to me. Can I finish getting ready now?"

Annie smacked his butt and walked away. Matt held onto his towel carefully because he wasn't totally honest about what was under it.

Daddy and Matt cleaned up the kitchen after breakfast, so Annie could shower and get dressed.

Detective O'Dell called Elisabeth.

"Hi, Keith. How are you this morning?"

"Doing fine. Annie made a delicious breakfast and she informed me we all want to go to the zoo today, then have dinner over here this evening."

"She must be a mind reader. I was thinking that very thing," Elisabeth said.

"Really?"

"No, not really, but it does sound like fun. I know Keyshon would like it. Not so sure if Mace will go along though."

"Annie wants to be there by eleven so we can get home early enough to use the grill."

"Keyshon and I will be ready, but I won't make any promises about Mace."

"I'll pick you up around ten fifteen. Keyshon can see my new minivan."

"I told him you were getting one and he's excited to see it. I don't know why."

Later, Keyshon came running outside as Keith O'Dell pulled into the driveway. "Hi, Annie! Hi, Matthew Sullivan! Hi, Mr. O'Dell! You got a new car. Can I see inside?"

"Sure, Keyshon. Hop in."

Keyshon jumped onto the passenger seat in front.

"It's a 1998 Dodge Grand Caravan Sport and it's white, as you can tell." Keith described the new minivan to Keyshon who was excited at first, but then wanted to talk to Annie.

"It's a nice minivan, but I like sports cars better. Like Annie's car." Keyshon ran in the house to find Annie. "Annie, will you show me the monkeys and can we see the lions and bears?"

"Sure, we can see everything you want."

Mace decided to go along since Erin was in Nebraska. "Nothing else to do. Might as well go with and make sure you and Matt behave."

"Thanks, Mace," Matt said. "You wouldn't believe how Annie attacked me this morning. I was just sleeping and not bothering anyone when she came into the room and jumped on top of me and tried to have her way with me."

"You poor guy. Did you manage to fight her off?"

"I was just barely defending my honor when her father walked into the room and saved me."

Annie scowled at Mace and Matt. "I guess I will just hang out with Keyshon at the zoo today. He always tells the truth."

Matt kissed Annie and she smiled.

"Are you going to kiss Matthew Sullivan all day long, Annie? If you do then I won't have as much fun," Keyshon said with his hands on his hips.

"I promise you and I will have fun, Keyshon, but I might need to kiss Matty once in a while just to make him happy."

"Okay. Once in a while you can kiss Matthew Sullivan."

Everyone was ready so they loaded into the van. Elisabeth sat in front with Keith while Keyshon pulled Annie into the rear seat with him. Matt and Mace sat in the middle row. They arrived at the Brookview Zoo shortly after eleven. Keyshon wanted to see the lions and tigers first.

"Let's take a look at the map and see what is first in line.

We can follow along this way and we'll see the lions and tigers after we visit some of the other animals," Annie suggested.

"Okay! Just so I get to see the lions and tigers before we leave," Keyshon said.

"Annie!"

"Yes, Daddy."

"Elisabeth and I are going to go on our own. Will you take care of Keyshon? I'm afraid we wouldn't be able to keep up."

"Of course I will. Matty and Mace will be around, too. We will all keep an eye on Keyshon."

"Let's plan to meet back at the entrance at three. Will that give you enough time?"

"More than enough. It will probably bore Mace and Matty, but they will survive."

"Three o'clock then. Have a good time," Dad said then he and Elisabeth walked away.

Keyshon got excited when he saw the lions and tigers even they though they were sleeping. Mace took Keyshon into the primate house so Annie could have a little time with Matty. After all, Sunday was the only day they were both off work.

"Are you thirsty, Annie?" Matt asked. "I could use a Coke or something."

"That would be great. Coke or even a bottle of water. There's a stand just up ahead. I'll sit here and wait for you."

Matt bought a Coke and a bottle of water.

"Are you bored out of your mind, Matty? I know this is our only day to be together."

"I'm all right. We are together, Annie."

"Yeah, but we're not alone. I was thinking about how perfect it would be if we were alone in the house right now. We could do whatever." Annie touched his thigh and grinned.

"It would be nice if we could just lie down and take a nap together. We wouldn't have to do anything but just hold each other."

"Maybe next Sunday we can figure out a way to do that."

# Chapter Seventeen

"Annie, I'm tired. Can we find Mom and your dad now?" Keyshon asked.

"Sure, we've seen everything," Annie answered.

"And some things twice," Mace added.

They turned around and headed back to the entrance. Annie saw her father and Elisabeth waiting on a bench.

"Mom! I had fun. I saw the lions and tigers, but I didn't see any polar bears," Keyshon said. "That's okay. I'm ready to leave."

"I'm happy for you, Keyshon," Mom said.

They returned to SoHam. Mace and Matt ran to the store with a list while Keith fired up the grill. Keyshon followed Annie into her room and saw the air mattress on the floor. He looked at it, then at Annie.

"Are you okay, little buddy?" Annie asked. "You look confused."

"Is this where Matthew Sullivan sleeps, Annie?"

"Yes, Keyshon. He sleeps on the floor when he stays overnight."

"So he doesn't sleep with you then." Keyshon walked around the room without stepping on the air mattress.

"No, Keyshon, he sleeps on the floor next to my bed, but not in my bed."

"Erin slept in Mace's bed one night when she was here," Keyshon whispered. "I'm not supposed to say anything to anyone, but I will tell you, Annie."

"It's a good idea not to tell anyone else, Keyshon."

Annie was aware everyone knew about Mace and Erin, but didn't want to make a big deal about it with Keyshon.

"If I spend the night here, can I sleep on the floor in your room?"

Annie held Keyshon's hand. "I don't think so. I'm sorry, but you are getting too big to do that now."

He nodded. "I understand, Annie. You love Matthew Sullivan like a boyfriend and you love me like a brother—just like Mace. It's okay. I will find a girlfriend someday and we will get

97

married and sleep together. You can be in my wedding."

"I would like that very much, Keyshon. Maybe we should see if Mom and Dad need our help."

Keyshon put his hands on her shoulders. "I still love you, Annie. You're like my sister now."

"I love you, too, Keyshon, and I always will. You're my favorite brother but don't tell Mace. It will be our secret, okay?"

Keyshon's eyes opened wide and lit up. "Okay! I won't tell him."

Mace and Matt returned from the store and a half hour later dinner was ready. They sat on the patio at the picnic table to eat. Grandpa came over because Annie called him and invited him.

"I'm glad you decided to join us, Grandpa," Annie said with a big grin.

Grandpa shrugged as he squeezed Annie's shoulders. "How could I refuse. Annie made me such a good offer."

"What was that?" Dad asked as he stared at Annie.

"She told me to get my butt over here and have dinner with everyone or else she was never going to see me again. I thought about it for a few minutes, then decided as good as it might be to never see Annie again, I was hungry."

"Grandpa! You know you would miss me too much."

Liam kissed Annie's cheek. "If you want to believe that, dear child, then go ahead."

Mace and Matt laughed because they knew how much Grandpa Liam loved Annie. She stuck her tongue out at the guys.

"All right, enough teasing, and Annie please keep your tongue inside your mouth at the table," Dad told her. He thought about what he said. "And later when you are kissing Matt, too."

Everyone laughed as Annie turned red.

"Daddy!"

"All right, let's eat before the food gets cold."

They passed around the food and everyone filled their plate. They talked as they ate and after a few minutes Annie noticed Matt being rather quiet.

"Are you all right, Matty? Is something wrong?"

"No, I'm fine. I was just listening. When I was growing up

we almost never talked at the dinner table. We seldom ate at the table together. As a family, I mean. My mother and father were always too busy with work or something. It's nice to sit and listen to everyone. Just one big happy family."

Annie kissed Matt then said, "Even if we aren't married, I consider you part of the family."

Mace sat across from Matt and Annie listening to their conversation. "Are you two gonna get all mushy now? You know there are still people eating."

Annie tried to kick Mace under the table but only managed to bang her shin against the table support. It started bleeding but she didn't realize it.

"She what you get for trying to kick me," Mace said. "Does it hurt?"

"I'll never tell," Annie said struggling not to grimace.

They sat at the table for an hour. Everyone felt stuffed, but happy. Finally, Elisabeth got up and started clearing the leftover food. Annie helped and Keyshon noticed her shin.

"Annie, you're bleeding. What happened?" he asked as he got on his knees to check her shin.

Annie glanced down. "Nothing, I just bumped my shin on the table."

Keyshon was concerned until Annie wiped away the dried blood and showed him that she was all right.

"Keyshon has never liked the sight of blood," Mom told Annie.

"I know. I didn't realize I was bleeding or else I would have cleaned it up before he saw it."

Keyshon said, "I'm going to watch TV."

"Okay, Keyshon. You can watch your shows."

Annie helped Elisabeth in the kitchen while the guys sat outside.

"Anyone need a beer?" Grandpa asked.

"Yeah! That would be good right now," Mace answered.

"Well, bring one out for everyone then, Mace," Grandpa said then chuckled. "Thanks for being so thoughtful."

Mace realized he had been suckered into getting the beers

for everyone. He went into the kitchen and opened the fridge. He grabbed four beers and his mother and Annie glared at him.

"Are you going to drink all those or are you sharing?" Elisabeth asked as she returned the condiments to the fridge.

Mace shook his head while holding two bottles in each hand. "Grandpa Liam wanted a beer so he volunteered me to get one for everybody."

"Are there any left for us?" Annie asked.

"Who says you can have a beer, young lady?" Mom asked semi-seriously.

"Please, can I have one?"

"All right. Since your father doesn't seem to mind his daughter breaking the law, who am I to care," Elisabeth said closing the fridge.

Annie put a finger to her mouth and looked up at Elisabeth. "If you don't want me to have one, I won't."

"It's all right, Annie. I don't mind since you aren't going anywhere tonight," Mom relented.

"Nobody says anything about Mace or Matty having a beer," Annie said with a hint of anger.

Elisabeth looked at her. "Isn't Matty twenty-one?"

"Not yet. He turned twenty in May. His birthday is on the eighth. Just three weeks before mine."

"Oh, that's right. I forgot. Mace will be twenty in January. It doesn't seem possible." Elisabeth thought back to when Mace was born and how pleased his father was. "I know Mace shouldn't be drinking, but he usually limits himself to one beer. You shouldn't be drinking either, young lady."

"I know, but I won't have more than three or four!" Annie joked.

Elisabeth shook her head. "Go have fun. The kitchen is just about done. I'm going to sit with Keyshon for a while, then I'll be out. I will probably have a glass of wine."

Annie joined the guys on the patio. Her father and grandfather were sitting in patio chairs talking to each other while sipping their beer. Mace and Matty sat across from each other on the picnic table benches. Annie sat beside Matt and he put an arm

100

around her waist.

"What are you guys talking about?" Annie asked.

"We were talking about you. Were your ears burning?" Mace asked.

"Yeah, do they look red?"

Matt moved her hair. "Nope. They look normal."

"Were you really talking about me?"

"Yes, we were talking about how to get rid of you," Mace joked.

She crossed her arms over her chest. "If you don't want me around, just say so, and I'll leave."

Matt tightened his hold on her. "I want you around, Annie. Mace is just kidding."

"Who says? I was serious, Annie."

Annie started to kick Mace under the table, but remembered what happened the last time.

"It's cooled off since a couple days ago," Matt said. "It's not as humid either."

"Yeah, it would be a nice night for camping out under the stars," Mace mentioned casually.

Annie looked at Matt and bit her lip.

Mace noticed the look and waved a hand. "Whoa! I didn't mean that for real. Your father won't let you do that."

"Why not? What's the difference if Matty sleeps in my room or we sleep outside?" Annie asked then took a sip of Matt's beer.

Mace stood up and pointed at the house next door with his beer bottle. "The neighbors for one thing. They can't see into your bedroom but they can see into your yard."

"No they can't. They can't see through the fence and we could set the sleeping bags back there by the garage so no one could see us."

"I'm not sure it's a good idea," Matt said waving a hand.

Mace nodded and sat back down. "I agree with Matt."

Nothing more was said about the sleeping bags.

Later, after the sun slipped below the horizon, Grandpa stood up and said, "Thanks for the steak and the beer and the pleasant company, but I'm going home."

"Can I go with you, Grandpa Liam?" Keyshon asked. "We could go fishing in the morning. I want to catch a whopper," he said with his hands spread out wide. "Bigger than this!"

Elisabeth looked at Liam. He nodded.

"Can I go, Mom?" Keyshon asked again.

"You can go, but you have to obey Grandpa Liam and help with the chores before you go fishing."

"I will. I promise."

Grandpa walked over to the picnic table where Annie sat between Matt and Mace. "I'll take him fishing in the morning, but I have things to do in the afternoon."

"Is it all right if I pick him up around noon?" Annie asked.

"That will work," Grandpa said.

Keith decided to go home with Elisabeth and walked over to tell Annie. She looked up at him with a disapproving expression.

"What?" Dad asked as he shrugged. "I've got to be in court in the morning and Elisabeth's house is closer to the courthouse."

"Sure, Daddy, if that's your excuse," Annie said.

"It is and I'm sticking to it." He pointed at Mace. "Maybe Mace would like to stay here with you and Matt."

Annie jumped off of the table and pulled her father a few feet away. "All right! I get the picture. You and Mom want to be alone. What kind of example are you setting for your sweet, innocent daughter though? Do as I say, but not as I do, huh? I'll remember to use that if I ever have a teenage daughter."

Keith tilted his head. "Now just who would that be?"

"Me! I'm still your sweet and innocent daughter."

"Of course you are. Just make sure you guys don't drink all the beer, or else I will have to call the cops."

Annie put her hands on her hips and frowned. "Fine! I'll stay here all alone with two horny young men who want to ravage my body."

Dad kissed her forehead. "That's my sweet girl. Don't let them ravage you all night long. You have to work in the morning, too. And don't drink all the beer!"

"I promise we won't drink all the beer, Daddy. I'll save you one for tomorrow and Keyshon is staying with Grandpa, so technically I don't have to watch him. I could stay in bed all morning and since Matty doesn't have to be at the Lion until the afternoon." She put her hands behind her back and bounced on her toes.

Dad put his hands on her shoulders. "If that's your decision, then I will accept it."

"Oh, Daddy," Annie sighed. "It's going to happen one of these days."

Keith and Elisabeth went inside and got ready to go back to her house. Annie returned to the top of the picnic table in between Matt and Mace.

"Annie, are you upset about your father staying with my mom?" Mace asked.

"It's a double standard. It sucks. Guys can sleep with their girlfriends and it's accepted. If a girl does that, she's looked down on."

"I won't look down on you if you sleep with Matt," Mace said.

"Stuff it, Mace."

Dad came back outside while Elisabeth waited in the minivan. "Night, Annie. Night, guys. Take good care of her and don't drink all the beer."

Annie sighed disgustedly, "Will you just go already? We aren't going to drink all the beer. I promise."

Keith kissed Annie's cheek and they left.

"Will you be upset if she sleeps with Matt?" Elisabeth asked.

"I don't know for sure. Sometimes I wish she was still a little girl, but I know she's all grown up for all practical purposes."

"It happens all the time."

## Chapter Eighteen

Annie waited until her father and Elisabeth were gone, then looked at Mace and Matthew and grinned. "Now, what about those sleeping bags?"

"What sleeping bags?" Matt asked.

"You still want to do that? What if it rains?" Mace asked.

Annie jumped down from the table and faced the guys. "It's not going to rain and we've been out in the rain before and you didn't drown or melt or anything."

"It would be a perfect night, Mace, and I would feel safer with you here," Matt said with a straight face.

"What is that supposed to mean, Matthew?" Annie asked.

Matt shrugged. "I meant if Mace is here you won't be as likely to ravage my body."

Annie stuck out her tongue. "You are so funny, Matthew Sullivan. Are we gonna do it or not?"

"Fine!" Matt said as he got down from the picnic table. "Might as well or else I'll never hear the end of it."

"Good! We can use the air mattress from my room and the sleeping bag from there. I know there are at least two sleeping bags in the basement. There might be another air mattress or something down there. You guys look downstairs while I get the stuff from my room." Annie walked into the house.

Mace and Matthew looked at each other.

"Do you know what she's talking about?" Matt asked. "I've never been in the basement."

"I know where the camping stuff is stored," Mace said. "Come on. I'll show you the basement. It's not too scary."

The guys headed inside and went downstairs.

"The basement's unfinished except for this room," Mace said as they walked through what Matt assumed was a small family room. "The camping stuff's in here."

Mace opened the large cabinet and found two sleeping bags. They looked around.

"Hey! Here's a couple foam mats that will work." Matt showed them to Mace.

"Yeah, these will work all right."

Mace looked at Matt and said, "If you want me to split, I will. I can crash with some friends if you don't want me around."

"What? No, I want you to stay," Matt said then shook his head. "We aren't going to do anything, Mace. We might kiss a little, but we're not going to sleep together."

"Are you sure?"

"Positive." Matt nodded. "I know Annie well enough to know that she doesn't want to do it with anyone else around."

"Exactly my point!" Mace exclaimed.

"No, I didn't mean it like that. You don't have to leave."

Matt and Mace brought the sleeping bags and foam pads outside.

"Good. You found a couple more bags." Annie inspected the foam pads. "There are two more of those in the garage. I'll get them and it will be even more comfortable for you guys."

"Why for us guys?" Mace asked.

Annie smiled as she poked Mace in the stomach. "Well, I get to use the air mattress since it was my idea in the first place. You two can use the foam pads. You can sleep on either side of me to protect me if prowlers come around."

Matt looked at Mace.

"Okay, I believe you now. Annie wants both of us here," Mace whispered to Matt.

"She really is sweet and innocent in a way, Mace."

"Yeah, should we get her drunk and ravage her body?"

"But of course!"

They high-fived each other and laughed because they were just joking. Annie came out of the garage in time to hear the last part of the guys conversation.

"Will you guys help me? The pads are too high."

"Ever hear of a thing called a ladder?" Mace asked.

"Very funny! Come and help me."

Mace and Matt followed Annie into the garage. Mace grabbed the ladder and positioned it.

"There you go, Annie. Now you can get the pads down."

Annie looked at Mace and frowned. She climbed up the

105

ladder with Mace standing behind her and Matt next to him. She tugged on the pads and nearly had them off the shelf when she slipped. Mace noticed Annie's slip, reached out and steadied her. She pulled the pads off the shelf and Matt grabbed them as they fell.

"Thanks for catching me, Mace."

"I'm sorry I made you climb the ladder, Annie. I should have done that for you."

"But then you wouldn't have had the chance to grab my butt," Annie teased.

"I tried to grab your hips more than your butt. I just saw you falling and grabbed you. Sorry if my hands ended up on your butt."

"I'm just teasing. I don't care that you touched my butt. Matt might be jealous though."

"No, I don't have any desire to grab your butt, Annie," Matt said without changing his blank expression.

"You don't? Don't you like my butt?"

"I'm kidding. You have a nice bottom and I like touching it."

Annie kissed Matt.

Mace rolled his eyes as he turned around. "If you guys are going to start that, I'm going inside."

"We're through," Annie said. "Let's get everything set up, then we can sit on the patio and have another beer and something to eat."

Mace looked at Matt and they smiled at each other. Annie wondered why.

They arranged the camping gear and since it was too early to go to sleep they sat at the picnic table. Annie and Mace drank another beer but Matt drank water.

"It will be so much fun to sleep outside," Annie said as she leaned against Matt's shoulder and chewed her chicken breast.

"What will you do if you get cold during the night, Annie?" Matt asked while adding a slice of onion to his burger.

Annie looked at Mace and grinned. "Did he really just ask me that or was I imagining it?"

106

"I heard it, too, Annie," Mace said as he scratched his jaw. "Is that really water or is he drinking vodka or something? You'd think a guy with his experience would know the answer."

Annie put a hand on Matt's back. "What do you think I will do, Matty?"

Matt realized what Annie would do. "I guess I'm out of practice."

"You have just changed the way you think, Matty. You're no longer thinking about sex every minute you're awake."

Mace took a quick drink of his beer then set the bottle down and grinned. "Maybe he's not, but I am!"

Annie giggled then said, "Well, don't look at me, Mace Franklin. We're practically brother and sister."

Mace reached across the table and grabbed Annie's hand. "I wasn't thinking about you, dear sister."

"You had your chance," Annie said then realized that both Matt and Mace were giving her a funny look. "I meant with Erin. Not me." She put a hand to her heart. "Mace was with Erin for almost a week and they didn't do anything."

They finished eating and Annie took their paper plates inside and dumped them in the trash. She grabbed another beer from the fridge, opened it and walked outside. She saw the guys standing by the sleeping bags.

"Are you sure you should have one more?" Matt asked.

She took a sip then nodded. "I'm sure because I'm not drunk enough for you both to ravage my body yet. I heard you guys talking before."

"You know we were kidding, right?"

"You were? Darn it! I was hoping you were going to deflower me tonight."

Mace decided to tease her back. "Well, if you insist, Annie. You wanna go first, Matt?"

Matt shook his head. "No, go ahead, Mace. You can go first. I insist."

"No, you should have her first in case she... has a disease or something," Mace said.

Annie glared at both guys.

"I know," Matt said. "Let's flip a coin and the loser has to do her first."

"Okay, that sounds fair." Mace reached into his pocket. "I've got a quarter. Call it in the air." Mace tossed the coin in the air.

Annie stood up and grabbed it out of the air. "Now neither of you wins, or loses."

Mace put an arm around her shoulders. "You better behave or I will tell your father and grandfather."

"Tell them what? That you guys got me so drunk that I couldn't resist your charms and you both seduced me."

"Maybe I'll tell your father about the time you got pulled over for speeding and flirted your way out of the ticket by nearly stripping for the cop."

"I did no such thing, Mace Franklin!" Annie exclaimed then punched his arm.

"Do you deny that you flirted with the cop?" Mace asked.

"No, I guess I did that, but I didn't do anything else. I swear it, Matty," Annie said as she looked up at him and crossed her heart.

"I was in the front seat with you, Annie," Mace said. "Do you deny that you unbuttoned your blouse while he was watching?"

"I just undid the top two buttons because I was hot."

Mace laughed. "I think the cop was getting hot while he watched you."

"He was not! That guy was older than Daddy."

"Not helping your case, Annie," Matt said as he crossed his arms over his chest.

"Matty, do you believe Mace or me?"

Matt shrugged then said, "All I know is that if I was a cop and I pulled over someone as pretty as you and they started flirting with me, I would arrest them and take them home to my special jail cell."

"Fine! I'm definitely sleeping by myself tonight. You guys can go to Matt's house to sleep."

"Okay, that sounds like a plan. All right with you, Mace?"

"Yeah, man. Sounds good to me."

"Why me, God? Why am I stuck with these two bozos?" Annie sighed as she looked into the heavens for an answer.

Mace put an arm around her waist. "Because you love us and you know it."

"I must not have any brains at all," Annie said.

They finally got tired enough to go to sleep. Annie went into the house and changed into her usual pajamas. Gym shorts and a sleeveless t-shirt. The guys slept in their boxers. Annie used the sleeping bag in the middle on the air mattress. She was the last one to get in the sleeping bags. She didn't see what the guys wore but could see they didn't have on a shirt. It didn't matter to her. She knew she was totally safe with both guys there.

"Night, Mace."

"Good night, Annie."

Annie turned to Matt and they moved close enough to kiss good night. Mace heard them kiss.

"Night, Annie. I love you," Matt whispered.

"I love you, too, Matty."

Mace used his elbow for support and asked, "Hey what about me?"

"Night, Mace. I love you, too," Matt said.

"Oh crap! I meant why don't I get a kiss?"

Annie turned to Mace. "Do you want a good night kiss?"

"As long as it's not from Matthew," Mace said with a grin.

"Fine, you big baby. I'll give you a good night kiss."

Annie leaned over and kissed Mace.

"What? No tongue?"

Annie smacked him hard but only succeeded in hurting her hand. It didn't hurt Mace at all. Annie swore because her hand hurt so much.

"Now, now. Let's not use that kind of language, young lady. Do I need to wash your mouth out with soap? Matt, does she often use that word around you?"

"No, but I think she should be punished for using it."

Annie repeated the word and directed it to both guys. She then ducked into her sleeping bag trying to hide from the guys. The

109

guys scrambled out of their bags. Matt unzipped Annie's bag, pulled her out and held onto her so she couldn't escape. Mace and Matt laughed as Annie used the naughty word again.

"Should we just spank her and be done with it?" Matt asked as he stood behind her with his hands on her shoulders.

Mace nodded. "Maybe we should. It might teach her a lesson on how to talk like a lady."

"I'll scream if either of you spank me. I swear it."

"That's why you need to be spanked. Because you are swearing. Will you scream if we both spank you at the same time?" Mace asked.

"You better not!" Annie squealed as she tried to get away.

Matt grabbed her around the waist. "Do you promise to behave and not use that word again?"

"I promise!"

"Okay, then we won't spank you." Matt released her.

"Thank you. Now can I go to sleep? I have housework to do in the morning."

"Go to sleep, Annie."

They climbed back into their sleeping bags.

"Night, guys," Annie whispered a moment later. "I promise I won't ever use that word again."

"Why don't I believe you?" Matt asked.

Annie used the word again.

Matt and Mace listened to Annie while she giggled.

"I knew we shouldn't have let her have that last beer," Mace said.

Matt sat up. "I think you're right, Mace. I think she's a little plastered."

"I'm not plastered. I'm just a little tipsy."

"Go to sleep, Annie!" both guys said.

Five minutes later Annie whispered softly, "I have to pee."

Mace and Matt groaned.

# Chapter Nineteen

When Mrs. Franklin got home from work on Wednesday, she sat down at the kitchen table and talked to Annie. "I know I told you I would need you to watch Keyshon on Monday, Wednesday and Friday, but I don't need you as many hours as I originally thought. I figured Mace would be working but since he isn't, he can take care of his brother. Would that be okay with you? I know you're trying to save up some money for school."

Annie checked the lasagna in the oven then sat down. "That's okay, Mom. Mr. Bushell actually asked if I could work a few more hours."

"That would work out just perfect. I know he pays you more than I do. Maybe you could watch Keyshon for a few hours on Monday and Friday. That way you can see Matt more."

Annie smiled. "I'm sure he would like that. We can be together on Wednesdays."

"Let's do that then. If you could watch Keyshon on Monday and Friday afternoons until I get home, I would appreciate it." Mrs. Franklin stood up. "Thanks for heating up the lasagna and putting a salad together, Annie. I'm going to change clothes. You're welcome to stay for dinner."

Annie said, "I might take you up on that because Daddy's working late and there's nothing to eat at home."

Annie informed Mr. Bushell of her new availability the next day.

"Would you mind working eight hours on Tuesdays and Thursdays?" he asked as he grabbed his suit coat from the rack. "And I could use you a few hours on Monday and Friday mornings if you have the time. Let me know when you decide. I need to meet a client downtown." He laughed and told Annie, "He got busted for petty theft again. Third time this year."

She called Matty to tell him about having a free day on Wednesday. "Mom doesn't need me to watch Keyshon as much, but I picked up a few more hours from Mr. Bushell's office. Wednesday I am all yours. We can be together all day."

Matt asked, "When are you going to study for your class? Why did you even sigh up for a summer class?"

"I only signed up because you're working late on those days. I wouldn't have been able to see you anyway and I can do some studying while I watch Keyshon and maybe Wednesday morning," she explained.

"That will work. You know I can help you study if you need. Just being together to study will be better than not seeing you at all."

"I don't have to work Friday morning because of the holiday, but I still need to watch Keyshon in the afternoon for a couple hours."

"I have a surprise for you," Matt said.

"What is it?"

"Dad gave me Saturday off. Can you believe it? I didn't even ask for it. He needs me for a few hours Sunday evening, but I get all day Saturday and most of Sunday to be with you."

"I love it!" Annie squealed. "We are going to have a big cookout at the farm. Daddy told me I could invite my friends."

"Are they both going to come?"

"Very funny. I'll have you know that I have more than two friends. I have four and I think they will all be there."

"Is it all right if I come over after work Friday night?"

"Sure! You can stay Friday and Saturday night. Oh, you can come over Sunday, too, if you aren't tired of me by then."

"Yeah, about Sunday, I'm not sure I want to see you three days in a row," Matt teased.

"Matty! You know if we ever move in together you will see me everyday."

"I'm teasing. I wish I could see you everyday and night."

Annie teased him back. "Let's not get too crazy. I need some time away from you to see all my other boyfriends."

"Oh, that's right." Matt slapped his forehead. "I forgot about those guys. Is it just the basketball team or did you add some football players to the list?"

"Just basketball players," she said. "Oh, and one golfer. He's really hot and swings a mean club."

112

Annie was tired after her class on Thursday night. She hadn't eaten since lunch and was just plain worn out both mentally and physically. She called Matt at the Hungry Lion, but he was busy and couldn't talk at that moment so she asked the hostess to ask him to call her back when he could. She got ready for bed, ate some dry cereal and waited until he could call back.

"Hi, Matty. I just wanted to hear your voice," Annie said when Matt finally called.

"Are you all right?"

"Just tired. It's been a long day. I'm going to sleep until noon tomorrow. I wish I hadn't signed up for this class now."

"Hang in there, Annie. You've only got this month to go, then the class will be over and we'll be on vacation. Have you talked to your father about that yet?" Matt asked.

"Not yet, but I will soon."

"Come on, Annie. You need to talk to him soon so we can decide where we want to go and make reservations if we need to."

"I know. I've been putting it off because I'm afraid Daddy will say no. He will probably threaten to ground me for life," she said.

"You're eighteen now, Annie. You don't need your father's permission to do stuff," Matt said then sighed. "But I know you will ask because you are such a good daughter. I hope Jennifer turns out as good as you."

"I'll ask him soon, Matty. I really will."

# Chapter Twenty

"Sweetie, you need to be waking up," Dad whispered on Saturday morning. "It's a little after noon. We have to pick up Matty pretty soon."

Annie groaned and turned over on her back. She didn't open her eyes at all. Her father decided to let her sleep and quietly left the room. He knew she needed the rest because she was worn out. She had been working a lot of hours and had been up late working on a paper the last two nights. He decided to run over to the Sullivan home and pick up Matt for her. He pulled his minivan into the driveway and saw Matt waiting outside. Matt hustled over, climbed in the front passenger seat and looked at the second row for Annie. Then he looked back at Mr. O'Dell.

"Morning, Matt. Annie was still sleeping so I came alone."

"Is she okay? She's not sick or anything is she?" Matt asked as he buckled up.

"No, she's just tired. She's been up half the night working on her paper for class. That and working the extra hours has finally caught up to her." Mr. O'Dell backed out of the driveway, straightened out and gunned the minivan. "Crap! I forget that this thing's not an unmarked squad car."

Matt said, "I offered to come over and help last night, but she told me to stay home. I hope she's not upset with me about something."

Mr. O'Dell shook his head. "She never said anything to me about being upset with you. I think she thought if you came over it would be too difficult to concentrate on the schoolwork. I agreed with her."

"I wish she wasn't taking that class, but it made sense at the time."

When they got back to the O'Dell house, Matt looked in Annie's room. She was still asleep. Matt left the door open as he walked away. He went into the kitchen and sat at the island.

"Still sleeping, huh?" Mr. O'Dell asked as he slapped some mayonnaise on wheat bread. "I'm making a sandwich to hold me over till later. You want one?"

"Thanks, but I'm good. I ate at home," Matt said as he waved a hand. "What time do we need to leave?"

"I guess we need to be there by three thirty. I think Annie told her friends we would eat around five."

Matt checked the clock on the wall. "It's almost one thirty now. She must be really zonked or else she's getting sick."

"I know she was still up at four this morning. I got up to take a leak and she was sitting at her desk swearing at the computer."

"That must have been funny."

"It was," Mr. O'Dell said then laughed. "Let's let her sleep until two thirty, then you can wake her up."

Fifteen minutes later a tired and sleepy looking Annie stumbled into the kitchen. She sat next to her father, closed her eyes and leaned against him. She didn't even notice Matt.

Dad put an arm around her shoulders and hugged her. "How are you, sleepyhead? Do you want something to eat?"

"I need coffee," she muttered. "What time is it? I told Matty I would pick him up by ten."

Matt chuckled. "You don't have to pick me up, Annie. I'm already here."

Annie opened her eyes, finally saw Matty and smiled. "Hi," she said quietly as she snuggled against her father even more.

"Good afternoon, Annie. Did you get enough sleep?"

She let go of her father and lay her head on the island. "I feel like I could sleep a few more hours. What time is it? Did I already ask that?"

"You did, but no one answered. It's about a quarter to two. We were going to let you sleep until two thirty. You can go back to bed if you want," Matt said.

She sat back up. "I should stay up. I'm sorry I slept so long, Matty. I've wasted half the day already."

"It's all right. Your father told me how late you've been staying up to finish that paper."

"It's finally finished. I can turn it in Tuesday. The rest of the class should be a breeze."

"Do you want me to make you anything to eat?" Dad

asked. "I made myself a sandwich." He held up half of his pickle and pimento loaf sandwich.

"You don't have to, Daddy. I'll eat some cereal and a banana."

Matt got up to fix her a bowl of cereal. He looked in the cupboard. "What kind do you want? There's three different kinds."

"Frosted Flakes, if we still have some."

Matt fixed the bowl of cereal and even sliced a banana for Annie. He placed it on the island for her. She was leaning against her father with her head on his chest and her arms around him. Her eyes were closed and she was close to falling asleep.

Dad kissed the top of her head. "You're still my little girl, Annie."

Matt looked at Annie then her father. "Should I eat this? It will get all soggy otherwise."

Dad whispered softly, "Annie, Matty has your cereal."

"Okay. Thank you, Matty," she said then raised her head.

"You're welcome, baby."

Annie woke up enough to eat, then dragged herself off to her bedroom. She found clothes to wear and went to take her shower. The shower seemed to revive her enough to start her day. She walked into the kitchen and stood behind Matt as he sat at the island. She put her hands on his shoulders, leaned around and kissed his cheek.

"Are you feeling awake now?" Matt asked.

"I feel much better. Are we ready to head out to the farm?"

"I'm ready if you kids are," Dad said.

It was five minutes before three when Keith pulled his minivan into the driveway at Grandpa Liam's farm. Matt and Annie jumped out and Annie ran inside. Keith and Matt walked around the front yard to inspect the new flower beds Grandpa had been working on.

"Grandpa, are you in here?" Annie hollered.

"I'm on the deck, Annie. Can you grab me a beer from the fridge and no you can't have one."

"I don't want one anyway," she answered.

Annie grabbed a beer for Grandpa and walked out the back

116

door. Keith and Matt walked slowly around the house to the backyard.

"Didn't the doctor tell you not to drink any more beer?" Annie asked as she handed Grandpa his beer.

"I'm not drinking anymore than I was. He told me to be careful."

"You're so stubborn, but I love you anyway." She kissed the top of his head.

"I love you, too. Where is Matthew?"

"I'm right here, Grandpa Liam."

"I need a favor, Matt."

"Sure, whatcha need?" Matt asked.

"Could you stack those bags of dirt and mulch on the cart for me and move them into the barn for the time being."

"No problem. I can handle that."

"Thanks, Matthew. I appreciate it."

Matt took care of the bags while Annie sat with Grandpa on the large deck. Dad made sure the new gas grill was operating properly. He would be responsible for the grilling later. Elisabeth arrived with Mace and Keyshon. Keyshon hurried around the house to the deck.

"Hello, Annie O'Dell! Hello, Grandpa! How are you doing this fine sunny day?" Keyshon asked as he climbed the steps.

"We are doing great," Annie said. "You seem to be in a happy mood. Why is that?"

"I have a new girlfriend and she's coming today." Keyshon grinned and his eyes sparkled.

"You never mentioned a girlfriend yesterday. When did you meet this girlfriend and what's her name?" Annie asked. "Are you keeping secrets from me now?"

"I didn't say anything yesterday because I wanted to surprise you. Her name is Lisa Miley and she lives down the street from me. She just moved in two weeks ago and she's a year younger than me. She is pretty, too." Keyshon made a motion like an hourglass. "She's got a great body."

"Keyshon Franklin, are you telling everyone about Lisa?" Mrs. Franklin asked.

117

"Yes, Mom. They will meet her today."

"Hello, Liam. How are you feeling?"

"I feel ten years younger than I did last year. You're looking as pretty as ever, Elisabeth."

"Thank you."

"Hey! Are you hitting on my girl there, old man?" Keith teased his father.

"Can't blame me for trying, can you?" Grandpa said then laughed. "Actually, the widow Hobbs might come over later. We ate dinner at The Hungry Lion last week."

Annie stared at Matt.

"What? I didn't do anything." Matt shrugged.

"Did you see Grandpa at the Lion?"

"No," Matt answered. "I don't see every customer who eats there."

Annie turned to her grandfather. "Will you stop calling her the widow Hobbs. I'm sure she has a name."

"It's Lucinda and I call her that if we're together."

A few minutes later, Mace saw Matt with the bags of dirt and mulch and walked over to help. "Need a hand?"

"I just about got everything. This is the last cartload."

"What's all this for, anyway?"

"Grandpa is doing some more flowerbeds. I think he just wanted this stuff in here for today."

Keyshon joined the other guys.

"Hi, Keyshon. How are you?" Matt asked as he wiped the sweat from his forehead.

"I'm okay. I have a new girlfriend, Matthew Sullivan."

"You do? What's her name?"

"Lisa Miley and she is supposed to come today."

"Where did you meet her?"

"She lives down the street. She just moved in and she's like me."

Matt looked at Mace and Mace gave Matt a little nod.

"Is she as pretty as Annie or Erin?" Matt asked.

"She's even prettier! You guys are going to be so jealous because my girlfriend is prettier than anyone's."

118

"She must be extremely pretty if she's prettier than Annie or Erin. I can't wait to meet her."

Keyshon walked back to the deck and Mace told Matt more about Lisa.

"She has Down Syndrome, too. Her family just moved in and I think her parents are both teachers. Mom met them, but I haven't. Keyshon and Lisa just seemed to hit it off."

By three thirty more guests started arriving including some of Keith's friends from the department and some of Liam's friends from school. Most of them brought meat to grill and something to drink. Grandpa placed three coolers filled with ice on the deck. Vice-Principal Kemmerick and his wife arrived and Annie saw them.

"Hi, Mr. Kemmerick. How are you and your wife doing?"

"Hello, Annie. It's good to see you. We're doing fine. We just got back from vacation. Have you been behaving yourself?"

"Always! I'm an angel, remember?" Annie grinned.

Mr. Kemmerick laughed as he remembered all the mischief Annie would get into. Most of which her father and grandfather were unaware of even to that day.

"Where did you go on vacation?" Annie asked.

"We went out to Utah. We wanted to see some of the national parks. They are beautiful. Have you ever been out west?"

"Not yet, but we're thinking about going out there in August," Annie answered.

"I highly recommend it. You'll have a good time."

Annie saw Elaine Novicki and Cindy Mackens so she excused herself and ran over to see her friends. "Hi, where are the guys?"

"They're over there with Matt and Mace." Elaine pointed.

Annie waved to the guys, then turned back to her friends. "I know Derrick and Kristen Keasling are coming and Tony Bertucci and Emmy Colasanti are suppose to come, too."

"Are Tony and Emmy still together?" Cindy asked. "I heard they broke up."

"Emmy called and said they were both coming."

"Good," Cindy said. "I hope they don't break up. They

119

make a good couple despite their differences in size."

Keyshon looked around anxiously as he paced back and forth next to the driveway. He hollered as he saw Lisa and her parents. He ran to Lisa and took her hand.

"I'm glad you could be here. I want to introduce you to my friends."

"Okay, but I want you to stay with me," Lisa said timidly.

Keyshon smiled. "I will stay right beside you all the time."

Keyshon introduced Lisa to Annie first, then to all the other kids. Lisa didn't say much and stayed close to Keyshon.

More guests arrived and Dad and a couple of his cop buddies started up the grill. Elisabeth and a couple of other women got the food out of the fridge and set it up on the picnic table on the deck. As soon as some of the burgers and hot dogs were ready, Liam told everyone to help themselves. Keyshon and Lisa were allowed to go first. Annie watched as Keyshon helped Lisa fill her plate. Keyshon found a spot for them to sit and even got a two cans of pop for them to drink.

Annie was about to get in line when she saw Derrick, Kristen, Tony and Emmy come around the corner of the house. She ran over to greet them. "Hi guys! You timed that just right. The food is ready and we are just getting ready to eat."

"Hi, Annie. It's good to see you. Mama made some potato salad and a chocolate cake," Tony said as he and Derrick held out the food.

"That was nice of her. She didn't have to do that, but I'm glad she did. I've eaten her potato salad before and it's so good. Would you mind setting it on the table up there on the deck?"

"No problem, Annie," Derrick said.

Annie talked to Kristen and Emmy while Tony and Derrick headed over to the deck.

"How have you been? Have you gone anywhere exciting this summer, Kristen?" Annie asked.

"No, we were going to Ireland but Dad postponed the trip because one of his managers passed away."

"That's too bad."

"We might be able to go later," Kristen said. "How about

you? Are you still working a lot of hours?"

"Yeah, but Matty and I have two weeks off in August. We might be able to go somewhere then. Are you still working full-time, Emmy?"

"So far. I thought I might get laid off, but it hasn't happened."

"I heard you got your own place. How cool is that?"

"It's pretty small, but I like it. Tony comes over a lot and Kristen stays with me sometimes."

"Oh, I should tell you happy birthday because I probably won't see you on the actual day."

"Thanks, Annie. Does it feel any different to be eighteen?" Emmy asked.

"Not really. I can vote but it's not much different otherwise."

"I should invite you and Matt over for dinner sometime," Emmy said as she looked around the farm.

"That would be fun. I'd like to see your place. I was joking with Daddy about Matty and I getting a place together."

"Really? Are you thinking about that?" Kristen asked.

"No, I just wanted to see what Daddy would say. He does let Matty stay over at the house with me though."

Emmy looked at Annie with surprise.

"We're not sleeping together. I know most people assume we are because of his reputation, but we're not."

"Tony and I haven't done anything either," Emmy whispered.

"I haven't had sex yet, either," Kristen added. "But I'm curious about how it feels."

"Then there are at least three of us left. Three virgins, I mean," Annie said then giggled. "I told Daddy I thought I was the only one in the whole college."

The girls laughed.

"I'm hungry! Let's go eat before the guys eat everything," Annie suggested.

There was plenty of food for everyone as it turned out. Grandpa placed several large logs around the fire ring and the younger group sat on them to eat. They talked about school and stayed away from talking about relationships, for the most part. Annie listened to Elaine and Adrien as they talked about raising a family. Elaine wanted to have kids right away, but Adrien wanted to wait a few years. Cindy and Bryce talked about moving to another state after they were married.

Annie looked at her friends and thought, *You guys have changed so much in the last year. You're more mature and so serious now.* She listened to Emmy and Tony carry on like kids. *I have more in common with you now.*

After they stuffed themselves with food, Emmy helped Annie gather up all the paper plates and empty cups. They came back to the fire ring and sat with Matt and Tony. In a few minutes Emmy was sitting on Tony's lap. Annie knew if she was sitting on Matt's lap, they would be kissing. Emmy and Tony weren't though. Emmy was just relaxing as Tony held her.

Annie looked at Matt and he smiled. "You can sit on my lap if you want, Annie. I'll behave."

"What if I don't want you to behave?" she whispered.

"I think we should for now."

Annie stayed next to Matt and they talked to Mace and Derrick. Kristen was sitting next to Tony and Emmy.

"Does anyone want to go over to the lake? Annie asked. "There is a dock where we could sit and talk."

"We could go swimming, too," Mace suggested.

"Did you bring a swimsuit, Mace?" Matt asked.

"Who needs a swimsuit?" Mace smiled. "We're all friends."

"And we want to stay friends, Mace Franklin!" Annie smacked his arm. "I'm not going skinny dipping with you so just forget it."

"Oh, Annie, you're no fun anymore."

"I've never gone skinny dipping with you so don't make it seem like we have."

Matt changed the subject by announcing, "I have some fireworks for later after it gets dark."

"You do?" Annie asked. "Does Daddy know?"

"Yes, I told him and he's okay with it. I don't have much. Nothing dangerous. Just some small stuff."

While many of the older guests left before it got dark, Annie's friends hung around. They got a small fire going in the fire ring mainly to keep bugs away.

"Are you looking forward to being at North Park, Kristen?" Elaine asked.

"I can't wait, Lainey. It will be so much fun."

"Do you know which dorm you will be in yet?" Cindy asked.

"Howe Hall, but I don't know who my roommate will be."

"We will all be in the same dorm," Annie said. "It would be nice if we end up on the same floor this year."

"Cindy and I are going to be on the first floor," Elaine said. "We're not sure which room yet, but we know the floor at least."

Annie interpreted that to mean Elaine and Cindy didn't care about Annie and Kristen or any of their other old friends.

By nine o'clock it was dark enough for Matt's fireworks. Mace helped Matt set them up and fifteen minutes later, it was all over. Elaine, Cindy and their guys headed home. Tony, Emmy and the Keaslings hung around.

"Hey, Tony, is it true that you are going to Notre Dame?" Mace asked as he poked at the fire with a piece of wood.

"Yes, I've already signed a letter of intent. My sister went to Notre Dame. She's still there. She's going to be a doctor."

"I'm grateful I got a scholarship to North Park otherwise I would be stuck at the junior college."

Annie smacked Mace on his arm—with some force.

"Why'd you do that?" Mace asked as he stared at Annie.

Annie glanced at Emmy who was sitting on the other side of the fire pit next to Tony then whispered to Mace, "Because Emmy goes to the junior college, you doofus! You made it sound like it was a waste of time. You should apologize."

"Aw, crap. Okay, I will. I just wasn't thinking." Mace walked around the pit to Emmy. "I'm sorry for putting down the junior college, Emmy. I didn't mean to offend you."

She looked up at him. "It's all right, Mace. I know it's not

123

as good as North Park."

"Do you think you will finish at North Park?" Matt asked.

Emmy looked at Matt through the fire. "Yes, but I'll just be a part-time student. I'll have to keep my job in order to pay for school and rent and utilities."

Emmy envied the kids who didn't have to worry so much about finances. She knew her parents couldn't afford to pay for junior college let alone North Park. She valued her independence too much to move back home though it would save some money.

"We need to take off, Annie," Kristen said. "Thanks so much for inviting us over."

"I'm so happy you came. I'm looking forward to seeing you in the dorm when school starts. We can spend more time together."

Derrick, Kristen and Tony said goodbye to Matt and Mace while Annie and Emmy talked.

"Thanks for coming today, Emmy. It was good to see you and happy birthday."

"Thanks, Annie. I'm happy you and Matt are together. I know he wasn't as bad as people thought and he seems to have changed for the better because of you."

"He is a nice guy. I think he had to go through a growing up stage. Maybe he had some peer pressure because of his father. Let's stay in touch, okay?"

"I would like that. I'll come over to see Kristen once in a while so we should see each other."

Annie gave Emmy a hug, then she and Matt watched as they got in the car and left.

"It's been a good day, Annie," Matt said as he put an arm around her waist.

"Yes, it has. Wouldn't it be nice to live out in the country when we are older."

"I was thinking the same thing. I think I could get used to the peace and quiet very easily."

# Chapter Twenty-One

"I need to talk to you, Daddy. Do you have a few minutes?" Annie asked on Thursday morning.

"I always have time for you, sweetheart. What's on your mind?"

"Matty and I have two weeks off in August before classes start. We want to go somewhere."

"Where do you want to go? I've got some vacation time coming."

Annie hesitated for a moment then just came right out with what was on her mind. "Daddy, we want to go on vacation together. Just me and Matty."

Dad looked at Annie and understood. "Oh! I see. You and Matthew."

"Daddy, I want to be with Matty. You know I went to the doctor with Mom and that I'm on the pill."

"I know you are old enough to do what you want, Annie. I'm glad you still care enough to ask me first. Do you need my answer right away?"

"Not this minute, but maybe in a couple days. If you give me your permission, we want to start planning the trip. We wouldn't object if you and Mom want to join us maybe during the second week. Mace and Grandpa could take care of Keyshon and you guys could have a vacation, too."

"Am I correct in assuming that you and Matty would be sharing a room on this vacation."

"Yes, Daddy, and a bed."

"I was afraid of that."

"You know it's going to happen sooner or later."

"You're only eighteen, Annie. You don't have to rush into anything."

"You know we haven't."

"I know. I guess I'm just trying to prolong the inevitable."

"It's not like it will be a honeymoon, Daddy."

"That's a good thing." Dad looked at Annie and sighed. It seemed his little girl had grown up so fast. "I'll talk to Elisabeth and let you know. Maybe we can take a week off together."

"Neither one of us has ever been out west. We were thinking about going to Colorado."

"The mountains are pretty, even in summer."

"I'm not sure we can afford to stay out there for two weeks though."

"I can help you with the expenses if you need. Grandpa would help if you ask him."

"Thank you, Daddy. If you do allow us to go, I want you and Mom to join us. I'm not just saying that. Matty said it was all right with him, too."

"It might be nice to go to Colorado."

Annie made it to Mike Bushell's office on time, caught up with her work and decided to call Matt. "Hi, Matty. I talked to Daddy about our vacation."

"How did it go?"

"Better than I expected, I suppose."

"Did he give you an answer?"

"No, because I told him he didn't have to answer right away. I could tell he was disappointed. I think it makes him sad that I'm not a little girl anymore. He's afraid of losing me."

"He won't ever lose you, Annie. You'll always be his sweet angel. We might make him a grandpa in a few years."

"I think that will be more than a few years away. Mace will probably have kids before I do."

"Do you think your dad would consider Mace's kids to be his grandkids?"

"He will for sure if he and Elisabeth get married. I think he probably would if they are just dating or even living together, too."

"I think you're right."

"Oh, I also mentioned we would like them to join us the second week. You're still okay with that, right?"

"Sure. It might be a little weird at first because we would be sharing a room but I think they will get used to it."

"I wonder if he will make you sleep on the floor when we get back from vacation?"

Matt chuckled. "Wouldn't surprise me if he does."

"Would you go along with it?"

"His house. His rules. I will do whatever it takes to be with you, Annie."

"I'll talk to you later. I might stop by the Lion after my class tonight."

That evening after work Keith and Elisabeth were having a late dinner at her house. Elisabeth watched him toy with his food for a few minutes.

"What's on your mind, Keith? I can tell something is troubling you."

"I talked with Annie this morning." He paused as he recalled the conversation.

"Yes, what about?" Elisabeth asked.

"She and Matty want to go on vacation together. They will share a room and a bed."

"Were you surprised?"

"No, I guess I wasn't but I was hoping they would wait a lot longer. She's still young..."

"She is eighteen and is old enough, according to the law, to make her own decisions. More than that though, I think she is mature enough to make sound decisions. You know she can't stay a little girl forever."

"I know and I'm not trying to keep her from growing up. I'm proud of her and I'm thankful she still wants my opinion or advice before she makes important choices. How can I tell her it's okay without making it seem like I'm giving her my blessing to have sex?"

"How old were you when you first had sex? And don't you dare say it's different because she's a girl."

"Okay, I get the point."

"They are in love and I think they will still be in love fifty years from now. They complete each other. I would say they are 'soul mates' if that wasn't such an obsolete phrase."

"They want us to join them the second week. They are thinking of going to Colorado. Would you like to go to Colorado? We could have Mace and Liam take care of Keyshon."

"I would love to take a trip out west with you."

"Should I tell her it's okay?"

"Yes. Do you want me to be with you?"

"No, I'll tell her by myself. I'll tell her in the morning."

Keith came home after spending the night with Elisabeth. He looked in Annie's room and she was still asleep. He was about to turn and leave when he noticed one of her old stuffed animals on the bed by her feet. He recognized it as the lion she used to call Samantha when she was a little girl. He smiled as he left the room.

He headed to the kitchen and made her favorite kind of pancakes—chocolate chip. He started the coffee and in a couple of minutes, Annie walked into the kitchen. Keith turned to look at her, and for a moment he saw her as a little girl carrying her favorite stuffed lion and her blanket with her.

"Good morning, sweetheart. Did you sleep well?"

"Yes, I slept like a baby."

Dad opened his arms and Annie moved close. He held her tightly and kissed her forehead. "I'm making pancakes. Are you hungry?"

"You know I can never pass up chocolate chip pancakes, Daddy."

"Have a seat and I'll bring you a plate. The syrup and the butter are already on the island."

Dad brought two plates over to the island and he sat beside her.

"I talked with Elisabeth last night about vacation."

"What did you decide?"

"We decided to join you the second week."

Annie looked up at her father and realized what his answer meant.

"Oh, Daddy, I love you. I'll always love you."

"I know you will and I'll always think of you as my little girl even though you are grown up."

Annie was quiet for a few minutes as they ate their breakfast. She looked at her father. She needed to tell him something but wasn't sure she could. He looked at her and could tell she had something on her mind.

128

"What is it, Annie? You can tell me."

"Please don't be mad, but there is something else."

Her father was sure she was going to tell him she had already slept with Matty.

He set his fork down. "It's okay. You can tell me."

"I want my first time to be here in my own bed. I don't want it to be in some motel room in Colorado or on the way to Colorado."

"Oh. Your first time, huh?"

Annie grinned. "You thought I was going to tell you that we've already done it!"

"Yeah, I guess I was," Dad admitted.

"We haven't broken your rule, but I want to. Soon," she said as she poured more syrup on her pancakes. "Sometime when you are over at Mom's so we can have total privacy."

Her father thought about it for a moment. "I guess I can understand that, sweetie. Is there a certain day you have picked out?"

"Daddy!" she squealed. "No! I haven't told Matty yet. Don't worry. I'll let you know after it has happened."

"Thanks, I think. I've got to get to the station. I'll see you tonight."

"Is there anything special you want for dinner?" Annie asked.

"Whatever you make will be fine with me."

"Okay, I was planning to make burned baloney sandwiches on moldy bread with lots of bacon grease."

"Could I have a side of smelly old cottage cheese, too?"

"You're pushing it, but I'll try to find some."

"That's my girl."

He kissed the top of her head as he left the kitchen.

After her father left for work, Annie got on the phone with Matty.

"Hey! What's up?"

"Daddy told me it was all right for us to go on vacation."

"Really?"

"Yes, and I told him I want to make love to you before we

129

go. I want my first time to be in my own bed."

Matt slapped his forehead. "You seriously told that to your father!? He's going to kill me."

"No, he won't. I think he understands how I feel."

"He's going to shoot me, I know it," Matt said as he walked out of his bedroom into the kitchen. He turned around and walked outside because he heard his father coming. "Is he going to be home in the morning when I come over to see you?"

"If you get here early enough."

"Maybe I should come over after he's gone and face him on Sunday."

"You can if you want, but wouldn't you rather see him tomorrow and get it over with?"

"Get what over with? Do you mean us having sex?" Matt asked.

"No! We have to wait until a night he is with Mom. I mean just seeing Daddy now that he has given his approval for us to go on vacation."

"I guess I should man-up and face him."

"Good. I think he will respect you more for facing him and not trying to avoid him. I'll talk to you later. Call me when you get a chance tonight, okay?"

"I will. Have a good day, Annie. I love you."

"I love you, too."

Annie went into the law office for a couple of hours, then over to watch Keyshon. Keyshon and Lisa wanted to go swimming so Annie took them to the pool. She stopped at her house first to get her suit. She spent a couple of hours at the pool with Keyshon and Lisa. She spotted a couple of high school kids staring at her, so she put a t-shirt over her bikini and sat on a chaise lounge. The two high school boys came over to talk to her.

"You're Annie O'Dell, aren't you?"

"Maybe. Why do you want to know?"

"I'm Chad Ahronson and this is Charles. We thought we recognized you. We're Diana's brothers."

"Oh my God! You guys have grown a lot since the last time I saw you."

"I'm going to be a sophomore and Charlie will be a freshman."

"Why are you guys here? You have a pool at your house."

"We had to shut down our pool for a week or so. Some kind of maintenance trouble, so Diana brought us over here."

"Is she here now?"

"No, she just dropped us off and is going to pick us up later. We're supposed to call her."

"Will you let me know when she gets here? I'd like to see her."

"Sure, Annie. Why are you here? Are you alone? I thought you're going out with Matthew Sullivan."

"I'm here with Keyshon Franklin and Lisa Miley. I watch Keyshon a couple afternoons to help out."

"We know Keyshon. He's all right as far as we're concerned."

"Yeah!" Charlie answered. "He's a cool kid."

Chad and Charlie hung out with Annie. They called Diana and she came over to pick them up. She spent some time talking to Annie as the boys went back in the pool.

"How has your summer been, Annie? How's Matt doing?"

"I've been working a lot of hours and taking a summer class on Tuesday and Thursday nights. Matt's working forty hours or more a week at The Hungry Lion, so we don't see each other as much as we would like."

"I know how that is," Diana said. "Damon is home for the summer at least. I watch Danica a couple of days, but the rest of the week she has a nanny. Damon and I are volunteering at the hospital two days. Daddy set that up for us."

Just then Chad and Charlie got out of the pool and splashed water on Annie and Diana.

"Sorry! We didn't mean to get you all wet."

"Have you been pestering Annie?" Diana asked.

"No, we talked to her, but we weren't pestering her."

Diana turned to look at Annie. "Were they bothering you?"

"No, they were behaving. They've grown so much. They're both taller than you now."

131

Diana watched as her brothers dove back into the pool. "I know. It's hard to believe they're both in high school already. Dad wanted to send them to St. Raymond's, but Mom talked him into letting them go to Roosevelt."

"I wonder if Roosevelt has changed much?"

"Not really. How are your grandfather and father, Annie?"

"They're both okay. Grandpa loves retirement. Daddy is still dating Mrs. Franklin. I call her Mom now."

"Oh, that's so sweet. I know she will never replace your mother, but I'm so pleased you feel that way about her. My parents know her and have always spoken highly of her."

"Daddy thinks she's special, too."

Annie and Diana both laughed.

"It was good to see you, Annie, but I need to get these guys home. I hope I see you more often this year. Maybe we will have a class together."

"It was nice to see you, too, Diana. Say hi to Damon for me. He probably won't remember me but..."

"He knows who you are, Annie. He knows Matthew, too. He always thought Matt would turn out all right and he has."

"Thanks for saying so, Diana."

"It's the truth, Annie. I wouldn't make it up just to please you."

Annie understood why Diana was so highly thought of by everyone she met.

# Chapter Twenty-Two

Annie woke up early Saturday morning. She looked at the clock and saw it was 7:06. She knew her father had to be at work at nine. Matty was supposed to be at the house around 7:30. She got out of bed to see if the bathroom was free. It was so she grabbed a clean towel and took her shower. She got dressed and started making breakfast. She heard her father go into the bathroom. Matty arrived a few minutes later.

"Morning, Annie. How was your night?" Matt asked after kissing her cheek.

"I got a good night of sleep. How about you?" Annie asked as she led Matt into the kitchen.

He shifted his weight back and forth. "I kinda tossed and turned more than normal. I think I was nervous about this morning."

"You know you don't have to be."

"I just put myself in your father's shoes and I know how I would feel if a guy told me he was sleeping with our daughter."

Detective O'Dell walked into the kitchen in time to hear what Matthew said to Annie.

"Morning, Matthew. Morning, sweetie. Breakfast sure smells good."

"Hi, Daddy. I thought you might want a good breakfast this morning. Are you hungry?"

"Yes, I could eat a small horse as long as it was covered in hot mustard."

"That sounds absolutely delicious," Annie said. "I'll see if I can find a recipe and we can have it this week."

Dad grabbed a cup of coffee and sat at the island.

"I heard what you told Annie about how you would feel if you were in my shoes. I'm glad you said 'our daughter.' That makes me feel you are committed to Annie for the long term. I'll admit it will be a little difficult for me, but I know you love her and she loves you."

"I do love Annie. I'd marry her tomorrow if we could," Matt said as he put his arm around her waist.

"Sorry, but I'm busy tomorrow. What about Tuesday?" Annie teased.

"Okay, I'm ready for breakfast. You guys can help yourself after I get what I want," Dad said.

What little tension there was in the room was now gone. Matt and Mr. O'Dell talked and teased Annie just like before. Annie knew that before too long, she and Matty would become lovers. She knew she would tell her father after it happened and she knew he would love her just the same as before—and Matty, too.

Later, Annie lay beside Matt on her bed. He was looking at a map of Colorado.

"How would you feel about starting the trip in Estes Park? That's where Rocky Mountain National Park is located," he asked.

"Matty, do you have your heart set on Colorado?"

"No, I suppose not, but I thought that's where you wanted to go. I'm willing to go somewhere else."

She rolled onto her back. "I was just thinking Colorado is so far away that we would have to drive close to three thousand miles for the two weeks. I mentioned that to Daddy and he suggested we take a look at Great Smoky Mountains National Park. I looked it up online and it's a lot closer. We could rent a cabin for two weeks and not have to drive nearly as much."

"I would consider it. What do you know about it?"

Annie showed Matt pictures of the national park and they looked at some cabins available to rent.

Her father walked in and sat on the edge of the bed. "What are you guys talking about?"

"I was talking to Matty about Colorado. He doesn't mind if we don't go there. Great Smoky Mountains National Park looks just as beautiful to us," Annie said.

"It would be closer and more affordable."

Matt grinned. "Not to mention easier on my car."

"There is that to consider."

"Would we be able to rent a cabin by ourselves?" Annie asked.

"I don't think that will be a problem. I was talking to your grandfather yesterday and mentioned the Smoky Mountains. He reminded me that an old friend of his actually owns several cabins in the area. Grandpa called him and he just happens to have a two bedroom cabin available."

"How much is it?" Matt asked.

"He told Grandpa we could have it for nothing," Dad answered.

"Are you kidding? For nothing?"

Dad shrugged. "Yeah, like I said, he's an old friend."

They moved from Annie's room to the kitchen so they could use the island to look at their maps easier. They all agreed a vacation in the Smoky Mountains would be even better than the Rockies. Matt and Annie started looking for attractions in the area. A ten minute phone call later and the cabin was rented and the dates set for August 9-22. Annie and Matt would be there the first week and Keith and Elisabeth would join them.

"We should save the Biltmore House for the second week so Daddy and Mom can see it, too," Annie suggested. "They will like seeing that. We can do a lot of hiking the first week and not have to go very far. The cabin is just outside Gatlinburg and close to the national park."

"I like the idea of staying in a cabin. We can cook our own meals and save money," Matt said.

"Grandpa's friend is saving us the most money. I wonder why he would let us have the cabin for free?"

"Mr. O'Dell, do you know why?" Matt asked as he rubbed Annie's back.

"You should ask Liam, but I know they went to college together."

"Oh, Matty, it will be so much fun planning all the things we should do," Annie said then kissed his cheek. "I need to buy some new shoes if we're going to do much hiking."

"I should probably buy some, too," Matt said.

"We should buy them soon, so we can break them in before we leave," Annie suggested.

# Chapter Twenty-Three

Elisabeth Franklin slipped home for lunch on Friday and caught Annie doing the laundry and cleaning the kitchen. "Annie, I appreciate it, but you don't have to do that for me. Wouldn't you rather be doing things with your friends?"

Annie rinsed out the Handi Wipe and hung it over the faucet to dry. "Maybe, but except for Mace, they all have jobs so they're just as busy as me. I haven't seen Lainey or Cindy since the Fourth out at Grandpa's. I have talked to Emmy a few times, but she's just as busy."

"I have a job," Mace sounded hurt.

"Oh yeah," Annie said. "Just what is your job? Don't say you have to watch Keyshon because he's spending most of his time with Lisa."

"I have to stay in shape for basketball. I have to work out and run for eight hours a day it seems," he said while twirling a basketball on his finger.

"Oh, you poor baby!" Annie exclaimed. "Is that why you sleep until noon everyday, then sit on your butt and watch TV and play games on that PlayStation thing?"

Mace feinted throwing the basketball to Annie and she flinched. "I'll have you know those games help improve and hand and eye coordination."

"I bet I could beat you with my eyes closed."

"Put your money where your mouth is, Annie O'Dell."

She frowned with her hands on her hips. "I don't have the time. I have work to do. Matty and I are still planning our trip."

"You mean your honeymoon," Mace teased.

Annie slugged Mace in the side. "It's not a honeymoon."

"What is there to plan? You won't even leave the cabin."

"Do you want me to slug you again?" Annie asked as she grabbed Mace's basketball from him.

Mace stole the ball right back. "Oh, excuse me. The hot tub is on the deck so you'll have to go outside to get in."

"Mace! Will you please leave Annie alone? Stop teasing her so much," Elisabeth said sternly.

"All right. Forgive me for teasing you. I didn't realize you were so sensitive nowadays."

"I'm just anxious for vacation," Annie said.

Mace grinned. "I know why, too."

"Mace!" Elisabeth yelled at him again.

Matt always called Annie in the morning, then in the evening when he got a break. Her job and night class kept her busy during the week. Since she and Matt were so busy, they were tired by Saturday night. Consequently, the chance for Annie to sleep with Matt had not happened—except for this Sunday when they did sleep together. Keith and Elisabeth came home from grocery shopping to find Annie and Matt sound asleep on the couch in the living room. After setting the bags of groceries on the island, Keith and Elisabeth walked out to the living room.

"No wonder they fell asleep. Baseball is boring enough to put an insomniac to sleep for a week," Keith said then chuckled.

"I thought you liked to watch baseball, Keith," Elisabeth said.

Keith put his arms around Elisabeth and kissed her. "I like to watch it with you because it puts us both to sleep."

"Hi, did you just get home?" Annie woke up at the sound of her father's voice, slipped from under Matt's arm and stood up.

"Yes, we did some grocery shopping. Did you eat lunch?"

"Not really. We ate breakfast but we skipped lunch. I did some laundry, then we were on the couch. Matty turned on a ballgame and we fell asleep."

Keith chuckled again. "I think that's why baseball used to be called the 'national pastime' because it put everyone to sleep."

"Would you like me to make some lunch for you and Matt?" Elisabeth asked.

"I guess I am hungry again."

"How about a sandwich? We picked up some roast beef and honey ham."

"Roast beef would be good. Do we have any cheese?" Annie asked.

"We have American, provolone and pepperjack."

"Pepperjack and mayo."

"Lettuce and tomato?" Elisabeth asked.

"Yes, please."

Keith and Elisabeth went back to the kitchen. Matty woke up and pulled Annie back onto the couch without realizing they were not alone in the house anymore. Annie turned to face him and he kissed her before she could stop him.

"We're not alone, Matty."

"Does that mean I can't kiss you?" Matt asked.

"No, I just wanted to let you know before you tried anything more than kissing."

Matt heard Keith and Elisabeth in the kitchen. "They're busy." Matt moved on top of Annie and kissed her again just as Elisabeth walked back into the room.

Elisabeth coughed to get their attention. "I was going to ask what kind of bread you would prefer, Annie. Would you like a sandwich, too, Matt?"

"Wheat bread is okay with me," Annie said.

Matt looked over his shoulder. "I'll take whatever kind of sandwich Annie is having, please."

"Would you like two sandwiches, Matt?" Elisabeth asked.

"Sure. I'm hungry enough for two."

"I'll let you know when they are ready. You can have them at the island. Not in here."

"Thanks, Mom," Annie said then waited until Elisabeth left the room. She whispered to Matt, "Mom sounded a little upset."

"Yeah, I got that impression, too."

"Maybe we should stop kissing and get off the couch."

"Maybe I should just get off of you, Annie."

"But I like having you where you are," Annie whispered.

They got up, walked into the kitchen and sat at the island.

"Are you upset with us, Mom? You sounded like it."

"I'm sorry, dear," Elisabeth said waving a hand. "I'm not upset with you or Matthew. It's Keyshon. I walked into his room and he was with Lisa. They were kissing and I yelled at them."

"He is too young to get serious about Lisa," Annie said.

"I know, but they are spending so much time together."

138

"Do you want me to talk to him?" Annie asked. "I will if you want."

Elisabeth shook her head. "I don't think it will do any good, Annie. He just isn't listening anymore. I talked to Lisa's mother and she was just as upset. I don't want to force them not to see each other. I think that would backfire."

Elisabeth made the sandwiches. Annie got some chips from the pantry. Keith grabbed a Sam Adams and three Cokes.

"I could try talking to Keyshon," Matt said. "I know I'm maybe not the best person to be giving advice to him."

"In a way, you might be the perfect person," Elisabeth said. "Keyshon likes you and he might listen to you more than Keith or me. It's worth a try."

"I'll talk to him when I see him later."

"Thanks, Matt. I hope you have better luck with him than I have been having. This is a difficult time for him."

Matt talked to Keyshon later that afternoon. Keyshon opened up about his feelings and promised to behave better and not to kiss Lisa unless an adult was in the room.

"I'll just give her one kiss as I'm leaving her house. Is that okay, Matthew Sullivan?"

"Yes, Keyshon. You can give her a quick kiss when you leave. You promise not to do anything else like we talked about, right?"

"I promise! I will wait until we are both older. I'm too young to be a father like you," Keyshon said.

Matt, Mace and Keyshon came back to the O'Dell house. Annie was hungry again so she ordered two pizzas. They ate them while watching a movie in the living room.

"Will that hold you guys for now?" Annie asked.

"I'm full," Mace answered.

"So am I," Keith said. "I need to pack some stuff."

He walked into the bathroom and was putting his electric razor into his bag when he spotted a bottle of Heavenly Nights bubble bath on the counter. He picked it up, opened it and held it up to his nose. "I've always loved the way this smells, Amy Catherine. It reminds me of fresh daisies and berries with a hint of lemon. Annie must have bought this. I didn't know they still made it." He set the bottle down, placed his toothbrush and deodorant in his bag and then understood. He stared at the bubble bath and whispered, "I know why you bought this, Annie. You bought it for Matt." He finished packing, walked out to the kitchen and smiled at Annie.

"What?" she asked while putting the pizza boxes in the trash can.

"I saw the bubble bath," he whispered.

"Daddy! You weren't supposed to notice," she said while blushing.

"I'm going to spend the night with Elisabeth. We're ready to leave."

"I kinda figured that," Annie said.

Mace walked into the kitchen and asked, "Hey, Annie, can I borrow your car to run Keyshon out to the farm? He's going to stay there tonight so he can go fishing in the morning."

"Be nice if you put some gas in it," she answered.

"I've got five bucks."

"Better than nothing," Annie said.

Mace took Keyshon to Grandpa Liam's house. He was about to leave and come back when he got a text.

"Why are you texting me now, girl? I'll bring your car back safe and sound," Mace said as he checked the message. "I'll even put gas in it." He chuckled as he read, "Stay away tonight!" *I know why you want me to stay away. Good for you, Annie girl.*

Annie took Matt's hand and led him outside to the patio. Matt didn't take his eyes off of her as he pulled her onto the chaise lounge. She leaned into him. He wrapped his arms around her and nuzzled her neck.

They were quiet for a moment, then Annie whispered, "I'm ready, Matty."

"Are you sure, Annie?"

"Totally! This is our last chance before vacation. I just texted Mace because he was planning to bring my car back."

"Do you think that's why your father was staying with Elisabeth tonight?" Matt asked.

140

"It might be, but I never said anything to him."

He rested his chin on her head. "I know how much this means to you, Annie."

"Am I being silly for making such a big deal about losing my virginity?"

He shook his head, moved her hair and kissed her neck while playing with a button. "It is a big deal."

She pressed his hand against her trapping it in place. "I love how you do that," she whispered. "It makes my heart go a hundred miles an hour."

"What? This?" He nibbled her ear.

"No! Yes! Don't stop," she said. "Just don't draw blood. I don't want to become a vampire like the girl in that story."

He smiled and slowly said in a deep voice, "But I need to suck your blood."

She giggled and offered her neck to him. "Are you trying to imitate that movie star who made all those old Dracula movies?"

"Is it working?"

"You're certainly erasing any nervousness I was feeling."

"I don't want you to be nervous, Annie. I want you to feel hot and... um..."

She turned over. "Hot and what, Matty?"

"Stop grinning like that. You know what I mean."

She kissed his lips. "I'm not nervous at all."

He returned her kiss, then flipped her over. He put his hands on her stomach.

"You can undo my buttons, Matty." She moved his hand to a breast.

"It's still a little light." He undid the top button.

"No one can see us here," she said while he did another button. "I'm definitely feeling a little... um... you know."

Matt caressed her neck with his lips and expertly unbuttoned her top completely.

"How did you do that so smoothly?" she asked.

"I've had a lot of practice," he answered.

She felt her heart beating faster as he put a hand on her bra and squeezed.

"I can feel something..."

"Hush," he whispered. "It's your fault. I can't help it."

She turned over and kissed him while lifting his t-shirt up and running a finger along his chest. "I think you need to lose this shirt."

He raised his arms and she pulled his t-shirt up.

"It's stuck. I need help," she said then kissed his nose through the t-shirt.

"Give me a second." He popped his shirt over his head, removed it and tossed it aside.

She touched a spot below his nipple. "When did you get this scar?"

"Several years ago. I cut myself shaving."

"Stop it," she said, then kissed the scar.

He kissed her again, put his hands on her shorts, pushed on them but then stopped. "I don't want to do it out here."

"I don't either, but you can start here."

He stuck his fingers in the pockets of her jean shorts.

"That tickles and why are you wearing a belt?" she asked.

"I didn't want my shorts to fall off."

"Oh, they're coming off," she said with a big smile.

He pulled her close and kissed her.

"I like it when you use your tongue."

"Just don't bite it," he said.

They stopped kissing to take a breath.

"I'm ready for my bubble bath now, Matty," Annie said.

He released his hold on her. "Okay. I'll start the water."

"Carry me, Matty," Annie said as she held out her arms.

Matt picked her up and carried her into the house. He started filling the tub with water and Annie added the Heavenly Nights bubble bath.

Annie kissed Matt and whispered, "It's kinda silly, but will you wait outside?"

"Call me when I can come back in."

Matt left the bathroom so Annie could undress. She slipped into the tub and hollered, "You can come back in now!"

Matt entered and sat on the toilet.

142

"Aren't you going to move closer? I want you to wash my back."

"Okay, are you nervous about letting me see you?"

"A little," she whispered. She covered her chest with both arms.

"You don't have to be. You are perfect."

"That feels so good when you rub your finger along my back. It makes me feel tingly in all the right places."

When she was ready to get out of the tub, Matt held her towel for her. He wrapped the towel around her without looking. He used another towel to dry her arms and legs.

"I'm pretty sure my butt is dry now, Matty."

"Yeah, I wanted to be sure," he said with a grin. "You smell so good, but not like a strawberry."

"I'm glad you like it," she said then giggled. "It's not the same bubble bath I used as a child. Daddy said it was Mom's favorite. She used to make him wait while she took a bath."

"I'm glad my wait is almost over," Matt said as he smelled her hair. "I'm going to take a shower now, Annie."

"Don't take too long. I'll be waiting for you." She let the towel fall open behind her then dashed to her bedroom.

"Nice butt," Matt hollered.

"Shut up, Matthew."

"That was quick," Annie said a couple of minutes later.

"I barely got wet in the shower," he said letting his towel fall to the floor. *Crap! Maybe I shouldn't let her see me yet.*

"Oooh! Let me look at you," she said as he stood beside the bed. Her eyes widened.

He shifted his weight from one foot to the other. "Come on, Annie. I feel weird."

"Don't cover up. I want to look." She bit her lip while staring. *Whoa! I didn't know it would be so big. That must be why everyone says it hurts the first time. I can't back out now. It can't hurt more than when I broke my arm.*

"Can I get in bed now, please?"

She nodded and scooted over holding the sheet to her neck.

"Thanks, I don't like being stared at."

"Aren't you forgetting something?" She pointed to the nightstand. "They're in there."

"Right. I didn't want to spoil the mood."

"You won't," she whispered, then giggled nervously.

He slipped into bed a moment later.

She still held the sheet to her neck. "I peeked at you putting it on."

"That's okay. I saw your butt." He pulled her close and reached under the sheet. "I'm going to kiss you until I can feel your heart pounding against my chest," he said while scooting closer and slowly tugging the sheet lower.

"I like feeling your heart beating against mine," she whispered.

"I don't ever want to be with another girl."

"You better not."

She closed her eyes when she felt his lips moving from her lips to her neck.

He paused there. "I love you so much, Annie," he said before moving his mouth to her breasts.

"I know and I love you even more." She took a deep breath, held it for a moment, then said, "You can keep kissing and touching me like that. It feels so good." She wrapped her arms around him and pulled him on top.

"Annie, are you..."

She put a finger to his mouth. "Don't say anything."

She closed her eyes and gasped when she felt him there.

He held himself above her and whispered, "Relax, Annie. I'll go slow." He waited for a moment before slowly continuing. "Does it feel better now?"

Annie opened her eyes and smiled.

## Chapter Twenty-Four

Annie was in the kitchen making dinner when her father arrived shortly after six.

"Hi, sweetie. I'm home. Something sure smells good."

"Hi, Daddy. I'm making pork chops and sauerkraut with red potatoes. How was your day?"

"Uneventful. I spent most of the day catching up on paperwork. Let me change and we can talk."

Five minutes later he was back in the kitchen with Annie. She stood on the other side of the island. He took one look at her and he knew. He opened his arms and she scooted around the island. He held her tight and she wrapped her arms around him and hugged him as tightly as she could. He kissed the top of her head.

"Are you all right?" Dad asked after they stopped hugging.

She looked up at him. "I'm fine. You know, huh?"

"Yes, I'm your father." He put his hands on her shoulders and squeezed them. "I know everything."

"Oh, Daddy," she said as she hugged him again. "It was so romantic and special. Matty really loves me!"

"I know he does, sweetie. I hope you're not letting the pork chops burn."

Annie turned around and walked around the island to the stove to check their dinner. She missed it as her father wiped a tear from his eye.

She lifted the cover and stirred the pan. "I think everything is ready. I hope you're hungry."

"It smells delicious."

As they ate Annie shared a few details. "After everyone left, we sat on the patio and cuddled. We talked about vacation and then I said I was ready. I took a bubble bath first."

"I noticed the bubble bath a couple days ago. It was your mother's favorite."

"I remember you telling me that a long time ago. You told me how you loved the way she smelled after taking a bath in that. I found some at the mall. I think I might like taking bubble baths."

"I'm guessing that means you enjoyed... everything."

"Daddy!"

"Sorry, that's none of my business."

"It's okay. I think I will enjoy 'bubble baths' more after I get more used to them." She used air quotes.

"So how was the office today?"

Dad changed the subject to avoid further embarrassment.

"It was not quite as boring as most days."

"Oh, why was that?" Dad asked while cutting his pork chop. "I like the thick center cut chops."

"I know you do. That's why I bought them," she said. "Matty stopped by with a dozen red roses and one white rose."

"He did? That was sweet of him."

"Daddy, is there any significance to the one white rose?"

Her father was silent for a moment as he remembered. "I might have mentioned something to Matthew a while back about sending white roses to your mother on the morning we got married."

"Oh, Daddy! I love you more than ever."

"I love you this much!" He held out his arms to his side the way he did when Annie was a little girl.

# Chapter Twenty-Five

Mr. O'Dell didn't see Matt until Wednesday evening when Matt came over for dinner. At first Matt was a bit nervous; totally understandable under the circumstances.

"Evening, Matthew. How was your day?" Mr. O'Dell asked as he sipped a Sam Adams at the kitchen island.

"It was all right. I worked six hours. Well, I guess I didn't have to, but Dad was short handed so I volunteered." Matt looked around for Annie.

"Annie's in the bathroom. She got home late," Mr. O'Dell said. "She's not taking a bubble bath, just a shower."

"That's good," Matt was more nervous now.

"That was sweet of you to take her roses, Matt. I remember how much Amy Catherine loved roses and how good she smelled after a bubble bath. I could never resist her... anyway."

"Thank you for telling me about the roses and the bubble bath."

"Thank you for... well... you know."

"I love her more now."

"Okay! Enough talk about Annie. Are you guys anxious to start your vacation?"

"I can't wait for Sunday to get here," Matt said feeling better since the conversation shifted away from the night.

"Liam called last night. He got a call from his friend. He's going to leave the keys to the cabin in the mailbox at the end of the driveway. He said they would be in an envelope."

"I still can't believe he's not charging us anything."

"Hi, Matty."

Annie walked up behind Matt and hugged him. Matt spun around and hugged her back. She was wearing a tank top and a pair of shorts. Her hair was still wet from her shower.

"You smell good, Annie," Matt said.

"What are we going to have for dinner?" Dad asked.

"We have the leftover chicken enchiladas from last night. I can warm up some more refried beans and I think we have enough stuff to make a decent salad," Annie answered.

"Sounds good to me," Dad said then finished his beer.

"Matty, will you help me with the beans while I put together the salad?"

"Should I warm up the enchiladas in the microwave?" Matt asked.

"If the dish fits. It might not fit."

The casserole dish was too large so Matt found a smaller one. He heated up the refried beans and enchiladas while Annie threw together a salad.

Dad watched them. *They seem to treat each other just the same as before.*

Matty teased her and smacked her bottom. She teased him back and they kissed. It didn't take long for dinner to be ready.

"Are we out of salsa?" Annie asked.

Matt pointed to the fridge. "It's on the door, Annie. Next to the ketchup and mustard."

"I see it. I'm used to it being on a shelf."

"Sorry, I guess I moved it," Matt said.

"It's all right. It probably makes more sense to put it where you did."

"We can put it back where you had it, sweetie."

Dad shook his head. "All right! Enough of this sweet talk. The fridge isn't so big that you won't be able to find the salsa no matter where it is."

"Daddy! We need to get used to being with each other."

"There will be plenty of time for that later. I mean a few years from now later."

They finished dinner, cleaned up the kitchen, then sat in the living room and talked about vacation. Annie went over the list of tourist attractions they wanted to visit. They were saving most of them for the second week when Mom and Dad would be there.

"I do want to visit the national park the first week. We can go back again. It looks so gorgeous," Annie said.

Matt added, "We can do most of the hiking the first week."

"That's a good idea. I know Elisabeth and I won't be able to keep up on any long hikes," Dad said. "Oh, Annie, I'm going to take your car in for an oil change and have it inspected in the morning. I'll take you to work."

"I can take Annie to work in the morning if that's all right."

"Are you sure?" Dad asked.

"Sure. I would like to spend the night if that's okay."

"I don't mind if you stay, Matt."

"Daddy?"

"Yes, sweetie."

"Do we still have to use the air mattress and sleeping bag?"

Keith had been expecting this question and had given it much thought. "I suppose it's okay if you put it away now. Just remember the walls are thin and I have excellent hearing."

Annie twisted her hair around a finger and said, "Just because we are in the same bed doesn't mean we will make love."

"Of course, dear. Oh, did I mention you still have to leave the door open?"

"For real? You're kidding right?" Annie asked.

"No, that's still the rule."

"That's okay, Mr. O'Dell. I wouldn't feel right otherwise."

Annie stared at Matt. "Are you saying you couldn't have sex with me because Daddy is here?"

"Geez, Annie! Are you trying to get me killed?"

"Daddy wouldn't hurt you."

"How about those Cubs?" Dad said as he slapped his knee. "They won another game yesterday."

Annie frowned at her father. "Daddy, stop doing that."

"Doing what?" he shrugged.

"Changing the subject whenever I talk about sex."

"Those Cubs are having a great year," Matt said.

"You men are impossible. You want to have sex, but the minute Mom or I talk about it, you change the subject."

"I can't wait for football season to start. How about you, Matthew?"

Annie tossed a throw pillow at her father.

"Me, too. I love football," Matt said.

"You can sleep on the couch tonight, Matthew Sullivan, and make sure you bring a sleeping bag with you on vacation."

Matt knew Annie was kidding as he kissed her.

# Chapter Twenty-Six

Annie was going over her list of things to pack for the trip at eight o'clock on Saturday evening. Matt and her father were sitting on the living room couch watching as Annie nervously paced back and forth.

"It's rather amazing," Dad said as he pointed at Annie.

"What's that?" Matt asked.

"Notice how she's concentrating on her list and not watching where she's going."

Matt watched for a few seconds. "Yeah, I see."

"If you or I were to pace around like that, we'd be bumping into the furniture," Dad said. "She stops and turns around just before she runs into anything."

Matt grinned. "It is amazing."

"I'm right here," Annie said. "I can hear you talking about me."

"Annie, you've gone over that list a hundred times," Matt said. "You've packed just about every piece of clothing you own."

"And half the towels we own," Dad said.

"Did not." She frowned at her father. "I'm just so nervous and excited. I probably won't get any sleep tonight and then I won't be able to help with the driving. Our vacation will be ruined before it even starts."

Dad grinned. "Maybe you should have a few beers. That will help you sleep."

"Very funny, Daddy! I would be so sick in the morning that I would have to stay home."

"Just try to relax, sweetie. You know they have stores in Tennessee just like we have here. If you discover you've left something behind, God only knows what that might be," he said then shrugged. "You can just buy it. Your car is all set. Oil has been changed, the belts and fluids are good, new tires all around. The battery is okay."

Matt added, "We have our maps and two copies of the letter with the directions to the cabin. I can't imagine we will get lost."

"I'm not worried about that," Annie said. "Grandpa has been there before and he told me it wasn't difficult to find. He said the only tricky part was the turn off the paved road onto the dirt trail. He said we have to turn at the place where there used to be a large oak tree."

"What do you mean 'used to be' a tree?" Matt asked.

Annie stopped pacing and looked at Matt. "Grandpa said the tree wasn't there anymore, but we would be able to tell where it was because they are always a couple cows hanging around."

"I think Grandpa is just pulling your leg," Dad said. "He does like to tease."

"I know he is. I'm not totally scatterbrained like some people I know," Annie said as she walked close enough to Matt for him to grab her and pull her onto the couch next to him.

"It's not nice to talk about Mace like that when he isn't here to defend himself."

"Did he drop off his Discman? He was going to let me borrow it for a small price." Annie asked. She looked at Matt then at her father.

"I haven't seen him, Annie. Did he say when he was coming over and what was the 'small price?'" Matt asked.

"He just said this evening and I hope he was kidding about the small price. He said I had to let him borrow my CDs."

"How many CDs are you planning to take?" Matt asked.

"I think that little case holds twenty-four. That should be enough."

Dad said, "You won't have much time to listen to them once you get there, sweetie."

Annie looked at her father to see what he meant by that remark.

"What? Why are you looking at me like that? I just meant you will be busy and won't be sitting around listening to music."

There was a knock at the door and Annie ran over to open it. Mace was standing on the porch listening to his Discman.

"Why didn't you just come in? Why did you knock?" Annie asked.

"I thought it might be safer if I knock from now on. If I just

151

walk in, I might surprise you and Matt."

"Do you want me to smack you?" She waved a fist at him. "Get in here and if you say anything to Matt I swear I will make you pay dearly. Who told you anyway?"

"Your father mentioned it to my mom and I kinda overheard it. Are you mad that I know?"

"No, you haven't told anyone else, have you?" she asked while stepping aside to let him pass. Then she slammed the door closed.

"Not a soul. Swear!" Mace raised a hand as if he were in a courtroom.

"Not even Erin?" Annie asked.

"Not yet. Is it all right if I tell her?"

"Just tell her not to tell anyone else, okay?"

Mace walked into the living room with Annie. "Here's the Discman and an extra battery, Matt."

"Thanks, Mace. If Annie breaks it, I'll make her buy you a new one."

"I'm not gonna break it," Annie said.

"Are you guys all packed and ready?"

"Yeah, except for some stuff we can't pack until tomorrow after we get ready to leave. Annie's checked her list a thousand times tonight alone," Matt said.

"She will think of something she has forgotten about the time you get out of Illinois," Mace joked.

Annie wrinkled her forehead as she frowned at Mace.

He made a face back at her and asked, "Did you pack any pajamas or aren't you going to need them?"

"You can kiss my butt, Mace Franklin! Don't expect to ever see your Discman again either!" Annie screamed at him.

"I'm sorry, Annie. I didn't mean anything," Mace said with his hands up in surrender.

"It's okay, Mace. Don't take it personally. She's been jumpy all day," Matt said.

"I should get home. I promised Erin I would call her tonight." Mace moved closer to Annie. "Have a good time and drive safely, okay?"

152

Annie moved close to Mace and gave him a hug. "Thanks. We'll have fun and I guess I'm not mad at you anymore."

"That's good," Mace said as he shook hands with Matt. "Be safe, Matt."

"Thanks. We'll be careful."

"Remember, Annie, if you see any bears, just try to outrun Matt."

"I'll remember," Annie said then giggled.

Annie walked outside with Mace and he gave her a hug before he got in his car and took off. Matt walked outside and joined Annie as she waved goodbye to Mace. He stood behind her and put his arms around her waist.

"He knows," Annie said.

Matt nodded. "I kinda figured that out. I didn't tell him if that's what you thought."

"I know. He heard Daddy talking to Mom. I hope he didn't tell Keyshon."

"I'm sure he didn't. Come back inside. We need to get some sleep tonight." Matt led Annie back inside and locked the door.

"I'm going to bed, Daddy," Annie said. "But I don't think I'll be able to fall asleep."

"Try to get some rest even if you can't sleep."

It took Annie nearly an hour, but she finally fell asleep as Matt held her.

# Chapter Twenty-Seven

Annie woke up before her alarm sounded. She looked at the clock and groaned. *Crap! It's only six thirty.* She lay her head on the pillow and stared at the ceiling for a few minutes. *There's no way I'm going to get any more sleep. I might as well get up.* She turned off the alarm and tried not to wake Matt, but he opened his eyes as she was getting out of bed.

"What time is it?"

"Six thirty," she answered. "You can go back to sleep while I take my shower."

"Don't let me sleep too much longer. We want to be on the road by eight," Matt said as he turned onto his side.

Annie took a quick shower, got dressed and gathered up everything she needed to pack. Matt woke up and took his shower. Annie heard her father humming as she walked down the hallway and into the kitchen.

"Morning, Daddy."

"Good morning, sweetie. Did you get any sleep?"

"It took me a while, but I finally fell asleep."

"There's coffee in that thermos and some donuts to get you started. I made some sandwiches and there's some fruit in the little cooler."

"Thanks, Daddy. We don't want to stop too many times."

"Just be careful. If you guys get tired, just stop. Better to get there a little bit later than to take chances."

"We'll be careful. If we get going at eight we should be there by eight tonight."

"There's an hour time difference, remember."

"Right. We are allowing for that and hopefully we will get there before it gets too dark."

Matt packed the last of the luggage into the car, then joined them in the kitchen. "We're ready, Annie. A few minutes early."

"Okay, Matty."

Annie hugged her father one more time. "I'll call when we get there if we have a cell phone signal. I love you, Daddy."

"I love you, too. Have a safe trip and Elisabeth and I will

see you in a week."

Matt shook Keith's hand. "I'll take good care of her, I promise."

"I know you will, Matthew. Drive safely. I'll walk outside with you."

Dad watched as Annie and Matt got in the car. He waved goodbye as Matt backed out of the driveway. His heart was a little heavy as he watched his little girl leave.

Six hours later Keith's cell phone rang. He looked to see who was calling. "Hi, Annie. Is everything all right?"

"We're fine. We stopped for gas so I thought I would call. We're making good time and Matty thinks we'll be there early. I'm not sure just where we are right now, but we just went through Lexington, Kentucky. Matt thinks we will be there in about four hours."

"Sounds about right to me. Just don't be in too big a hurry, okay?"

"We'll be careful. I love you."

"I love you more," Dad said. He stared at his phone after ending the call. *It makes me feel good to know she's still not totally grown up.*

Matt's prediction was just about right. Just before seven Eastern time. Annie called her father.

"Hi, Daddy."

"Hi, sweetie. Where are you guys now?"

"We're in Gatlinburg," she answered. "We stopped to buy pop and stuff. I thought I should call now because I might not get a signal at the cabin."

"You're probably right. The cabin is in a kind of remote area. Any problems on the trip?"

"None! We didn't get lost and the car is running great."

"That's good to hear."

"If I can't call from the cabin, I'll try calling when we are back in town, okay?"

"Okay. Have a good time and I'll talk to you soon."

"Bye, Daddy. Love you!"

Annie read the directions to Matt as they made their way

through the city. They found the county road leading to the dirt road where the cabin was located. Matt slowed the car as they approached something weird looking.

"What the devil is that?" Annie looked and began to laugh. "It's cows! Look! Grandpa wasn't kidding when he said there would be cows hanging around."

Matt stopped the car as they looked to see four black and white, flat, plywood 'cows' hanging from the large maple tree alongside the road. The names of the cabins were painted on the cows.

"I guess we're close, Annie," Matt said.

"Grandpa said it was about a mile up this road, then we turn to the right."

Matt checked the mileage as they drove slowly along the gravel and dirt road. After traveling nearly a mile, Annie saw another 'road' on the right.

"I think this is it, Matty."

"Are you sure?"

"I think so."

"I'd hate to be out here after a heavy rain."

"Maybe that's why we see a lot of pickup trucks," Annie said.

Matt turned onto the side road and after two tenths of a mile Annie saw the sign for their cabin. Matt pulled into the gravel driveway.

"This is it, Matty. It's in that clearing and there are woods all around. There's a swing hanging from that tree."

He parked the car and they jumped out. They looked around and couldn't see any signs of civilization. Annie saw the mailbox on top of a stump near the end of the driveway. She walked over and found an envelope inside. Annie opened it and inside were two keys and a note.

Annie read it, then told Matt, "Mr. Rulabaughn says to have a good time and to say hi to Grandpa when we get back. He left a phone number in case we need anything. Otherwise, he will leave us alone."

"Let's check it out!" Matt shouted.

From the outside the cabin appeared to be a quite a few years old. There was a porch across the entire front with wooden stairs right in the middle. Annie ran up the stairs ahead of Matt and tried the door.

"It's locked. Can you open it, Matty?"

"Just give me a second."

Matt unlocked the door, grabbed Annie and picked her up.

"Are you going to carry me across the threshold like we are married?"

"Just practicing in case I ever get married to anyone."

"If you get married to anyone it better be me, Matthew Sullivan!"

Matt carried Annie inside and they looked around.

"Wow! This is even nicer than the pictures made it seem," Matt said. "It smells so good, too. Like we're in the forest or something."

"I agree," Annie replied. "Matty?"

"Yes, sweetie," he said with a big grin.

"You can set me down now."

"If you insist," Matt said.

"The knotty pine looks better in person," Annie said.

Matt walked over and plopped down on the couch. "I like the fireplace and the open rafters."

Annie pointed to the other end of the room. "I like how the kitchen is open to everything. This dining room set looks like it was custom made for this cabin." She turned around and said, "The bedrooms and bathroom are over there."

Straight ahead were French doors leading to the back porch.

"Let's check out the hot tub." Matt led the way.

"I thought you'd never ask," Annie replied.

They walked out onto the deck in back and the view was just as breathtaking. In addition to the hot tub there were deck chairs and even a grill. Matt stood behind Annie with is arms around her waist. She looked over her shoulder at him.

He looked into her eyes. "Are you thinking about something romantic?"

157

"Not exactly," she said as she spun around. "I need to use the bathroom, then we can check out the bedrooms."

Matt laughed. "I'll grab some stuff from the car." He grabbed some luggage from the car while Annie took care of business. They checked out the bedrooms together.

"They look about the same size and they each have a queen-sized bed."

"Which one should we take?" Matt asked. "Do you have a preference?"

"I think I should take the one in front so I can have the sun in the morning."

"What about me?" Matt asked.

"You can use the other bedroom until Mom and Daddy get here."

He shook a finger at her. "No way I'm going to do that, little Missy."

Annie took a deep breath as she put a finger to her mouth and pulled on her lip. "You mean you expect to share a bedroom with me? What would my father think if he knew?"

"Okay, I'll use the other bedroom."

Matt started to walk in the other bedroom, but Annie grabbed his arm.

"Where do you think you're going?"

"Oh, so you want to share your bedroom with me, huh?"

"As long as you sleep on the floor."

Matt put their gear in the room while Annie checked out the kitchen. She found everything they would need in the way of plates, dishes, glasses, pots and pans—everything. She opened the fridge and found a casserole dish covered with foil and a note on top.

"Matty, there's a note and some lasagna."

"What does it say?"

"It says. 'We thought you might be hungry when you arrive so my wife made some lasagna. Hope you like it.' That was so thoughtful. Should we eat it tonight or save it for tomorrow?"

"I'm hungry. Let's eat it tonight and maybe have leftover lasagna tomorrow."

There were heating instructions in the note. Annie soon had the oven going and the lasagna warming up. After unloading the car and unpacking their suitcases, they sat down to eat. They enjoyed the homemade lasagna but saved some for the next day.

"Should we use the hot tub tonight?" Annie asked as she cleaned up the dishes. "Mr. Rulabaughn mentioned in his note that he checked it this morning and everything was all right."

"Yeah, let's try it. I'll go put on my swim trunks."

"I don't think that will be necessary, Mr. Sullivan," Annie whispered as she twirled her hair around a finger.

"Oh, so that's the way it's gonna be, huh? You want me to get naked so you can take advantage of me."

"The thought did cross my mind," Annie said.

"Give me a minute to turn on the jets. I'll be right back."

Matt uncovered the hot tub, turned on the jets and raced back inside. "It's ready."

They watched each other as they stripped naked.

"I'll bring the towels and I found these fluffy white robes in the closet." She handed them to Matt.

He buried his nose in one. "They smell like the ones you get in expensive hotels."

"When have you ever stayed in a fancy hotel?" she asked while they walked outside.

"When I was in Chicago with my father."

They got in the hot tub and were soon used to the warm swirling water.

"I could get used to this, Matty. Think how nice it would be to have a hot tub back home to use in the winter."

"We would have to wear clothes at home, Annie."

"Why? If we put in in the right spot and put a fence around it we would have enough privacy," she said as she splashed some water at him.

"What about you father? I just thought of something."

"What? Are you gonna tell me?"

"What if your father and Mrs. Franklin want to use the hot tub like this?" Matt asked.

"I can't see that happening. Especially if we are here."

"What if we want to use the hot tub..."

"It wouldn't bother me."

"It wouldn't?"

"No, do you remember about three years ago when I got hurt?"

"Yeah, I remember."

"I needed help getting dressed. I couldn't do much of anything without help."

"I get the picture."

"There wasn't anyone around to help me except Daddy."

They spent twenty minutes in the hot tub before they got out. They dried off and put on the fluffy robes.

Matt held her close and managed to slip his hands under Annie's robe.

"Are you going to take advantage of me," she asked.

An hour later they were back on the deck in their pajamas.

"Are you sleepy now?" Annie asked with her arm around Matt's waist.

Matt nodded. "I'm tired from the drive and actually the hot tub kinda made me drowsy."

"We can go to bed for real if you want, but I'm not real sleepy now. You kinda woke me up."

"You seemed to be more... I don't know... relaxed, maybe, tonight."

"I guess I know what to expect now. I think I'm going to like it a lot, Matty."

Matt smiled. "I'm sure happy to hear that."

They headed back inside and Matt went out the front door to make sure the car was locked. Annie was in bed when he returned.

"Night, Matty. I love you."

"Good night, Annie. I love you more than ever," he said as he leaned over to kiss her.

# Chapter Twenty-Eight

"How about we head back into town and grab breakfast? Then we can visit the park. Maybe skip lunch and do some grocery shopping and come back here to make dinner. What do you think?" Annie asked.

"That sounds like a plan to me. Do we have to get out of bed right away?"

"Why? Do you have something in mind?"

Annie smiled at Matty. A half hour later they were ready to get out of bed. Matt showered and dressed first so Annie could take her time in the bathroom. He made sure all their hiking gear was in the car while Annie got ready. They got in the car and headed back into Gatlinburg.

"Wanna try the Pancake Palace?" Annie asked. "It's up there on the right or we can do McDonald's."

"Let's try to eat at places we don't have back home, okay? I mean, we can always eat at McDonald's."

Annie nodded. "Let's do the Pancake Palace."

They stopped at the local restaurant. Matt ordered biscuits and gravy. Annie wanted to try their chocolate chip pancakes so she could compare them to what she made at home.

"Well are they any better than yours?" Matt asked.

"If I say no, does that seem like bragging?"

"You do make good pancakes, Annie."

"Well then, I guess mine are just as good, but I don't have to clean up afterward here."

They finished breakfast and headed into the Great Smoky Mountains National Park stopping first at the Sugarlands Visitor Center. They spent enough time at the center to get better acquainted with the park. They planned to visit Cades Cove first. The drive to Cades Cove took them through wooded areas as they wound their way up the mountain. They finally reached the cove and drove around the loop road until they reached the visitor center.

"Matty, look! Those deer act as tame as cows," she said after hopping out of the car.

"Yeah, they've been fed too many times by people."

Annie laughed and Matt wondered why. "What is so funny?"

"I was just imagining the deer on Grandpa's farm coming up to the house wanting to be fed and Grandpa making pets of them instead of wanting to shoot them so he could eat them."

"You can be goofy sometimes, but I still love you anyway."

Matt and Annie spent several hours exploring Cades Cove. Annie took pictures of the houses, churches and even some 'wildlife.' She tried to imagine what it must have been like to live here a hundred years ago.

"You know we could build a small cabin back in the woods at the farm."

"Do you think you would like that, Annie?" Matt asked.

"Maybe it could be a place to get away on the weekends. We could use solar energy and have our own well for water."

"And a wood burning stove and you could cook the animals I bring home for dinner. You could make homemade butter and make our own clothes."

"All right! I just think it would be nice to have a place away from the traffic and congestion of the city. I would like to keep some of the modern conveniences we have."

Matt kissed the top of her head. "Grandpa was telling me he was thinking of buying the fifty acres next to his place. They are almost all woods and hills. No one has ever farmed that land and it's too far away for developers to be interested."

"I heard Grandpa talking to Daddy about it and I think they are going to go ahead."

"I think your father would like to live out there when he retires from the force."

After the visit to Cades Cove, Matt and Annie headed back to Gatlinburg to do their grocery shopping. They bought enough supplies to last for the rest of the week. Annie had made a list of what they might want to eat for dinner. They planned to have breakfast at the cabin and dinner most evenings. They bought Powerbars to take on their hikes because they figured they would be too busy for lunch stops.

162

Over the next two days they visited several interesting places in the park. They saw Clingman's Dome, Laurel and Rainbow Falls and other features. They hiked several miles each day. While hiking in the Roaring Fork area Matt spotted two small black bears. Annie tried to get a picture but the bears disappeared before she could get her camera out.

Thursday they used the entire day to visit Cataloochee. The area was similar to Cades Cove because it was once home to a thriving community, but it was more remote and away from the crowds. Again, Annie took lots of pictures and they hiked several miles.

"Matty, we could live in a place like the cabin in this picture. It's the Daniel Cook cabin according to this."

"You are talking about out on the farm right?"

"Yeah. Wouldn't it be so cool to live in a log cabin?"

"As long as we don't have a bunch of kids."

"Do you think we will have lots of kids together?" Annie asked as she looked into his eyes.

"Who knows how we will feel when we get older. I do know I would like a son and a daughter."

"You already have a daughter."

"I mean with you. Wouldn't you like to have a little girl?"

"When I'm older. Not anytime soon."

"Maybe after we finish college and have careers," Matt said.

They stopped for dinner that evening in Gatlinburg. They decided to try the Cherokee Grill even though it looked expensive. They wanted to see if it was a place where they might have dinner next week when Mom and Dad arrived. Matt ordered a steak and Annie chose salmon. Annie decided it would be a good place to have dinner again. As long as Daddy was paying.

# Chapter Twenty-Nine

When Annie woke up Friday morning, she heard the steady rhythm of the rain on the metal roof of the cabin. She got up and walked out onto the front porch. To her it looked like one of those days when it might rain all day. She crawled back in bed with Matt and they decided to sleep in. It was after ten when they woke up for good.

"It's still raining, Matty. Looks like we might be stuck here all day. Is that all right with you?" she asked.

"What will we do all day, Annie?" he asked with a straight face.

Annie grinned as she moved on top of Matthew. "I'll think of something."

It was nearly noon when Annie got out of bed. After using the bathroom she joined Matt in the kitchen. He had gotten up a half hour earlier, showered and dressed in shorts and a t-shirt. Annie was still in her pajamas as she hugged Matt. She heard the rain and ran back to the bedroom. When she returned she had on her old  sneakers. She took Matt's hand and pulled him outside onto the back porch. They watched as the steady rain kept falling. The air smelled so clean and woodsy. Annie turned to Matt and smiled. He knew she was up to something.

"What are you going to do?" he asked. "I know that grin means you're up to something."

"I want to enjoy the rain. Wanna join me?" Annie removed her pajamas and walked out into the rain.

"Annie! What are you doing?"

"What does it look like? I'm going 'rainy dipping.'"

Matt laughed at her as she looked up and let the rain caress her face and body.

"It's warm. Come on!"

"What if someone sees us?" Matt asked as he looked around.

"We haven't see another person or car all week. It's as though we're the only people left in the whole area."

"I already took a shower and got dressed."

164

"You aren't going to melt and the rain won't get you dirty. Come on!"

Matt decided it might be fun and joined Annie. He ended up chasing her all around the cabin in the rain. Annie squealed like a little girl as Matt caught her in the front. He put her over his shoulder and carried her to the tree swing.

"We used to have a swing like this in the backyard when I was a kid." She climbed into the swing and said, "Can I have a push to get started?"

"I suppose so," he answered and began pushing her. "I kinda like going... what did you call it?"

"Rainy dipping," she answered then giggled.

They were dressed, sitting on the back porch drinking Dr Pepper and watching the rain when Annie thought about running around the cabin.

"We could never do that back home."

"Where would we ever have the privacy?"

Annie grinned. "Maybe out at the farm."

"Grandpa Liam would probably think we were crazy to be outside in the rain.

"We would have to be away from the house to make love like we did here," she said. "Maybe by the lake."

"Now I see why you want a cabin in the woods. You want to be able to run around naked all the time."

"That's not why, but it might be fun to do."

"I'm going to tell your father what you did," he teased.

"You were naked, too. Should I tell your father?"

"Like he would care. He would congratulate me."

"I like your father now that I'm not intimidated anymore," Annie said.

"He's always liked you, Annie. I remember the first time you ever met him. You weren't even in high school and you didn't seem afraid of him at all."

"I was probably too scared to let it show," Annie admitted.

"He never tried to intimidate you like he did other people," Matt said.

Annie got up, walked to the edge of the porch and held out

a hand. "I think the rain is stopping. Maybe we can go for a hike around here. There is an old deer path through the woods. We can see where it leads."

"Can I keep my clothes on?" Matt asked with a grin.

"If you must," she teased.

The rain stopped and Matt and Annie decided to see where the 'trail' led. They walked for fifteen minutes and discovered a small stream. They walked along the stream until their way was blocked by a small waterfall. There was a small pool at the base of the falls which were eight to ten feet tall.

"This is cool," Annie said. "Can we get down there somehow?"

Matt found a way to get to the bottom of the waterfall.

"If this was in the park there would be a hundred people here watching the falls," he said.

"Maybe no one has ever been here before. We should name the falls."

"What should we call them, Annie?"

"How about Annie Falls?"

"How about Matt's Falls since I saw them first?"

"What about Grandpa's Falls since it's his friend's cabin."

"You're goofy!" Matt said. "We should call them the Rulabaughn Falls since he probably owns the land."

"They're our falls so we should name them after one of us. Not a guy we have never met."

"Sssh! Annie, look over there." Matt pointed to the other side of the stream where four deer had appeared. They kept quiet and still and the deer didn't notice them at first. Then one deer raised its head. The others did the same. Matt and Annie could see them sniffing the air. Suddenly, the deer bounded away.

"I think they smelled us, Annie," Matt said.

"I told you to change your underwear," Annie teased. "We can name them Deer Falls since that's who really found them."

"Okay, you can call them that, Annie."

They headed back to the cabin.

"We have the stuff for tacos. Would you like tacos for dinner?" Annie asked.

166

"Okay. Don't we have some leftover pasta salad, too?"

"We can have tacos and salad."

"Are you ready to eat?" Matt asked. "I'm kinda hungry considering all I've had all day was a Powerbar."

"You had a Powerbar and didn't share it with me! I haven't eaten anything all day."

They decided to have an early dinner and ate on the back porch.

"Since it's stopped raining, do you want to run into Gatlinburg to maybe see a movie or something? I could call home, too."

"If you want. I'll have to check the road to see if it's passable. We could do some more grocery shopping if anything is open."

The road was muddy but passable so they headed into town and Annie called home. She left a message. She and Matt saw the movie *There's Something About Mary*.

"I think Brett Favre should stick to football. He sucks as an actor," Matt said. "Otherwise, it was funny."

"I agree," Annie said. "He might have a couple years of football left in him, but he's getting old."

Annie's cell phone rang and it was her father calling back.

"Hi, Daddy! How are you? Do you miss me yet?"

"Are you gone? I thought maybe you were just at work."

"You are so funny."

"How are you, sweetie? Are you and Matt still getting along? You're not fighting, are you?"

"Oh yeah! We were getting along great until we went hiking Tuesday. There was this big bear on the trail and I took off running. I haven't seen Matty since then. I did hear some screaming though," Annie said as she grinned at Matt.

"Was that the bear or Matthew screaming?" Dad asked.

Annie laughed. "We are having such a good time. It rained most of the day today and we had a blast."

"You did? In the rain?"

"Yes," Annie said but then was quiet as she looked at Matt.

"Is this something I don't want to hear about?"

167

Annie turned her back to Matt. "It might be."

"Tell me you guys have been out of the cabin at least."

"Daddy! We've been seeing a lot of the park and doing a lot of hiking. Today was the only day we stayed at the cabin. We're in Gatlinburg now though. We saw a movie and we're going to do some more grocery shopping."

"How are you guys doing with money?"

"We're all right, but if you want to bring more we won't argue. We ate dinner at a nice place yesterday. I thought you and Mom would like it. We would go back there if you want."

"You mean it's expensive and I have to pay, huh?"

"Exactly!"

"Elisabeth and I are leaving tomorrow around noon. We're going to stay overnight somewhere around Lexington. We should be there around noon on Sunday just so you guys know."

"We have a list of places we think you and Mom would like to see."

"Meaning they are too expensive for you and Matt to pay for, right?"

"We are just being careful how we spend our money."

"That's okay. I don't mind paying for your vacation, honey. I know we want to go to Asheville to see the Biltmore House."

"There's stuff in Pigeon Forge to do, too."

Annie and her father talked for another fifteen minutes.

"We'll be expecting you around noon then. Love you!"

"Love you, too. Say hi to Matthew for me."

Matt and Annie did the grocery shopping and returned to the cabin before it got dark. They put away the groceries and were sitting on the back porch when it started raining again. Annie looked at Matt and grinned. She got up and was soon having more fun in the rain as Matt watched. She tried to get Matt to join her, but he was content to sit on the porch and watch as she danced in the rain again.

# Chapter Thirty

Saturday morning Matt and Annie returned to the park for more hiking. They wanted to see Abrams Falls so they went back to Cades Cove. On the way back from the falls they got caught in a sudden downpour and were both soaked to the skin.

"Oh, no way, Annie," Matt said as he saw the look on Annie's face. "Don't you dare do anything like yesterday. There are other people around."

"Where?" Annie shrugged. "I don't see anyone else out here."

"Annie!"

"Oh, don't worry. I'm not about to do anything foolish. Of course if we were back at the cabin..."

Because it was Saturday, there were so many other people in the park and the area of Cades Cove was rather crowded. They stopped to look at the tame deer again and when they were ready to leave Annie commented on the crowded road.

"Look at this!" Annie said as they began the drive back to the cabin. "A traffic jam in Cades Cove. They need to widen these roads to three lanes in each direction and put up traffic lights. A mini-mall would be nice, too. Some shopping areas and a couple nice restaurants. Maybe a hotel and a golf course."

Matt looked at her like she had lost her mind. "You are kidding, I hope."

"What? Don't you think a golf course would fit?"

"What am I gonna do with you?"

"I can think of..."

Matt slammed on the brakes to avoid colliding with the camper in front of them. "You need to take a cold shower."

"I thought that only worked on men," she teased.

It took twice as long to get back to the cabin because of the traffic. Even after they were away from the traffic it took longer. The road to the cabin was a mess because of the rain.

"I hope we don't get stuck!"

"We won't, but I have to be careful." Matt tried to avoid the puddles. "I think we just ran over a Mazda Miata in that pothole."

They made it to the cabin without getting stuck. Annie took the sheets off the bed and replaced them with fresh ones. She looked at all the dirty clothes in their room. "We should have done laundry today," she said as Matt walked into the room.

"Why? You can't be out of clean clothes. You brought enough to last a month or more."

"I will be needing clean underwear soon. Can we go back into town in the morning before Daddy gets here? Or maybe I could go and you can stay here."

"Not a chance of that happening," Matt said.

"Why not? You could sleep late."

"I'm not letting you out of my sight. I promised your father I would take care of you."

"Oh, Matty, that's so sweet, but I'm not a child. I can manage on my own."

"If we were back home it would be different," Matt said as he stuffed his pillow into a fresh pillowcase. "I'll get up early and go with you. I actually need clean underwear. This pair is getting dirty. I knew I should have brought two pairs."

Annie made a face. "Oh, you are so gross! That sounds like something Mace would say."

"Speaking of Mace, how do you think he will do taking care of Keyshon this week?"

"He has Grandpa to help him. Keyshon is starting to become more difficult now that he is older. He and Lisa are always together and I worry they might become too serious."

"You mean they might 'experiment' a little," Matt said as he walked out of the bedroom.

"Is that what it's called?" Annie gathered up all the dirty clothes and stuffed them into the large bag she brought just for that purpose. "Anything else you need washed?" she hollered as she carried the bag out to the open great room.

"Maybe these shorts."

Annie smiled at Matt. "Then take them off. I can't wash them if you're wearing them."

Matt walked past Annie into the bedroom and changed into the boxers he had been wearing to bed. He came back out and

170

Annie looked at his boxers.

"Have you worn the same pair all week?"

"Yeah, why?" he shrugged.

"Don't you have another pair you could wear?"

"I was saving them for next week."

"Go put them on and let me have those unless you want to sleep outside tonight."

"Okay! Geez, Annie, they don't smell bad."

"Then what is that I smell? Did a skunk wander in here?"

"Fine!"

"I still love you, Matty."

"I love you, too. Even if you make me wear clean underwear."

Matt moved close to Annie and tried to hug her.

"Go away, you gross man! No more hugs or kisses until you have clean clothes on."

He kept moving toward Annie.

"I mean it! Go away," she ordered.

"I think I'll sleep outside with the skunks and other critters tonight."

"I won't stop you. The wildlife may leave the area though. They have more sensitive noses than I do."

"Do you want me to toss you in the hot tub?"

"Maybe later, but after I get all the dirty laundry together I want to eat dinner. What are you making tonight?"

"Shoot! That's right. It is my night to cook. I almost forgot. Good thing I picked up a frozen pizza at the store."

"You are such a gourmet chef. Can you turn on the oven or do you need my help?"

"Would you turn it on while I change clothes. It probably needs to be at 400 degrees but would you check please just to make sure."

"Fine! Go change and I'll get the pizza started."

She found a pizza pan in the cupboard and checked the pizza for the correct temperature setting.

"How's this?"

She turned and saw Matt. "That's better. I like that t-shirt.

Let's sit on the porch while the oven heats up."

"Okay, do you want a Dr Pepper, Annie?"

"Thanks, Matty. Could I have a glass with ice, please?"

Annie sat outside while Matt got her pop. He grabbed one for himself, too. He put the pizza in the oven after a few minutes and set the timer.

"Did you see a pizza cutter?" Matt asked.

"Yeah, I saw one in the drawer next to the one with the silverware by the sink."

They sat and relaxed while the pizza cooked. Matt checked on the pizza after the timer went off. He gave it a couple more minutes to brown up. Then he sliced the pizza and grabbed a couple of slices for Annie and two for himself.

"It's still hot, Annie. Be careful."

"Thanks, sweetie."

They sat quietly listening to the sound of nature.

"I didn't realize how noisy it can be in the quiet outdoors. Does that make any sense?"

"I know exactly what you mean. It is noisier than I expected. A different kind of sound though. No car engines or police sirens. No loud music from drunk teenagers."

"I know! Isn't it just so childish for those young teenage hoodlums to play their rock and roll music so loud. We never did that when we were that age, did we, Grandpa Matthew?"

"Did we even have anything to play our music on when we were teenagers?"

"I can't remember that far back, but I doubt it. We just listened to string quartets play proper music for dancing. None of that gyrating and bumping against each other like kids do nowadays. It's so disgusting."

"Wanna do some 'dirty dancing,' Grandma Annie?" Matt asked. He raised his eyebrows like Groucho Marx.

"Okay. As long as your don't hurt your hips. You might have to replace them again."

Matt laughed at Annie and she grinned at him. They finished the pizza and Matt brought out a bag of chips.

"I hope we don't attract any bears by eating outside."

"I think we're safe as long as we don't leave anything outside."

"Are we gonna use the hot tub tonight?" Annie asked. "It might be our last chance to use it."

"You mean our last chance to use it naked," Matt teased.

What?" Annie put a hand to her mouth. "You mean you have not been wearing your trunks. I am shocked. I was too shy to look to see what you were wearing."

"Is that what you are going to tell your father?"

"Do you think he'll buy it?" she asked as she stuffed a handful of chips into her mouth.

"Sure! And while you're at it try to sell him some swamp land in Florida."

"If you remember there is this place called Disney World that was built on that swamp land I used to own," Annie said.

"Did you sell it for a good price?"

"Sure thing," Annie said then hesitated while she tried to come up with a comeback. "I got nothing."

"That's all right. Every comedian tanks once in a while."

She punched his arm.

Later, after spending some time in Matt's arms in the hot tub, Annie was getting sleepy.

"Stop yawning. It's contagious," Matt said.

"I'm ready to fall asleep, Matty. Will you take care of the hot tub and lock up the cabin?"

"Okay, I'll be coming to bed shortly."

Matt kissed Annie and she got out of the tub and went inside after wrapping a towel around her waist. By the time Matt got in bed, Annie was sound asleep. He kissed her cheek and whispered, "I love you, Annie. See you in the morning."

# Chapter Thirty-One

Annie opened her eyes as the bright sunshine moved across her face. She stretched out her arms and touched Matt. He was still asleep. She looked at the alarm clock on the nightstand next to the bed. It was just after seven o'clock. She decided to sleep a little longer so she moved next to Matt and he placed an arm over her. An hour later they both woke up. Annie turned over to face Matt.

"Morning, Matty. Are you gonna stay in bed all day?"

"I might if you stay with me."

"That sounds good, but you know Daddy and Mom are coming today."

"I know but they won't get here before noon. We can stay in bed a little longer."

"Maybe a little longer, but then we need to get up. We have to do laundry today, remember?"

Thirty minutes later Annie was in the shower. Matt showered and dressed after Annie then took the dirty laundry out to the car. They planned to grab some breakfast in town. They had noticed a laundromat close to a McDonald's. Annie stayed at the laundromat while Matt ran to grab breakfast. There was only one other person doing laundry, so Annie used two machines.

By eleven they were back at the cabin. Annie put the clean clothes away. Matt tidied up the cabin.

"Let's go for a walk, Matty. Maybe we will meet them on the dirt road."

"Give me a second and I'll go with you."

A couple of minutes later Annie and Matt began walking along the road. They reached the main dirt road and needed to make a decision.

"Which way should we go?" Annie asked. "We haven't been this way. We know there are more cabins along here somewhere."

"We've got time to check it out."

They went to the right which was uphill. They followed the road as it wound around and climbed higher. They saw two turnoffs that lead to other cabins but couldn't actually see the cabins. The road ended at a parking area for a trailhead.

Annie checked out the sign with some trail information. "Maybe we can come back here and explore the trail later."

"It looks like it keeps climbing."

"That's all right," Annie said then giggled. "It just means the way back will be downhill. Maybe we should get back to the cabin. Daddy might get here sooner than he said. He usually gets up early."

They got back to the cabin and were sitting on the front steps drinking pop when Dad's new van pulled up. Annie jumped up and ran over to greet Dad and Mrs. Franklin. Dad hugged her, then she gave Mom a hug. Matt came over and shook hands with Mr. O'Dell.

"You found the place. I was afraid you would get lost," Matt said.

"It wasn't that hard to find the right turnoff."

"Right. The hanging cows. Need any help unloading the van?"

"Sure."

Dad opened the tailgate and he and Matt grabbed the luggage while Annie took Mom inside to show her the cabin.

"Matty and I have been using this room, but we can switch if you and Daddy want."

"It doesn't matter to us. You can stay in that room. We'll use the other one. They look like they're about the same size."

Matt and Mr. O'Dell dropped the luggage in the bedroom.

"I need to use the bathroom," Elisabeth said.

"It's right there." Annie pointed.

Elisabeth came out and said, "It's nicer than I imagined. The shower is nicely tiled."

"Yeah, but it's kinda crowded for two people," Annie said without realizing what she revealed.

Elisabeth looked at her and smiled. Keith met them in the hallway a moment later.

"Come on!" Annie said. "Let me show you guys the back porch and deck. There's a hot tub."

"Have you been using it?" Dad asked.

"I think we've used it every night for a little bit. It helps me fall asleep."

"How has the weather been? Has it rained?" Elisabeth asked.

"It rained almost all day Friday and we got caught in a shower yesterday afternoon," Matt answered. "How was the ride down here? Where did you stay last night?"

Mr. O'Dell answered, "We stayed in Richmond just south of Lexington at a Days Inn. We made better time than we expected so we got a little further south. We didn't have any rain on the way down here. What have you guys been doing?"

"Should we have some lunch, and we can tell you about our week?" Annie asked. "We can sit on the back porch to eat."

"Sounds good to me. I'm hungry."

Annie and Elisabeth made sandwiches while Dad and Matt sat on the porch and drank bottled water.

"This is nice, Matt. I could get used to living out in the country, but Elisabeth likes living in the city."

"Annie talked about building a cabin out on the farm. I think she was serious."

"Yeah, she's talked about that before."

"Here are some sandwiches and chips. Help yourself," Annie said.

Annie told her father about their week. She got excited talking about the national park and the places they visited. She mentioned the different places they ate dinner.

"Maybe we can go into town for dinner tonight. There's a place called the Cherokee Grill you would like," she said smiling at her father.

He laughed. "Meaning it's too expensive and you want me to buy dinner there."

"Yes, Daddy! That would be so sweet of you."

Dad shook his head because he knew Annie was going to expect him to pay for everything the next week—not that he minded. He told her he would pay for everything, but she wanted to pay for as much as she and Matt could afford.

"What did you do Friday when it rained?" Elisabeth asked.

176

Annie looked at Matt and they grinned at each other. "I went 'rainy dipping' and Matty chased me around the cabin."

Matt got embarrassed and even more so when Elisabeth asked, "What do you mean, Annie?"

Dad answered for her. "It's like skinny dipping without being in the water. She used to do it when she was little."

"Annie! Do you mean you were running around in the rain naked?"

"There's no one else around here, Mom. We haven't seen another person or car all week."

Matt was grateful Annie didn't mention he was doing the same thing.

"Do you guys want to do anything this afternoon, or do you just want to hang out here and relax?"

"It might be nice to get out for a hike."

"Matty and I found a trailhead at the end of the dirt road. We could drive over there and see where the trail goes. It's uphill going out but that means it will be downhill on the way back."

"I think they understand that, Annie," Matt teased her.

"We could just go as far as you want, Mom, then turn around and come back."

"I've been doing a lot of walking to get ready for this trip so I can try to keep up with everyone."

Matt drove Keith's minivan to the parking area.

"I've got a couple bottles of water in the backpack. Should I bring it?" Matt asked.

"Maybe we could just carry the water. I don't think we'll be gone too long," Annie said as she looked back at her father and Elisabeth.

They started up the trail which was all uphill at first. They lost sight of the trailhead as they walked around the side of the mountain. For a time the trail meandered up and down but for the most part it was uphill. Trees provided shade and the trail felt soft and easy on their feet. Surprisingly, it was mostly dry. After they had gone about a half mile, they came to a small meadow. On the far end were the remains of a log cabin. The trail continued past the old cabin but climbed more steeply now.

Dad arrived at the cabin and said, "I think we will stop here, but if you kids want to keep going we will wait."

"Should we give you the keys and you can go back to the cabin?" Annie asked. "Matty and I will walk back."

"Are you sure?" Dad asked.

Annie nodded. "We want to see where this goes."

"Just be careful, okay?"

"We will. We'll see you back at the cabin. Don't forget about dinner tonight."

Keith and Elisabeth walked back to the minivan and returned to the cabin while Matt and Annie climbed up the trail. They reached the end after another quarter mile. The trail ended on a point of exposed rock with a view of the valley below. There was a bench of sorts. Actually, the ledge was a couple slabs of rock which people obviously used to sit on to enjoy the view.

"I bet the sunsets are nice up here," Matt said as he sat down.

"No doubt. Maybe we can come back during the week to see."

"That might be romantic," Matt said as he put an arm around Annie.

"Should we get back? I'm getting hungry and Daddy usually likes to eat an early dinner."

"I'm ready if you are."

The return trip was quicker and they made it back to the cabin just as Dad was coming outside.

"How far did you guys go?"

"We found the end of the trail. It wasn't much farther, but it was steeper."

Annie described the end of the trail to her father.

"Are you ready to go into town and have dinner?"

"We're ready whenever you and Matt are."

"Just give us a few minutes to clean up," Annie said.

Forty-five minutes later they were seated at their table at the Cherokee Grill. They ordered drinks and appetizers.

"The steak Matty devoured the other night was good and I ordered the salmon. It was all right, but tonight I'm going to have a steak. I feel carnivorous." Annie grinned.

"Make sure you order a large steak, Annie."

"Why?"

Dad grinned. "Because you won't be able to eat it all and I can finish it later."

"Maybe I will want to have it tomorrow."

"It won't taste as good tomorrow. I'll have to finish it tonight."

"Maybe I'll surprise you and finish the whole thing."

Everyone ordered a steak. Matt ordered fries while everyone else chose a baked potato. Annie and Elisabeth needed a box because they couldn't finish everything. Keith and Matt finished their meal without any trouble. They decided against dessert figuring they could buy a pie and ice cream at the store.

"Maybe we should stop and get some beer for you, Daddy," Annie said as they walked out to the minivan. "You'll probably want to have some in the cabin."

"You mean you want some," Dad said then laughed.

"Daddy! I'm too young to drink beer."

"You are, but that hasn't seemed to stop you before. Didn't you bring your special ID?"

"No! You took it away remember."

"Just checking to see if you had another one."

"I didn't bring mine either, Mr. O'Dell," Matt mentioned.

"We can make a stop for dessert and beverages."

It was still light when they got back to the cabin. Matt put the groceries away while Annie changed into her bikini. She put shorts and a t-shirt on over her suit. Soon everyone was sitting on the back porch.

"Did Grandpa ever tell you why his friend was letting us use the cabin for free?"

"Yeah! This will make you laugh. Grandpa introduced John Rulabaughn to Gertie Gentry while they were at college. John and Gertie got married and Grandpa loaned him the money to buy a house. I guess John never paid Grandpa back for several years and always felt bad about it."

"Are they still married?"

"Still married and they live in the same house," Dad said.

"But now he owns a bunch of cabins, too."

"He owns more than just a few cabins, Annie. He also owns several hotels and other real estate."

"I guess he can afford to let us stay for free then."

Matt was soon ready for dessert. Annie helped Elisabeth get the apple pie and ice cream ready.

"Apple pie a la mode anyone?" Annie asked out the back door.

Dad rubbed his stomach. "I think I have enough room."

Annie brought out the dessert for her father and Matthew.

"This is so good," Matt said a moment later.

"Yeah, and it didn't cost an arm and a leg like in the restaurant."

"Oh, Daddy! It was only six dollars for dessert."

Matt took the dishes into the kitchen after they were finished. They relaxed on the porch until ten o'clock when Annie asked, "Do you and Mom want to try out the hot tub?"

"Are you and Matt going to use it?"

"Yes, I've already got my suit on."

Dad looked at Elisabeth.

"We might as well make use of it, Keith."

"We are paying for it. Sort of," Dad said. "Give us a few minutes to change."

"There are extra towels in the bathroom," Annie said. "I'll meet you out there after I do the dishes."

Matt, Keith and Elisabeth were already in the hot tub when Annie finished in the kitchen. She took off her shorts and t-shirt and got in the hot tub. She slipped under the water and adjusted her bikini top.

"Annie, what are you doing?" Matt asked.

"It slipped, okay? I needed to fix it before Daddy saw anything."

Matt looked at her father. "I guess so."

"Oh, Matty! It's no big deal. At least I'm wearing it."

"I won't be using the hot tub without my bathing suit," Elisabeth said.

"Maybe the kids will be gone one evening and we can use the hot tub then," Dad suggested with a grin.

"Matty and I are going to watch the sunset from the end of the trail one night this week. You will have some privacy then."

Annie got out of the hot tub first and ran to the bathroom to dry off and put on her pajamas. She rejoined everyone on the porch. Elisabeth went inside and changed back into the clothes she was wearing earlier. Matt and Dad stayed in their swim trunks. They stayed up until midnight making plans for the coming week.

"Let's go to Cades Cove tomorrow," Annie suggested.

"But you've already been there, Annie," Elisabeth said. "Wouldn't you rather go somewhere new?"

"We saw a trail we thought would make for an interesting hike. We could do that while you and Daddy explore the valley. There's lots to see," Annie said.

"Sounds good to me," Dad said to settle the matter.

Annie and Matt headed off to bed and Keith and Elisabeth followed soon after.

When Keith and Elisabeth were in bed, she asked, "Are you okay with Matt and Annie sharing a room?"

"I guess it must be hard for any father to know his little girl is growing up or is grownup. I know they love each other and they are being careful."

Elisabeth grinned as she moved closer to Keith. "Can you picture Annie running around in the rain like that? The way she looked at Matt made me wonder if he wasn't running around in the nude, too."

"When I picture her doing that it's as a little girl, not as a grownup teenager," he said as he pulled her closer. "And I refuse to picture Matt doing the same."

Elisabeth laughed. "I bet it was fun."

"We might have some rain later this week."

"Don't even think about it!" Elisabeth said. "It won't happen. Not even out here."

# Chapter Thirty-Two

"Breakfast is almost ready. If you want any you better get your butts out of bed," Annie told Matt and her father.

"I hope you have coffee ready."

"Yes, Daddy. Your coffee is ready."

"That's my sweet girl."

The men got up and made it out to the kitchen to eat.

"We have scrambled eggs, bacon, sausage and some hash browns," Annie said. "If you want something else, you guys will have to make it yourself."

Everything smells good," Matt said as he kissed Annie and patted her bottom. He turned and saw her father staring at him.

After breakfast they got ready and headed to Cades Cove. Matt and Annie were going to hike to Abrams Falls because they thought it was worth another trip. They agreed to meet back at the visitor center at three o'clock. Keith and Elisabeth took their time and explored all the sights around the Cove. Annie and Matt arrived at the visitor center twenty minutes early.

"What did you think of the place?" Annie asked her father when he and Elisabeth returned. "Could you picture living here?"

"I would get rather lonesome," Elisabeth said. "But I know your father would love living in the valley."

"Tonight I will make dinner on the grill," Keith said as they arrived back at the cabin. "Matt, would you mind if I did the grilling?"

"Not at all. We used it last week, but I experienced a little trouble getting the heat just right."

For dinner Keith grilled chicken breasts, potatoes and ears of corn. They ate dinner then sat on the porch.

"I'm rather thirsty," Dad said.

Matt went inside and brought out three beers and a Dr Pepper. He handed the pop to Annie.

She frowned. "If you're old enough for a beer, so am I."

Matt looked at her father.

Dad shrugged. "I'm not on duty"

"But you are her father," Matt said.

"If you kids are old enough to sleep together, you can make your own decisions about having a beer. One beer," he said as he pointed at Annie.

"I'm all right with the Dr Pepper, Matty. I just wanted to make a point," Annie said.

After using the hot tub again, everyone went to bed early. They hoped to make an early start in the morning to Asheville and Biltmore House.

They arrived at Biltmore, purchased tickets and were ready to start by 9:30. They listened to audio cassettes on the self-guided tour. They also bought tickets for the two o'clock 'behind the scenes tour.' Matt and Annie soon got ahead of Keith and Elisabeth, but they planned to meet in the Courtyard Market after finishing their tour.

Annie and Matt were sitting at a table when she stood up and waved. "There they are, Matty. Over here, Mom and Dad."

Dad and Elisabeth joined them.

"Well, what did you think of the place?" Annie asked.

"Pretty amazing."

"Can you imagine what it must have been like to actually live here?"

"No way!" Matt said. "I wouldn't trade places with George Vanderbilt for all the money in the world."

Dad mentioned, "He was rather young when he died."

"Yeah, and he had to change clothes four or five times a day. I could never get used to that," Matt said.

"How would you feel about having a servant dress you, Matty?"

"Not a chance in hell, but I wouldn't mind being a servant and helping you get dressed, Annie."

"I can dress myself, thank you very much."

"Just letting you know I'm willing to provide assistance."

"You just want to help me out of my clothes!"

"Wow! Look at the gardens. Aren't they spectacular?" Dad said even though they could barely see them.

"Oh, Daddy! You're just trying to change the subject."

183

"I heard the gardens are spectacular," Elisabeth said. "I'd like to see them if we have time."

After eating lunch and walking around the gardens, they met their guide for the next tour. For ninety minutes he showed the group some unrestored bedrooms and other areas of the house.

"I liked that tour better than the regular one," Dad announced while they walked back to the van.

"It was interesting. I enjoyed seeing the unrestored bedrooms," Elisabeth answered. "It proves that even with all their money, the Vanderbilts struggled to keep up the house. It must be impossible in this age."

"I want a bedroom as large as Mrs. Vanderbilt's," Annie told Matt.

"Okay, but you will have to rent a warehouse, Annie," Dad said as he unlocked the van.

"Matty will build me a huge house someday and I can have my own private bedroom."

"No I won't," Matt insisted. "If I'm going to build you a house you better believe I will be sharing your bedroom."

"Even when I'm old and gray?" Annie asked.

"Yes! Even after you get old and wrinkled. You know, after you turn thirty," Matt teased."

Annie glared at him. "I hope you enjoy sleeping on the porch tonight, Matthew Sullivan!"

Matt smiled at Annie and kissed her. "We can sleep outside and count the stars."

"You just want to sleep outside because you are afraid to make love to me now that Daddy is here," Annie whispered.

Matt smiled as he nodded. "I have a very fine-tuned sense of self-preservation."

"You are so silly. Daddy wouldn't hurt you unless you get me pregnant, then he will chop off your..."

"I get the picture."

# Chapter Thirty-Three

"What do you have there?" Dad asked as Annie set a piece of paper next to her plate while they ate dinner Friday night.

"This is the list of tourist attractions I made before we left home. I've been crossing off the items as we visited them."

"Do we have any more to see?" Matt asked.

Annie picked up the list and held it out. "After this afternoon's adventure I have crossed off the last item. We managed to see a few more than I even knew about. I would say it's been a very successful vacation."

"Elisabeth and I have certainly enjoyed it," Dad said. "I love this cabin and the privacy."

Annie grinned at her father. "I noticed someone used the hot tub while Matty and I were hiking this morning. Did you take advantage of the privacy like Matty and I did?"

Dad pointed a finger at her. "That's privileged information, young lady. You work for an attorney. You should know better than to ask."

After dinner on Friday Annie and Elisabeth cleaned the cabin while the guys sat on the back porch.

"I'll let you slide tonight, Matthew, but this will not happen once we get our own place," Annie said.

"Do you need some help, Annie?" Matt asked as he jumped up from his chair.

"Your timing is perfect," Annie replied. "Mom and I just finished."

Everyone slept late on Saturday. All they needed to do today was pack up, load the cars and head home. Keith made breakfast while Annie wrote a thank you note to Mr. Rulabaughn.

"Breakfast is ready," Dad hollered. "Come and get it before Matt eats everything."

"Be right there, Daddy."

"Elisabeth, breakfast is ready," Keith told her through the bathroom door before walking back to the kitchen.

"Do you want to read the note I wrote to Mr. Rulabaughn?"

Annie asked while holding it up.

Dad took the note from Annie. "Sure, did you make reservations for next year?"

"Should I?"

"I would like to come back again. I know Elisabeth had a good time even though she likes the city better."

After breakfast Matt and Keith loaded Annie's car and Dad's minivan and by ten o'clock they were heading home. They planned to drive straight through to South Hampshire since it didn't matter how late they arrived. They managed to stick together on the Interstate. The only times they stopped were for gas and once to have dinner, just outside of Indianapolis. They pulled into the O'Dell driveway just before nine o'clock. The vehicles were unloaded and the suitcases soon unpacked. Keith grabbed four beers and they sat outside on the patio. Annie sat next to Matt on the picnic table bench and Keith and Elisabeth sat across from them.

Annie said, "I had a wonderful vacation, but I'm happy to be home. It will feel so good to sleep in my own bed tonight."

Matt looked at her and grinned.

She poked his side. "I mean that. All I'm going to do is sleep."

"Do you need any company?"

"Yeah, maybe I should call Mace. I'm sure he has missed me," Annie teased.

"I'm sure he has. I can sleep on the couch."

Dad looked at Matt, then Annie.

"I'm just teasing him, Daddy. We didn't have a fight or anything."

"It's okay if Matt sleeps on the couch," Dad said.

"Keith!" Elisabeth said as she frowned at him. "You promised you would treat Annie as a grownup young lady."

"All right, but the door has to stay open."

"Does that mean we have to keep your bedroom door open as well?" Elisabeth asked Keith.

"No!"

"So you have a double standard when it comes to..."

"Yes! Absolutely! And I will until they are married."

"I don't mind leaving my door open. We are both too tired to do anything other than fall asleep tonight."

"I'm not all that sleepy, Annie," Matt said.

Annie replied, "You will be after a few beers."

"Are you ready for another one, Mr. O'Dell, Mrs. Franklin?"

"Yeah, thanks, Matt."

"Can I have one more, too?"

Matt looked at Mr. O'Dell to see if Annie could have another beer. He nodded his head and held up one finger meaning Annie could have one more, but that was all.

"I don't need another, Matt, thanks anyway," Elisabeth told Matt.

Matt headed into the kitchen and grabbed three more beers.

The front door opened and Mace entered. "Hey, Matt, what time did you guys get back?"

"A little before nine. We're having some tasty beverages on the patio. Wanna join us?"

"How could I refuse an offer like that? Did you guys have fun?"

"Oh yeah. It was just about perfect. I'm sure Annie will fill you in on the details."

"I don't need all the details. Just some of them," Mace said.

Mace grabbed a beer and followed Matt outside.

"Howdy y'all! I was just checking the house. I wasn't sure if you were coming home tonight or in the morning."

"Hello, son. How are you and how is Keyshon? Did he behave for you?"

Mace walked over to his mother and kissed her cheek. "He did. Lisa was gone all week so he was all right. I mean he missed Lisa, but he called her a couple times a day. He and Grandpa Liam went fishing everyday. That wore him out. He was already sleeping when I left Grandpa Liam's farm."

"Annie missed you, Mace. She won't admit it but she did," Matt said.

"I did not!" Annie poked Matt's side. "Don't believe him."

187

"I'm sure you were too busy sightseeing to even think about me."

Mace walked around the table, sat next to Annie and they looked at each other. Annie wondered what Mace was thinking. She grabbed his hand and squeezed it under the table. Keith and Elisabeth stayed outside for another ten minutes before heading inside.

"We're going to bed. See you kids in the morning. Don't stay up all night and no more beers for you, Annie."

"Night, Daddy. Night, Mom. We'll be quiet, and this is my last one, promise."

"Are you going to spend the night, Mace?" Elisabeth asked.

"Maybe. Depends on how long we stay up, I guess."

"Well, you know where the extra blankets and pillows are if you decide to stay."

After Keith and Elisabeth were out of hearing range, Annie turned to Mace. "Matty wouldn't do it after Daddy and your mom got there. He was too afraid."

"Too much information, Annie."

"Hey, now!" Matt exclaimed. "Maybe I was just tired after the first week and needed time to recuperate."

"Bull poop!" Annie swore. "You want to ask me for details. I know how your perverted mind works, Mace Franklin."

"Okay. So give. Was it worth the wait?"

"Oh, yeah! At least I think so," Annie said.

Mace looked at Matt. "Are you gonna keep her around?"

"I'm not sure yet. I mean she was all right in bed but..."

"Maybe I just need more practice. I'm not as experienced as either of you Romeos."

"What do you think, Mace? Is she worth hanging onto?"

Mace took another sip of beer as he thought about the question. "She does have a few good qualities. Kinda small though."

"If you are talking about my breasts..."

"I wasn't thinking about them," Mace said.

"I can't help it if they're not as big as Erin's."

Annie looked at Matt, then at Mace waiting for them to

make a smart comment.

"You are absolutely perfect the way you are, Annie."

"You better say that, Matthew Sullivan."

She kissed Matt tenderly while Mace watched.

"Do I get a kiss?" Mace asked.

"Did you miss me while I was gone?" Annie asked.

"Was I supposed to?" Mace asked.

Annie poked him in the ribs. "Yes, you creep. I missed you when you went to see Erin."

"All right. I missed you. Happy?"

"Yes!" Annie turned to Mace, kissed his cheek then said, "It rained one day and we ran around the cabin naked."

"Inside or outside?"

"Outside. Matt wasn't going to at first, but he changed his mind. It was fun. The cabin was so secluded. We didn't see another soul around all week."

"Sounds like a great place for a honeymoon."

"It was not a honeymoon," Annie insisted.

They stayed up until midnight. Matt listened to Annie and Mace talk about the trip. He added comments occasionally. It didn't bother him that Annie shared some details with Mace.

"I'm ready for bed," Annie said as she leaned against Matt's shoulder and looked at Mace. "Are you crashing here or going home?"

"I have two options," Mace said while holding up three fingers. "Sleep in my own comfy bed, or crash on your lumpy couch."

"You don't have any options, Mace Franklin," Annie said as she dug in his pocket for his keys. "You aren't driving anywhere tonight, buddy."

Mace looked at Annie and grinned. "Could I use the air mattress since Matt doesn't have to sleep on the floor anymore?"

Annie checked with Matt. He shrugged.

"Okay, but you better stay on the floor, or else I'll murder you dead," Annie threatened.

189

# Chapter Thirty-Four

Annie's cell phone rang early Wednesday morning. She checked to see who was calling and rolled her eyes.

"What's up, Mace? Why are you calling so early?"

"Are you still in bed? It's almost nine. Get your lazy butt up already." He paced in a circle around his bedroom.

"I was up late, okay? Why are you up so early? You never get out of bed before noon."

"I need a favor," he said then took a deep breath.

"Explain," Annie said. She sat on the edge of the bed and stretched her arms over her head.

"Erin and Franny are coming and I promised her parents you would stay with them out at the farm. Will you?"

"It's a little late to be asking, isn't it?"

"Please?"

"Okay, but it will cost you big time."

"What do you want?" Mace asked.

"I'll think about it. When are they arriving?"

"Tomorrow afternoon. Don't worry, I'll pick them up at the train station. Can I borrow your car?"

"You are such a loser!" She stood up and shouted. "Are you ever going to get your own car? I do like to use mine occasionally."

"Why should I? I have you to take care of my infrequent transportation needs."

"Ha! You're lucky I like you."

"I'm such a lovable guy."

"How long are they staying? You did ask Grandpa if they could stay, right?"

"Well... I was kinda hoping you would do that."

She kicked some dirty clothes on the floor. "You are going to owe me so much. You didn't even ask Grandpa if they could stay. Are you afraid he would tell you no?"

"Kinda, but I know he won't refuse you since you are his favorite grandchild."

"You do realize I'm his only grandchild, right?"

190

"Of course I know that. I'm not totally dense."

"I beg to differ, but we'll discuss that at a later time. You do know Grandpa is not going to let you stay out there with us."

"Yeah, I suppose so. He will let me see them though, won't he?" He walked into the bathroom, closed the door and raised the toilet seat.

"Maybe, but I won't promise anything. I can't believe you didn't even ask Grandpa. What are you going to do if he says no?"

Mace shrugged. "Can they stay with you?"

"You are so pushing your luck." She listened for a second. "Are you taking a leak?"

"Not now. I'm finished," he said.

"You are a total... a total... I don't know what, but you are so gross."

Mace grinned. "How's Matty?"

"He's fine and quit trying to change the subject. I know part of what you owe me for this."

"What?"

"You have to move all my stuff into the dorm. Daddy's back has been bothering him so you and Matty have to move all my stuff and Erin's."

"No problem."

Annie rolled her eyes. "You knew you were going to move her stuff anyway. I'll think of something else you owe me."

"Do you think I could sneak upstairs..."

"No way! You are not sneaking upstairs at the farm so you can spend the night with Erin."

"But isn't Grandpa Liam's room downstairs?"

"Yes, but..."

"Maybe I could convince him to take Keyshon on an overnight fishing trip. Keyshon would love that."

"You are impossible."

"No, just horny."

"Call me later after you have taken a long cold shower."

Annie hung up and stayed in bed for awhile. She knew how much Mace missed Erin this summer. She got out of bed and took her shower before calling Grandpa.

191

"How is my favorite granddaughter this morning."

"I'm all right. How are you? I miss you."

"I'm okay. What do you need, Annie? I know you need something by the way you are acting."

"All right, I'll tell you. Mace promised Erin's parents she and Franny could stay at the farm with me only he was too afraid to ask. They're coming tomorrow. Is it okay if we stay at the farm while they're here?"

"Of course you can, sweetie. Just so you know though, I'm taking Keyshon on a fishing trip. We'll be gone Friday and Saturday nights."

"Just when did you plan this trip, Grandpa?"

"Keyshon called me earlier and asked if we could go fishing somewhere other than the lake."

"I'm going to kill Mace when I see him!" Annie screamed.

Grandpa laughed. "Just make sure you hide the body in a place where it won't be discovered for a long time."

"When I get through with him there won't be much of anything left. I'll talk to you later, Grandpa," Annie said as she hung up.

Grandpa stared at the phone, chuckled and said, "At least now I know why Keyshon insisted on fishing somewhere else and who put him up to it. I sure wouldn't want to be in Mace's shoes when Annie gets hold of him."

# Chapter Thirty-Five

"What time are they arriving again?" Annie asked on Thursday as she sat at the reception desk at Mike Bushell's office.

"Three o'clock. Can I use your car?" Mace asked.

"Sure. I'll pick you up and we can both meet them at the station. I'm only working until one."

"Are you sure you don't mind?"

"Anything for you, Mace honey!"

Mace stared at the phone after Annie hung up. "I don't like how that sounded."

Annie drove to the Franklin home at two thirty. She ran into the house and looked for Mace. "I'm here. Where are you?"

"In the kitchen. Is it time to go?"

Annie walked into the kitchen and saw Mace eating.

"You son of a bitch!" she shouted as she smacked the sandwich out of his hand. "You talked Keyshon into asking Grandpa to go away this weekend so you can be alone with Erin."

Mace held out his hands. "I did not."

"Don't lie to me. I talked to Grandpa and he told me about the fishing trip."

"Oh, you did," Mace said and then sighed.

"Yeah! I did."

"I just mentioned fishing to Keyshon and about how Grandpa Liam needs to get away from the farm sometimes. I don't think I specified it had to be this weekend."

"Yeah, right." Annie shook her head. "Well, come on. We need to get to the station so they aren't wondering where we are."

Annie dropped Mace off at the station and he headed inside while she parked the car. By the time she found a parking spot and walked to the terminal, Mace and the girls were waiting.

"Took you long enough," Mace said.

Annie walked up to Mace and pinched his arm while smiling at Erin and Franny. "Hi, Erin. How was the trip?"

"Boring," Erin said as she rolled her eyes. This is Franny."

"I kinda figured that. I'm Annie."

Mace rubbed his arm. "That hurt."

"It's nice to meet you, Annie. Erin has talked about you a lot."

"She has, huh? Did she say anything nice about me?"

"A couple things," Franny teased.

"Erin, did Mace mention making me ask Grandpa about staying at the farm?" Annie poked Mace in the other arm.

"No, he didn't say anything about that. He asked me to come back to SoHam early and I asked Franny to come with me." Erin turned to Mace. "I thought it was all set. You asked us when you came out to see us."

"I sorta kept putting off asking Grandpa Liam and the time just snuck up on me."

"It is all straightened out though. Grandpa told me it was all right. He even promised to let Mace see you for a few minutes Sunday afternoon."

Franny looked confused. "What's going on?"

"Mace just told me you were coming yesterday. Kinda short notice, but that's Mace for you." Annie punched his arm.

Erin frowned at Mace.

"I knew Grandpa would let you girls stay at the farm," Mace said as he rubbed his arm.

Annie drove out to the farm and introduced Franny to Grandpa Liam.

"It's a pleasure to meet you, Franny, and it's good to see you again, Erin. Have you had a good summer?"

"It was all right, but I missed Mace."

"I can understand why he would miss you, but are you sure you missed him?" Grandpa asked.

"Thanks a lot," Mace said as he set the luggage down.

Grandpa Liam laughed. Mace carried the luggage upstairs and Erin followed. He had a chance to be alone with Erin for a couple of minutes and they kissed each other passionately.

"Are we going to have any time by ourselves?" Erin asked.

"Grandpa Liam will be gone on the weekend if that's what you mean."

"Franny and Annie will be here though."

"Yeah, does that make a difference?" Mace asked as he set

194

Franny's suitcase in one of the guest bedrooms.

"I guess not. They both know about us sleeping together."

Grandpa asked, "What would you girls like for dinner? I can make chicken breasts or hamburgers or whatever you like."

"I thought we would go into town for dinner tonight, Grandpa. I have to stop at the house to get my stuff anyway. You can cook for us tomorrow morning, okay?"

"Sure, just let me know what you would like to have."

"See you later, Grandpa. Don't wait up," Annie said. She ran to the bottom of the stairs and hollered, "What are you guys doing? How long does it take to put some suitcases in the bedrooms. Do I have to come up there and separate you?"

"Be right there," Erin said as she pushed Mace away.

Annie drove back into SoHam and they ate dinner at La Cantina. Annie persuaded Mace to pick up the check since she was holding the upper hand right now.

"Annie, did you tell Erin about your vacation with Matthew?" Mace asked hoping to gain the upper hand.

"Not yet."

"What vacation? Did you go somewhere with Matt Sullivan?" Erin asked.

Mace nodded. "They spent their honeymoon in Tennessee at a cabin in the woods."

Erin and Franny looked at Annie with big eyes.

"It wasn't a honeymoon. Mace is exaggerating as usual."

"It was like a honeymoon because all they did was stay in bed and have sex all day."

"We did not!"

"Annie! Did you and Matt make love?" Erin asked.

Annie smiled. "I was going to wait to tell you later. Thanks, Mace." She kicked his shin for spoiling her surprise.

Franny looked at Annie. "Was he your first lover?"

"Yeah, I got a late start."

Mace looked at Franny and wondered if she was still a virgin. "Franny, are you still dating that guy I met..."

"No way! I dumped him shortly after you left. He was going out with another girl. He kept pressuring me to sleep with

195

him and I kept telling him I wasn't ready."

"You'll find someone better."

"I think I'll date some college guys this year, but I'm not going to get serious yet. I'll wait until I get to North Park."

"Are you coming to North Park for sure?" Annie asked.

Franny nodded. "Unless something disastrous happens."

"You'll love it here. The campus is beautiful."

When they left the restaurant Annie ran by the house to pack up some clothes. She left a note for her father on the island countertop.

"Where's Matt?" Erin asked.

"He's working until midnight tonight and tomorrow, but he's got the weekend off."

"Great! We can double on the weekend."

"Hey! What am I supposed to do? Sit at home and knit sweaters," Franny asked.

"You can go with us, Franny," Erin said. "We aren't going to leave you behind."

Franny looked at the backyard. "It would feel too weird to hang out with you if you're going to be making out all the time."

"Mace won't be doing anything like that while you're here, Franny," Annie told her.

"What do you mean I won't?" Mace asked. "I think Erin wants to make out so I should accommodate her wishes."

Erin walked up to Mace and grinned. "I'll be all right if we just talk and maybe hold hands."

Mace looked stunned. "What? Are you mad at me?"

"You're a doofus, Mace. Can't you even tell when you're being conned?" Annie laughed at him.

"I knew you were kidding, Erin."

"I'm ready to go," Annie said. "We should drop Mace off at his house, then head back to the farm."

"Very funny. You can fool me once but not twice." Mace thought Annie was kidding.

"Who says we're kidding, Mace. You can't spend the night with us and I'm not taking you out to Grandpa's then bringing you back later."

"Can't we stay here longer? Your father's still at work. It's still early. Please, Annie. I'll owe you," Mace pleaded.

"You already owe me."

Mace looked at Annie with such sad puppy dog eyes that she caved.

"All right, we can hang out here for another hour, but that's all. Then we have to go."

"Thanks, Annie."

Mace put his hands on Annie's shoulders and asked, "Do you mind if Erin and I use your room for a while?"

"You're pushing your luck," Annie said thinking Mace wasn't serious.

"Please?" Mace was almost begging.

"Are you serious? You're actually asking to use my bed to have sex. Really?"

Mace shrugged. "Well, yeah. I'd let you use my bed if you and Matt needed a place."

"You are unbelievable, Mace Franklin." Annie looked at him and for some reason gave in to his request.

"All right, but if you guys do it then you're washing the sheets. I'm not sleeping in my bed after you guys have been screwing in it. Got that?"

"I'll do the laundry if we mess up the bed," Mace said then kissed Annie on the mouth.

Annie pushed him away. "Stop that, you creep. You owe me plenty, buster. Come on, Franny. Let's go for a walk around the neighborhood. I'll show you the sights."

Franny looked at Mace then at Annie. "You must be really good friends with Mace to do this for him."

"It's not just for him. Erin is my friend, too."

"How long have you known Mace?" Franny asked.

"Way too long!" Annie said and Mace laughed.

Annie shrugged. "We've known each other since second grade, I think."

"I think he really loves Erin and I know she loves him," Franny whispered as she watched Mace kiss Erin.

"Yeah, he does. His first girlfriend dumped him for an

older guy. It rocked his boat for some time, but then he met Erin and instantly fell for her. I introduced them by the way," Annie said as she grabbed her house key. "We're leaving now. Don't take all night," Annie shouted.

Franny followed Annie out the front door, heard some birds squawking and looked at the mature trees in the front yard. "I know. Erin told me. She said he made her first time special."

"Mace can be considerate when he wants to be."

Franny looked at Annie. "Did you and Mace ever... you know?"

"We've never had sex!" Annie said. "We did feel an attraction for each other at one time but nothing happened."

"Nothing?" Franny asked as she grabbed Annie's arm.

"Do you promise not to tell Erin?"

Franny put a hand to her heart. "I swear!"

"Mace and I made out in bed once."

"Is he a good kisser?"

"Oh yeah!"

They both giggled as they walked along.

"Erin told me a little about Matthew Sullivan. What's he really like?"

Annie paused to let one of the neighbors back out of his driveway. She waved at him then said, "Matty is the sweetest, sexiest guy in the world—and those are his bad qualities."

"Oooh! The sexiest, huh? I can't wait to meet him. Not that I want to kiss him or anything."

"Lots of girls would like to kiss him and he's been with several. He has a daughter. Did Erin mention that?"

"No! Does he really?"

"Yes, her name is Jennifer and she lives with her mother and her girlfriend."

"Girlfriend?" Franny stopped walking.

"Yeah, Joni is a lesbian or maybe bisexual. Anyway, she has full custody of Jennifer."

"That must be hard for Matt," Franny said as she hurried to keep up with Annie.

"Yeah, he tries to help financially, but I know he would

like to see her more often."

By the time Annie and Franny got back to the house, Mace and Erin were in the living room. Annie looked at Erin, then at Mace. By the look on his face Annie knew what happened.

"There are clean sheets on the bed and the other ones are in the pile of dirty clothes in the corner. Thanks, Annie."

"Shut up, Mace." Annie frowned at him. "I don't want to hear about it. Are you ready to go home now?"

"Please don't be mad at us, Annie," Erin said.

"I'm not. Just don't think you can use my bed for sex anytime you want."

Mace gave Annie a funny look. She noticed and poked him in the ribs then whispered, "You squandered your chance."

He shrugged. "I guess it wasn't meant to happen."

"Guess not."

Annie dropped Mace off at his house, then she took Erin and Franny back to the farm. Grandpa was still up so they sat in the kitchen and talked to him until he got tired.

"I'm going to bed. Will you make sure the windows are closed, Annie. It might rain tonight."

"Night, Grandpa. We'll see you in the morning."

Grandpa waved and said, "I'll make breakfast if you girls get up before noon."

"I'm sure we will be up before then. Maybe even by eleven."

"Go on with ya!"

Annie kissed him good night as she laughed. "We're going upstairs. We'll try not to disturb you."

"I won't hear a word. Stay up as long as you want."

The girls headed upstairs and gathered in the room Annie used whenever she stayed at the farm. Even now she kept some clothes and some of her older stuffed animals there. Erin showed the room to Franny.

Annie noticed Franny looking around. "This has been my room since I was old enough to sleep in a room by myself. I'm the only grandchild, so Grandma and Grandpa kinda spoiled me when I was little."

"He still does, Annie," Erin said.

"I suppose so, but I still miss Grandma."

"Is that a picture of her?" Franny asked as she pointed to the dresser.

"Yeah, that's me with Grandma and this one is Grandma, Mom and me."

Erin noticed a sad look on Annie's face as she looked at the picture. "What should we do now? I'm not sleepy yet."

"You can tell us what happened in Annie's room," Franny said as she sat on the edge of Annie's bed. "I want to know."

"What do you think happened?" Erin said rather sternly.

"I know what happened. I just wondered if it was special."

"It's always special, Francine."

"Oooh! Pardon me. I am so inexperienced, you know."

"Can we not talk about Mace for now?" Annie asked.

"Sorry, Annie. I know you are upset with us for taking advantage of you like that."

"I'll get over it by tomorrow."

"Tell us about Matt. How was your first time?" Erin asked.

Annie smiled and shared the details of her first night with Matthew.

"That sounds like a movie. So romantic!" Franny sighed.

"A bubble bath and roses. Who could ask for more?" Erin asked dreamily.

"Daddy told Matty that Mom liked bubble baths and white roses."

"Oh, Annie! Matthew sounds so special. I can't wait to meet him." Franny wrapped her arms around Annie and almost tackled her onto the bed.

Erin looked at Franny. "Just remember he's Annie's boyfriend, little sister."

"I just want to meet him, Erin. I know he loves Annie and she loves him."

"You'll like him, Franny. He's so good looking," Annie sighed.

The girls stayed up talking in Annie's room until after one, then headed off to bed.

200

"Good morning, sweetheart. Did you sleep well?" Grandpa asked without taking his eyes off of his paper.

"I always sleep like a baby in my room." Annie walked over and kissed Grandpa on the cheek as he read his paper and drank his tea. "You need a shave and a haircut."

"Are the other girls up?"

"They are taking showers and getting dressed. They should be down in a few minutes."

Grandpa set his paper down and drained his cup of tea. "What would you like for breakfast?"

"I told them you make the best chocolate chip pancakes in the world."

"Flattery will get you everywhere. Chocolate chip pancakes coming up. There is juice in the fridge if you want some. Apple and orange juice, I think."

Annie looked in the fridge, saw some Guinness and grabbed a bottle. She used her best look of innocence as she asked Grandpa, "Can I have a bottle of this Guinness juice please, Grandpa?"

"Not for breakfast, young lady. I thought you didn't like Guinness."

"I like other kinds better, but I'm learning to like it."

Grandpa shook his head.

Erin and Franny made it downstairs a few minutes later.

"Are pancakes all right with you guys?" Annie asked.

"Sure! You said your grandpa makes the best chocolate chip pancakes in the world. I want to see if you're right."

"I'll start on them straight away," he said.

Annie got up from her chair. "I'll be back in a jiffy. I want to shower first. Don't let them eat all the pancakes, Grandpa."

"I'll make sure they save one for you, sugar."

"Do you put a secret ingredient in your pancakes?" Erin asked.

"I've always told Annie I do, but not really." He shrugged. "I do make them from scratch if I have the time."

Annie hurried and was back before the pancakes were ready. Her hair was still soaking wet and she was wearing shorts and an old t-shirt from Roosevelt High.

Grandpa noticed and grinned. "Are you still wearing that old shirt?"

"It's not that old," Annie said. Then she explained to Franny, "Grandpa was the principal at Roosevelt until he retired. I was always getting in trouble and got to know the vice-principal rather well. Usually he wouldn't tell Grandpa about the mischief I would get in."

"He told me more times than you realize, Annie Mercer. I just didn't tell you, or your father, unless it was serious."

"Can you tell us some stories about Annie in high school, Mr. O'Dell?" Franny asked.

"I might be able to do that very thing."

They sat at the table and ate the pancakes as Grandpa told stories about Annie.

"When she was a freshman she got caught making fake IDs..."

"I wasn't a freshman, that happened when I was a junior."

"That was the second time. The first time was when you were making those school ID cards for freshman boys."

"Oh, yeah. I forgot about that."

"Then there was the time she broke into the coaches office to steal Playboy magazines..."

"They belonged to a friend's older brother and he would have gotten killed for losing the magazines."

"Did you look at them?"Franny asked.

"Yeah, but there were just pictures of girls."

"What were you expecting?" Grandpa chuckled.

"Can we talk about something else, please?"

"How about the time..."

Grandpa told a few more stories that embarrassed Annie, but then he hugged and kissed her on top of her head. "I still have the best granddaughter in the whole world though."

"Thank you, Grandpa. I love you, too."

"Do you like the pancakes?" he asked Erin and Franny.

"They are fantastic!" Franny squealed as she actually clapped her hands.

"Do you have a secret recipe?" Erin asked. "I bet you do."

"Okay, I confess," he raised his hands in surrender. "I have a recipe my grandfather used and it has been passed down through the years but it's still a secret."

Annie snorted. "Don't believe that bull! Grandpa uses whiskey in the pancakes."

"Annie, dear, if you are going to spill all the family secrets, I will have to disown you."

After they finished eating breakfast Annie helped Grandpa clean the kitchen while Erin and Franny talked to their mother.

"Okay, what are we gonna do today? I have to pick up Matty at midnight."

"Can we go into town and see what Mace is doing?"

Annie shook her head. "Absolutely not!"

Erin looked crestfallen.

"I'm just kidding. God, you are so easy sometimes, Erin. You fall for everything."

"Annie, I just want to remind you I'm going to pick up Keyshon for lunch and we'll be gone until Sunday evening," Grandpa said as he looked at Erin and Franny. "I'm taking Keyshon fishing, but Keith and Elisabeth will be here to take care of you girls."

Annie looked at Erin who couldn't believe her ears.

"Thanks, Grandpa Liam," Erin sighed.

Grandpa chuckled then rubbed his jaw. "That's my story and I'm sticking to it. It's not my fault if I forgot to mention it to your father now, is it? I am getting old and senile."

The girls understood and smiled. Erin and Annie hugged Grandpa.

"I was young and in love once a long time ago. Now I expect you to behave yourselves while I'm gone, although I don't have any idea how kids are supposed to behave in this day and age. Oh, and I know exactly how much beer is in the house, Annie Mercer," he said pointing a finger at her.

"Do you know how much is in the fridge in the garage?"

"What garage? What fridge? I'm getting so forgetful."

The girls hung out at the farm for the rest of the morning. Annie showed them around the buildings and the lake.

Erin asked, "Did your father grow up here, Annie?"

"No, he grew up in SoHam. Grandpa lived in town until Daddy got married. I'm not sure of the exact dates, but I know Daddy never lived on the farm."

Grandpa made some chicken salad sandwiches for the girls before he took off to pick up Keyshon.

"Have a good time, Grandpa," Annie said. "Tell Keyshon I said hi and don't worry about us. We'll behave."

"I know you will. At least you'll try to behave. Say hi to Matthew for me. He promised to help me clean out the barn before school started."

"I'll remind him."

Grandpa headed into SoHam to get Keyshon. Annie and the girls hung out around the farm until lunchtime. They ate the sandwiches, then headed into town shortly afterward. Mace was waiting for them.

"What are we going to do this afternoon?" he asked after kissing Erin.

"I thought we could show Franny the campus," Erin answered. "She hasn't been here before."

Mace smiled. "Sounds all right to me. Annie can show Franny the campus while you and I walk along the river."

"Just remember you will be watched at all times," Franny said.

Erin shuddered. "That sounds creepy, Franny."

"I only meant there are probably other people going for a walk."

Annie showed Franny around the campus and even sneaked her into Howe Hall where Annie and Erin would live. They checked out some of the classrooms and the library.

"Do you know how to get into every building on campus?"

"Pretty much," Annie said.

Franny looked around the mostly deserted campus. "What if we get caught?"

"I know the security guys pretty well. They're friends and a lot of them know Daddy."

Annie took Franny to the area where the new football stadium was being built.

"Right now we are using the SoHam stadium until our new one is finished. It will be so convenient when it's done."

"Is the football team very good?"

"Not really. They usually lose as many games as they win. The basketball team is better. They made it to the NCAA tournament last year and this year they should be even better."

"How good a player is Mace?" Franny asked as she looked up at the construction site.

"He's getting better every year. He works hard, probably harder than anyone else on the team."

"He's a good match for Erin."

"Yeah, he really loves her."

"Erin told me he's a good lover, too." Franny looked to see how Annie reacted to her statement.

"I guess so from what I've heard."

"Where are we supposed to meet those guys?"

"In the quad. We should head over there now."

Annie and Franny walked over to the quad to wait for Mace and Erin.

Mace and Erin had been walking along the river.

"You are going to stay at the farm tonight, right?" Erin asked.

"If you want me to, I will. Do you want me to stay?"

"What do you think?" Erin responded by putting her arms around Mace and kissed him passionately. "I missed you this summer."

"I missed you, too, Erin. Maybe next summer you can find a job in SoHam and stay here instead of going back to Nebraska."

"I don't know if my parents would let me."

"They might if you stay with Annie."

"I'm sure they wouldn't let me live with you, Mace."

"I know that. I wouldn't even suggest it. Who knows what will have happened a year from now. Mom and Mr. O'Dell might even get married. They could be living in our house and you and Annie could live in his house."

"You're just hoping that will happen so you could stay there with us."

"Wow! What a great idea. I'm glad you thought of it."

Erin shook her head. "Won't happen."

Mace grinned at Erin.

"Maybe Matt will be living with Annie and I could share a room with you."

"Don't even think that way. You're just horny."

"Well, can you blame me? You're the most beautiful girl in the world and I love you. That's why I want to be with you all the time."

"I love you, too, but we have to get through school before we do anything."

"What do you mean by anything? You're not talking about sex are you?"

"I mean living together or getting married. I don't want to give up sex anymore than you do."

"That's a relief." Mace kissed Erin and held her close. They walked a little farther before turning back to the campus. "We need to meet the girls in the quad."

A few minutes later Mace saw Annie talking to Franny on a bench in the quad. Annie saw Mace and Erin coming and jumped up to meet them.

"Did you guys have a nice walk?"

"Yes, did you show Franny the campus?"

"Yeah, she did, Erin. She took me into Howe Hall and some of the other buildings." Franny pointed at the dorm. "I wish I was out of high school already. This is a beautiful campus. I can't wait till next year."

"Have you ever thought about graduating early?" Annie asked. "I did. I graduated a whole year early just so I could start college with my friends."

"I probably could graduate in January. I might just look into that. There's nothing to do in Kearney."

Erin said, "I think Mom and Dad would agree to it."

"Would it bother you if I started school here in January?"

"Of course not. It would just give us more time together."

"It would allow Franny more chances to watch me play basketball," Mace said.

"Do you think you're Michael Jordan or something? Why would Franny want to watch you play ball?" Annie teased.

"Because I am such an exciting player, that's why."

"Yeah, right!"

"Are we gonna head out to the farm soon?" Erin asked.

"Are you getting anxious for something, Erin?" Franny asked as she grinned.

"I'm just hungry and I know your grandfather made some food for us."

Mace rubbed his tight, flat stomach. "I'm hungry, too."

"You're always hungry, Mace," Annie said as she rolled her eyes.

"You're gonna get it, Annie O'Dell."

Annie took off running and Mace chased her. He caught her and threw her over his shoulder and carried her back to where Erin and Franny were laughing at them.

"Put me down this instant, you creepoid!"

"What did you call me?"

"You're a creepozoid."

"Are you going to behave?"

"I might, but I guarantee I will get even sometime when you least expect it."

They headed back to the car and out to the farm.

# Chapter Thirty-Seven

"I could fix hamburgers and Grandpa made some potato salad yesterday. How does that sound?" Annie was in the kitchen looking through the fridge for something for dinner.

"Sounds good to me," Mace answered enthusiastically, "Annie is a good cook."

"Does she cook for you a lot?" Franny asked.

"Not a lot but sometimes. Why?"

"Just wondering." Franny shrugged.

"Franny, I told you Mace and Annie have been friends forever." Erin got after Franny.

"I'll help you make dinner, Annie. That way Mace can show Erin around the farm."

"Erin has been here before. She knows her way around the.... Oh, I get it."

Annie realized Franny wanted to give Erin and Mace a chance to be together before dinner.

"Fine! Franny and I will make dinner while you guys do whatever."

"Thanks, Annie," Mace said as he grinned.

"Stick it in your ear, Mace. Now get out of here. We'll let you know when dinner is ready."

An hour later Annie had everything ready. Franny helped by setting the table and putting the food out. Annie grabbed a beer. "Do you want one, Franny?"

"No thanks, I'll just drink water. Should I let Erin know dinner is ready?"

"Do you know where they are?"

"I think they're on the back porch. I'll go see."

Annie sat at the table and finished her beer while she waited for everyone to come inside and grab a chair.

"Everything smells good, Annie," Erin said.

"There is beer in the fridge if you guys want one. Will you bring me another one, Mace?"

"Sure. Do you want one, Erin?"

"Okay, but one is my limit."

Mace entertained Erin and Franny with stories about growing up in SoHam. He noticed Annie was being quiet and seemed to be upset about something. After they finished dinner, Mace helped Annie clean up. They were alone in the kitchen while Erin and Franny watched TV in the family room.

"Are you pissed at me for some reason, Annie?"

"What makes you think I'm pissed at you? Just because you and Erin have been fooling around like rabbits doesn't mean I'm pissed at you."

"I knew it was that. We've just missed each other."

"You're an ass! You couldn't even wait. You had to use my bed."

Mace realized this was what was really bothering Annie. "I'm sorry, Annie. I shouldn't have asked to use your room."

Annie moved close to Mace and looked up at him. "It will take me a while to get over the fact you and Erin used my bed."

"Will it make you feel better if you slug me?"

"You deserve it, but I'd probably just hurt my hand if I hit you. Don't ever ask to use my room for that again."

"I won't, I promise. Will you forgive me?"

"Maybe tomorrow. I just want to be mad at you tonight."

"Are you just missing, Matty? Is that why you're upset?"

"Probably. I would never ask to use your bedroom."

"Yeah, I know. I was wrong. Do you want another beer?"

"Not yet. I've already had two. If I drink another one now, I'll get drunk, then Matty will be mad at me. I might have one later after Matty gets here."

"You don't have to pick him up, do you?"

"No, he's got his car and he's got the weekend off. We need to clean out the barn this weekend for Grandpa."

"I'll help Matt with that tomorrow morning. You girls can do whatever you want and we can do something together in the afternoon."

"We need to make sure Franny isn't left out."

"We won't. I like Franny. She's a lot of fun to be around. She won't have any trouble finding guys when she starts at North Park."

209

Annie looked at Mace and he smiled at her.

"Ah, screw it! I can't stay mad at you until tomorrow."

"I knew you couldn't. It's my irresistible personality." Mace kissed Annie's cheek. "Do you still love me, Annie Mercer?"

"I must be insane but, yes, I do." Annie punched Mace in the stomach and it didn't hurt her as much as it did him.

"I wasn't expecting that."

"I know." She grinned. "That's why I did it. Now let's go see what Erin and Franny are watching."

Annie was upstairs in her room changing into pajamas later when Matt walked in the front door. He saw Mace, Erin and Franny in the family room watching TV so he assumed Annie was with them. He walked into the room and looked around.

"Hey, Matt. We didn't hear you come in. How was work?" Mace asked.

"So, so." Matt waved a hand. "Hi, guys. Where's Annie?"

"Hi, Matt. Annie's upstairs in her room," Erin said.

"Hi, Erin. It's good to see you again. This must be Franny." Matt stood in front of the couch where Erin and Franny were sitting. "Hi, Franny. I'm Matthew Sullivan."

Franny put a finger to her mouth. "You guys are right, he is good looking."

Matt grinned and shook hands with Franny. "Thank you, Franny. You look very pretty yourself. You look a lot like Erin."

"So does that mean I'm pretty, too?"

"You know I think you're pretty, Erin," Matt told her just as Annie walked into the room.

"And what about me?"

Matt turned to see Annie and smiled. They moved close to each other and Matt held Annie in his arms.

"You are the prettiest of all. I missed you."

"I missed you, too."

Annie jumped into his arms and they kissed passionately as everyone watched.

"Don't watch, Franny," Mace said. "They are going to be all over each other now. They'll probably make out right in front of us."

"We're not going to do that. I'm not like you, Mace," Annie told him as Matt set her down. "Are you hungry, Matty? I made burgers earlier and there's some potato salad left, unless Mace ate it all."

"I didn't eat it."

"I'm not hungry, Annie. I ate dinner around nine. I am kinda thirsty though."

"Do you want a beer?"

"Sure! Anyone else want one?"

Everyone decided to have one so Mace and Matt went into the kitchen to grab the bottles. They returned and Matt sat on the love seat with Annie. Erin and Franny stayed on the couch and Mace made himself comfortable in Grandpa Liam's recliner.

"I think this is the first time I have ever sat in this recliner."

"Grandpa always sits there," Annie explained to Franny and Erin. "You better be careful, Mace. If you break his recliner, Grandpa will shoot you."

"I'm not going to break it. I'm not huge like Ryder Keselowski."

"Who is that?" Franny asked.

"Ryder is going to be Mace's new roommate. He plays football and weighs over three hundred pounds," Erin explained.

"Ryder is huge but he's not fat. He's as strong as an ox and quick on his feet. He's probably the best lineman ever to play at North Park. He'll probably be drafted in the first couple rounds."

"Is this your first visit to the area, Franny?" Matt asked.

"I think we might have been here when I was real young. Other than that, it's my first trip here."

"What did you think of the campus?"

"I love it. I definitely want to go to school here."

Annie added, "Franny might graduate early and start in January if everything works out."

Mace and Erin decided to call it a night and headed upstairs. Annie decided to have another beer.

"Anyone else want another one?"

"I'll take one."

"Are you sure, Franny?" Matt asked.

"I'm sure. I've never had two beers before. Daddy doesn't know I ever drink beer at all."

Annie grabbed a beer for her and Franny, but Matt switched to Dr Pepper. He moved to the couch. He sat at one end and Franny was at the other end. Annie sat in the love seat and watched as Franny talked to Matt. Franny finished her beer and moved next to Matt. Franny seemed to have a crush on Matt even though she knew he was Annie's boyfriend. Franny giggled and touched Matt as he told her about growing up in South Hampshire.

"Erin told me you have had a lot of girlfriends. She said you have a baby girl, too."

"That's true, but I've changed. Now I have the best girlfriend in the world and I don't even look at other girls."

"Matty! I know you still look at pretty girls. I don't mind as long as you don't do anything more than look."

"Do you still think I'm pretty?" Franny asked though she slurred her words.

"You are pretty, Franny."

Franny looked at Matt, then over to Annie. She moved back to the end of the couch away from Matt. "Oh God! I'm sorry, Annie. I was flirting with Matt. I didn't mean to."

"It's all right, Franny. I know how charming Matt can be."

"I won't do it again. I think maybe I shouldn't have had any beer this late at night."

"Will you be all right?"

"Yeah, I'll be okay. I'm sorry I was flirting with you, Matt. Will you both still be my friend."

The two beers were obviously affecting Franny now as she talked to Matt and Annie.

"Of course we will. Maybe we should go upstairs. Are you ready for bed now?"

"I'm ready to go to sleep now. Will you forgive me for how I acted? I won't let it happen again, I promise."

"Let's go upstairs, Franny. I'll help you."

Annie went upstairs with Franny. Franny sat on the side of the bed with Annie next to her.

"Do you need any help, Franny?"

212

"No, I can get ready for bed by myself. I'm sorry for how I was flirting with Matt, Annie. Matt is lucky to have you for a girlfriend."

"I'll see you in the morning, Franny. Do you remember where the bathroom is?"

"Yeah, I remember. I feel so stupid. I mean, all I had was two beers and I wanted to kiss Matt."

"You'll feel better in the morning."

"Thanks for understanding, Annie. I won't ever try to kiss Matt. I swear it!"

"You'll find a new boyfriend soon and you can kiss him all you want. I'll check on you later before I go to bed, okay."

"Thanks, Annie."

Annie went back downstairs and sat beside Matt.

"Is she okay?"

"She'll be all right. I'll check on her before we go to bed."

Matt and Annie stayed up for another thirty minutes before they headed upstairs. Annie looked in the room where Franny was sleeping. She was still in her clothes on top of the bed. Annie looked at Matt.

"We should at least take off her shoes for her, Matty."

"I'll pick her up while you take her shoes off and pull down the covers."

Annie removed Franny's shoes, then Matt picked Franny up. Annie pulled down the covers and Matt placed Franny on the bed.

"Will she be all right?"

"I'll just cover her with the sheet so she doesn't get too hot."

Annie covered Franny with the sheet, then looked at Matt.

"I'm so tired," Annie said then yawned. "You might need to help me get undressed."

"That sounds like fun."

# Chapter Thirty-Eight

"Are you awake, Matty?" Annie asked as she lay on her side next to Matt.

"I am now. What time is it?"

"I'm not sure but it's light outside."

Matt turned on his side and faced Annie. He kissed her as they lay in her bed upstairs at Grandpa's house.

"Did you enjoy last night?"

"It was fun. I couldn't help but laugh when you started tickling me."

"Yeah, up until then you were doing a good job of being asleep."

"If you hadn't tickled me you could have undressed me all the way," Annie let Matt know.

"We should get out of bed and see if anyone else is up."

"Are you sure you want to get out of bed? Wouldn't you like to cuddle for a while?"

"I can think of something else I would like to do," Matt teased.

Annie moved onto her back and asked, "What might that be?"

"I want to make funny noises on your belly!" Matt began to make weird noises by blowing on Annie's stomach.

She giggled and tried to make him stop. "Stop it before Mace and Erin hear you."

Just then there was a knock on her door. "We can hear you guys. Are you decent? Can we come in?"

"No!" Annie yelled.

"You can come in. We're still in bed though."

Mace and Erin open the door cautiously. "We're hungry. Are you guys gonna stay in bed all morning?"

"What time is it anyway?"

Mace pointed at the alarm clock. "It's nine thirty. Get your butts up."

Matt got out of bed. He was wearing his boxers but not a shirt. Annie covered up because she didn't want Mace to see her.

214

"I'll get up if you get out of here, Mace."

"Are you naked?"

"No, but I don't want you to see me like this."

Mace rolled his eyes. "Throw some clothes on and meet us in the kitchen. You have to make breakfast."

Mace and Erin left the room. Matt dressed and headed downstairs. Annie got out of bed and threw on shorts and an old sleeveless sweatshirt. She went into the bedroom where Franny was sleeping.

"Franny, are you awake?"

Franny yawned and stretched her arms.

"What time is it, Annie?"

"After nine thirty. Are you hungry? Everyone is up and Mace is hungry. I'm gonna make breakfast."

"I am hungry now that I think about it."

Franny finally realized she was still dressed except for her shoes. "I guess I fell asleep before I could get undressed."

"Yeah, you did. Matty and I checked on you before we went to bed. I took your shoes off and we put you under the sheet. Are you all right?"

"My head hurts a little but I'm okay. I'll meet you guys downstairs in a couple minutes."

Annie ran downstairs to the kitchen. Mace and Erin were sitting at the table. Matt was making coffee.

"What time did you guys get up?" Annie asked because Mace and Erin were both dressed and Erin's hair was wet.

"We woke up around eight. Don't know what time we got out of bed. We were..."

"I don't want to hear about what you guys were doing. I can guess," Annie said.

"We showered, got dressed and came to see if you were awake," Mace told them.

"Is Franny awake yet?" Erin asked.

"I just checked. She's awake and should be down in a minute. What do you guys want to eat?"

"Bacon, eggs, sausage, biscuits or any combination of those," Mace touched a fingertip for each one of those options.

"Whatever you can make quickly."

"Oh, for crying out loud, Mace. You aren't going to starve," Annie said as she made a face. "Let me see what Grandpa's got."

Franny joined them in the kitchen and Annie made breakfast. Soon everyone was satisfied with a full stomach except for Mace. Annie made him two more eggs and more bacon.

"You're a pig, Mace Franklin," Annie said as she set his plate in front of him. "No wonder Mom spends so much for groceries."

"Keyshon eats just as much as I do. Maybe even more," Mace said as he poured ketchup on his scrambled eggs, then shoveled half of them into his mouth.

"Mace, will you help me clean up the barn for Liam?" Matt asked. "I promised him I would get it done."

"Sure, no problem. I've eaten enough of his food, so that's the least I could do." He looked at Erin and Franny. "What are you girls going to do this morning?"

"I thought we might work on the flower beds. They need to be weeded."

Franny surprised Erin and Mace when she said, "Thanks for putting me to bed last night, Matt."

Erin looked at Franny, then Matt and Annie. "What do you mean, Francine?"

"Not anything bad. I fell asleep on the bed and Matt picked me up so Annie could pull back the covers. That's all."

Erin tilted her head and stared at her sister. "You made it sound like something else happened."

"Well, it didn't!" Franny insisted.

Matt and Mace headed out to the barn. The girls cleaned up the kitchen, then found some work gloves and headed outside to the flower beds in the front of the house.

"Do you always call Mrs. Franklin 'Mom?'" Erin asked. "Did she ask you to?"

"Most of the time. I didn't always, of course, but now that she and Daddy are a couple, it just seems natural."

"If Mace and I ever get married, I guess I will call her Mom, too."

216

The girls finished with the flowers before the guys were done with their job. They headed to the barn to check up on the guys. It took two hours of steady, dirty work for Matt and Mace to get the barn totally cleaned. They were dusty and dirty when they finished.

"You need a shower, Matty. Use the one in the basement. I'll make sure there are clean towels down there. You need a shower, too, Mace. You guys are both covered in so much dust and dirt that you look like brothers."

"I'm not going to take a shower with Matt," Mace said.

Annie smacked his arm. "I didn't mean for you to shower together."

"You are dirty, too, Annie," Mace said. "You've got dirt on your forehead and face plus your arms are filthy. You haven't showered yet, have you?"

"No, I was waiting till after the chores were done."

"I need to take a shower, too," Franny stated.

"I guess I'm the only one who doesn't need a shower," Erin said. "I'll make some sandwiches and get lunch together while everyone else gets cleaned up."

"Sounds like a plan," Annie said. "Franny and I can shower upstairs and you guys use the one in the basement. I don't care if you shower together or not. I'll make sure there are clean towels."

"What about clean clothes or are we supposed to shower, then walk around in just a towel?" Mace asked just to be annoying.

"All right! I'll bring clean clothes to you guys while Franny is in the shower. What a creepozoid."

Franny went upstairs to shower, Erin started on lunch, Mace took a shower, Matt waited outside in the yard and Annie brought clean clothes for both Matt and Mace.

Annie hollered to Mace, "I've got your clothes. Where do you want them?"

"Just set them outside the door unless you want to join me in the shower."

"That would be fun, but I think I'll pass. Your clothes will be by the door."

"Chicken! Are you afraid to..."

"I'm not afraid of anything. I just don't want Matty or Erin to be upset because I took a shower with you."

The basement shower was in an unfinished bathroom in the corner. Two sides of the bathroom were the concrete walls of the foundation. A third wall was made up of concrete blocks. The fourth wall was constructed of wood and drywall with a door. Inside the bathroom were a sink, toilet and the free standing shower in the corner. Grandpa used it when he was too dirty to use the modern bathroom upstairs. If Annie were to open the door to give Mace his clothes, she would see him as he showered.

"I'm just kidding. I wouldn't want to get in trouble with Erin or cause you any problems with Matt."

"Good! The clean clothes will be outside the door," Annie hollered.

Just then Matt walked up behind Annie.

"Are you talking to Mace?"

She jumped. "I didn't hear you. Yeah, I wanted him to know where his clean clothes were."

"Why didn't you just put them in the bathroom for him?" Matt asked.

Annie put her hands on her hips and looked up at Matt. "You have used this bathroom before, haven't you?"

"Yeah, a few times."

"So you know there isn't a curtain around the shower or anything. If I open the door I would see Mace showering."

"Haven't you seen him naked before?"

"No! I've never seen him naked and he's never seen me naked. Why would you think we have?"

"I'm just teasing you, sweetie. Don't get all mad. You look like an angel with a dirty face like that James Cagney movie we saw a few weeks ago," Matt said then kissed Annie.

"Could I watch you take your shower?" Annie asked without realizing Mace had turned off the water.

Just then the door opened and Mace stood there in just a towel. "I heard that. You guys can have the shower after I get dressed." He grabbed his clothes and closed the door.

Eventually, everyone was showered and dressed. They met

in the kitchen to eat the sandwiches Erin put together.

"Grandpa will be pleased his barn is clean. Thanks, guys, for doing that for him. He's getting too old to do all the work around here," Annie said.

"I don't mind helping him, Annie. I like working on the farm better than working at the Lion. I get to work in the fresh air and sunshine."

"What about when it's pouring and there's work to be done."

"Or in the winter when it's freezing outside," Erin asked.

"Still better than the Lion." Matt smiled.

"What are we gonna do the rest of the day?" Franny asked. "It's gonna be over ninety degrees this afternoon."

"Erin, did you and Franny bring swimsuits?" Annie asked.

"Yeah, we did."

"We could go swimming in the lake," Annie suggested. "Let's take a cooler of beverages, a radio so we can listen to tunes and spend the afternoon working on our tans."

"Yeah, I need to work on my tan!" Mace laughed.

"You're lucky you don't have to use sunscreen," Erin said.

Annie shook her head. "I remember coming out here to swim years ago and Mace got sunburned."

"Sorry, I thought... never mind. I shouldn't make assumptions," Erin said.

"There's a big cooler in the basement. We should use it otherwise we will have to keep running back to the house for more beer."

"We should drink more water than beer. We might get dehydrated otherwise," Erin said.

"Don't we have to wait an hour before we go swimming because we just ate?" Franny asked.

Annie shook her head. "I don't think we ate enough to cause any trouble, Franny."

Matt got the cooler out of the basement. Mace grabbed a bag of ice from the freezer in the garage. They filled the large cooler with bottled water, a few bottles of beer and some cans of Dr Pepper. The girls went upstairs to change into their swimsuits.

Matt and Mace changed into swim trunks. Matt had been keeping some clothes at the farm and Mace just happened to toss a pair in the bag he brought.

"I'm going to wear a t-shirt and shorts over my bikini," Erin told Annie and Franny.

"We should all wear something over our bikinis so the guys don't get too excited and attack us," Franny squealed.

"You're just hoping Matt attacks you, Francine. You better behave," Erin warned.

"I will. It's you and Annie who will probably misbehave."

*Oh, I plan on misbehaving.* Annie grinned. "I'll bring the sunscreen and towels. We should bring a couple blankets to spread on the ground."

"I'll carry the blankets," Franny volunteered.

"Will you carry the radio, Erin?"

"Okay, as long as it's not too heavy."

"It's not. See you in the kitchen in a couple minutes," Annie said then dashed out of the room.

"Should we bring anything to eat?" Erin asked. "Mace will get hungry."

"He can wait until we get back. He won't starve."

The guys used Liam's four-wheeler so they didn't have to carry the heavy cooler. Matt drove the ATV over to the lake while everyone else walked. Matt parked next to the dock and set the cooler on the it. He got back on the ATV and passed the other kids.

"I'm going back to the house and load up the smaller cooler. I'll be right back."

Annie nodded. "See you at the lake."

By the time Matt returned to the lake, the other kids had the blankets spread out, the radio playing and were drinking a bottle of water. The girls still wore their t-shirts and shorts. Mace decided he was ready to go swimming.

"I'm going in. Are you coming, Annie?"

"Give me a minute. I want to tell Erin and Franny about the depth of the lake."

"Don't take long," Mace said. He jumped into the lake from the dock.

"The deepest part is right there in the middle. It's probably fifteen feet deep there. It's kinda deep right by the dock but most of the shoreline is pretty shallow. The section by the dam is steep but not as deep as the middle."

"We've been swimming in our uncle's lake before, Annie. Erin and I are pretty good swimmers, so we'll be okay," Franny said.

"Just be careful, okay?"

Mace was getting impatient so he hollered, "Are you coming in the water, or do I have to drag you in?"

"I'm coming! Keep your pants on."

Annie slipped off her t-shirt and shorts and joined Mace in the water. Erin joined them a couple of minutes later. Matt sat on the edge of the dock with his feet in the water watching. Franny took off her t-shirt and shorts and sat next to Matt. Her feet just reached the water.

"Are you going in the water, Matt?" Franny asked.

"I will. I just wanted to watch Annie and Mace for a minute."

Franny watched as Mace and Annie horsed around. Mace dunked Annie, then she did the same to him. Annie tried to swim away but Mace caught her. He grabbed her around the waist and held onto her.

"They are acting like little kids," Franny said as she leaned closer to Matt.

"Yeah, it's fun to watch. They treat each other like brother and sister sometimes," Matt said and then looked at Franny. *You look very sexy in your bikini.* "Are you ready to get in the water, Franny?"

She smiled. "I am if you are."

Matt grinned and grabbed Franny around the waist. She squealed as Matt picked her up and tossed her into the lake. He jumped in after her and swam toward her.

"Are you all right?"

"I'm okay. I didn't expect you to do that."

"Sorry, if I scared you."

"I don't mind. Should we swim over to Annie and Mace?"

"I think Annie is coming over here."

Annie, Erin and Mace swam over to join Franny and Matt near the dock.

"About time you got in, Matty. I was starting to believe you were afraid of the water," Annie said just before Mace dunked her under the water. She popped back up and spat water at Mace.

"I may not swim like a fish the way you do, but I can certainly swim fast enough to catch you," Matt said as he reached out and grabbed Annie. He pulled her close and kissed her.

"If you want to kiss me again you have to catch me!"

Matt reached out and kissed her again.

"No fair. You didn't give me a chance to get away."

"That's enough kissing, you guys. I'm going to get out and have a beer. Anyone else ready for a tasty brew?" Mace asked.

"I'll take one."

"I knew you would want one, Annie. How about you, Erin?"

"I'll take another bottle of water."

Mace, Erin and Annie got out of the water and sat on the dock. Mace and Annie drank a beer while Erin sipped her water. Matt and Franny were still in the water, but they stayed close to the dock.

"I'm going to work on my tan. Do you want to join me, Mace?" Erin asked.

"A royal command," Mace told Annie. "I must do what my queen commands."

Annie laughed and grabbed the string on the front of his trunks. "Just remember you're not alone out here so keep your trunks on."

"Can't make any promises." Mace shrugged. "Erin might attack me."

"You've got a vivid imagination," Annie said as she laughed.

"Just make sure you and Matty behave. You've got Franny with you and she's young and impressionable."

"What do you mean we've got Franny with us?"

Mace pointed to the water. "I don't think she's going to

222

stray too far away from Matt."

Annie turned to look and saw Franny touch Matt's shoulder. "Should I be worried?"

"I don't think so. Matty is so in love with you and Franny is just having fun."

"I'll be keeping my eye on you two, so behave," Annie said.

"Yes, Mom, I'll try to fight Erin off if she tries to rape me," Mace replied.

"Yeah, you wish, creepozoid."

Matt and Franny got out of the water and joined Annie on the dock. Mace sat beside Erin on one of the blankets. Erin lay on her back for a while, then turned over. She undid her top and could feel the warm sun on her back. Later, she turned over on her back without fixing her top. She looked at Mace and he looked to see if the rest of the kids were watching. Matt, Annie and Franny were still sitting on the dock drinking a beer. Mace slipped a hand under Erin's top. He moved his body between Erin and everyone else. Erin removed her top and Mace shielded her from view. Mace put a hand on Erin's belly. She smiled at him as he moved his hand to her bottoms. Erin grabbed Mace's hand and shook a finger at him.

"Should we get back in the water?" Mace asked.

"No, let's sit on the dock with everyone," Erin answered. "But I need to put my top on."

They sat on the dock and talked for an hour.

"Is anyone else hungry?" Mace asked. "I could eat a horse."

Annie laughed. "That's just what I was planning to make for dinner so you're in luck."

"I wondered what happened to Blackie," Matt said.

Franny looked at Mace and asked, "Who's Blackie?"

"They are just kidding, Franny. There is no Blackie," Erin explained.

"What are we having for dinner, anyway?" Mace asked.

"I took some more hamburger out of the freezer. We can grill some burgers and have potato salad and maybe some baked beans. There is still a lot of potato salad, so we need to finish it."

223

Mace said, "I'll get the grill going when we get back."

"Are you sure you can handle starting the grill, Mace?" Annie asked. "It's complicated."

He laughed. "Sure, I'm an expert."

Franny stared at Mace.

"It's a gas grill, Franny," Annie said. "All Mace has to do is light it up."

"Oh, I guess I'm still not use to your sense of humor."

"It takes a while to get used to Mace and Annie," Matt told her.

Mace and Matt took care of the burgers while Annie heated up some baked beans and brought out the leftover potato salad.

"What are we gonna do tonight?" Mace wanted to know later.

"We could stay here and watch movies," Matt said.

Erin shook her head. "No, it's too nice outside to stay indoors. How about doing something outside?"

"We know what you and Erin want to do outside," Annie teased.

"Oh, like you and Matt aren't thinking the same thing," Erin said as she blushed.

"We could use the fire ring and roast marshmallows," Annie suggested.

"Do we have to sing silly old folk songs, too?" Mace asked. "Should I have brought my guitar?"

The other kids glared at him.

Annie poked his side. "You don't have a guitar."

"Fine! We can sing Beatles songs."

"Stop being such a doofus, Mace," Annie said.

"Hey! I'm not a doofus. I'm a creepoid, remember?"

"How could I forget? You remind me every time you open your mouth," Annie said.

Annie found a bag of old marshmallows in the cupboard. They sat on logs around the fire pit, roasted the marshmallows and talked about plans for the rest of the summer.

"I've never been to Chicago," Franny said. "Could we spend a day in the city? Would it be worth it?"

224

"It's not much different than Kearney," Mace teased. "Should I start singing now? I want to sing 'Michael, Row Your Boat Ashore' to start my concert."

Erin slugged him hard enough to knock him off his log.

"Okay, I'm open to other tunes," Mace said as he got up.

"Don't listen to him, Franny. I think it would be fun to spend a day in the city. We could take the train, so we don't have to drive," Annie suggested.

"Sounds all right to me," Matt said.

"I can check the train schedule later," Annie said.

"I want to go up in the Sears Tower," Franny said.

"We could take a boat ride," Erin suggested.

"We will have time to do a bunch of stuff," Mace said. "We just need to get out of bed early enough to get going."

"Will you remember that in the morning when you wake up next to Erin?" Annie asked.

"Hey, girl! We weren't the last ones out of bed this morning," Mace said as he pointed at Annie and Matt.

Everyone hit the sack early so they could get an early start in the morning.

# Chapter Thirty-Nine

"I would like to see the museums by the lake and I want to go to a Cub's game," Franny said at the breakfast table the next morning.

"I can understand the museums, but why on earth do you want to see the Cubs?" Mace asked.

"We don't have any major league teams back home so I've always been a Cub fan," Franny said as she covered her pancakes with maple syrup.

"We can check the schedule to see if they're playing at home. It might be too late to try to get to a game today, but we can see about tomorrow," Annie said.

Matt checked the Cub's schedule. "They're playing the Pittsburgh Pirates at home Monday."

"I've still got Nick Whitaker's number in my phone. Should I call him? He might be able to get us tickets. He has a connection," Annie said.

"Sure," Mace said.

She called, but had to leave a message. He returned her call ten minutes later.

"Hi, Nicky. How have you been?"

"I'm doing great. How are you, Annie?"

After talking for a few minutes, Annie asked Nick about Cub tickets.

"How many do you need?"

"There are five of us who would like to go to Monday's game."

"I can get you the tickets, but only on one condition."

"What's that, Nicky?"

"I want to go with you guys. I'd like to see you again. Is Matt going to be with you? I'd like to see him, too."

"Yes, Matty is coming along," Annie said.

Nick and Annie worked out the details about the game and where they were going to meet. Nicky bought all the tickets in spite of Annie telling him it wouldn't be necessary.

They took the train into the city on Sunday and spent the

226

day along the lakefront. They visited the Field Museum, the Art Institute and ended up at Navy Pier. They caught a late train back home. Grandpa and Keyshon were home when they got back.

Keyshon heard Annie talking to Matt so he ran to see her. "Annie, I caught more fish than Grandpa. I'm an expert now."

"Good for you, Keyshon. Where are they?" Annie asked.

"We put them back in the lake so we could catch them the next time we go fishing," he said.

"I'm glad you had a good time, Keyshon," Annie said as she smiled at him then looked at Grandpa.

"Do I need to count the beer?" Grandpa asked.

Annie put a finger to her mouth.

Grandpa shook his head. "It appears you all survived, so I don't need to hear any details."

Later, Matt took Mace and Keyshon home.

They got up early Monday morning. Matt picked up Mace. When Keyshon learned about the trip to the Cub game, he became upset because he wasn't included.

"I'm sorry, Keyshon, but I will make it up to you. How about I take you and Lisa to a SoHam Hammers game?"

"Will you buy us hot dogs? I want a t-shirt."

"Okay, I'll even buy one for Lisa," Mace said.

"Good. We want hot dogs and nachos and maybe even one of those big pretzels."

"You drive a hard bargain, little buddy, but I'll agree as long as you don't get sick."

Keyshon seemed pleased by Mace's promise.

Matt and Mace picked up the girls at the farm. After Grandpa made breakfast for everyone, they took Matt's car to the train station. By eleven o'clock they were standing in front of Wrigley Field. Annie and Matt were looking for Nick. Annie spotted him first.

"There he is!" She ran over to him and Nick gave her a hug. They walked over to where the rest of the kids were waiting. Annie introduced everyone.

"Was it hard to get the tickets, Nicky?" Annie asked.

227

"No, both the Cubs and Pirates are having lousy years, so tickets are pretty easy to get. About the only time Wrigley sells out is when the Cardinals are in town. When they are in town there are more Cardinal fans at the game than Cub fans," Nick explained.

"That's probably because the Cardinals have won the last two World Series," Mace mentioned.

They made their way inside the ballpark. Their seats were along the third base line between third base and the bullpen ten rows from the field. Since Nick bought the tickets, Annie and Matt wouldn't let him buy anything once they were inside. Nick sat next to Annie so they could talk. He told her about Stephanie's baby and how much he enjoyed being an uncle.

"How is Avanna?" Annie asked.

"She's doing great. Right now she's in California with Drew and Leslie. She got a small part in Leslie's new movie." Nick talked about Avanna, then they were both quiet for a minute.

"Have you talked to Reid lately?" Annie finally asked.

Nick nodded. "I talked to him this morning. I told him about the game. He told me to say hi."

"That was nice of him."

Nick leaned closer to Annie. "I should tell you he and Hannah are engaged. Did you know that?"

"No, I haven't talked to him since we broke up. When did that happen?" Annie asked.

"About a month ago, I guess."

"Please tell him I am happy for him when you see him."

"I will, Annie." Annie looked at Matt who had been listening.

He smiled at her and said, "Don't be getting any ideas, Annie. We have to finish college first."

"I know. I just wanted to see how you would react."

The game was rather boring. Neither team scored until the eighth inning when Tevin Young hit a homerun for the Pirates. In the bottom of the eighth Mark Gosnold was batting. On the second pitch he hit a pop-up toward the third base side of the field. It was hit high and the wind carried it out of play. Annie was watching the ball and screamed at Matt as the ball appeared to be coming down right at them. Everyone around them stood up. Mace, Matt and two guys in the row in front of them appeared to have a chance to catch the ball. The ball hit eight hands at the same time, then glanced toward Annie. She grabbed the ball with both hands and didn't let go. Matt and Mace looked at her in disbelief. She smiled and teased them as the TV camera caught all the action.

"You couldn't catch it because you are used to a basketball, Mace."

Mace shook his head. "You were just lucky, Annie. I would have caught it if we all hadn't been fighting for it."

"Yeah, sure."

Matt held onto the ball for Annie.

After the game, Nick made sure Annie and her friends made it to the Addison station to catch a train headed south. He told them where to make a connection to get back to SoHam.

Annie gave Nick a hug. "Thanks for everything, Nicky. It was great to see you again. Say hi to Avanna and Reid for me, okay?"

"I will. You take care of yourself, Annie, and call me again sometime, or I'll call you. Maybe we can go to a concert or something. You can bring Matt and I'll bring Avanna."

"That would be fun. Take care, Nicky."

By the time they got back to SoHam, everyone was hungry. Matt took them to the Hungry Lion for dinner. Annie proudly showed Cormac Sullivan the baseball she caught at the game. After dinner Matt dropped Mace and Erin off at Mace's house. He then took Annie and Franny to the O'Dell house. Her father was in the kitchen when they got home.

"Did you have fun at the game? Did the Cubs win?" Dad asked.

"They lost, but look what I caught." Annie showed her father the ball. "I grabbed it after it bounced off the hands of Mace and Matty and a couple other guys."

"Did you really catch it, Annie?" Dad asked as he looked at Matt.

"She really did, Mr. O'Dell." Matt gave Annie a high-five.

They moved to the living room and Annie told her father

about the last few days. Franny was surprised and a bit embarrassed when Annie told her father about swimming topless in the lake. Matt wasn't surprised, though, since Annie always told her father everything.

"Are you going home or are you staying here, Matty?" Annie asked.

"Is it all right if I crash here tonight? I'm kinda tired."

"You can stay here," Dad said.

"I'll sleep on the couch tonight so you and Franny can have the bedroom. I don't mind."

"I can sleep on the couch, Matt. I don't mind. That way you and Annie can share her room," Franny whispered.

"You wouldn't like the couch, Franny. You can have the bed and I'll sleep on the air mattress."

In the morning after breakfast, Matt took Annie and Franny to pick up Mace and Erin. They spent the day at Grandpa's farm. He put them to work and they finished all the chores on his list. Keith, Elisabeth, Keyshon and Keyshon's girlfriend, Lisa Miley, came out to the farm for dinner. Keith and Matt grilled steaks and burgers. Keyshon wanted hot dogs so Matt grilled some just for him. That night Annie, Erin and Franny stayed at the farm. Keith and Elisabeth said goodbye to Franny since they wouldn't see her before she left for home. Matt had to work the next day so he said goodbye also. Franny gave him a hug and a kiss on the lips. Matt looked at Annie to see what her reaction would be.

"It's all right, Matty. You can give Franny a hug back."

"I'm sorry, Annie. I didn't mean to kiss him, but he's just so irresistible."

"Just remember he loves Annie," Erin said.

The girls stayed up talking until one o'clock in Annie's room. Finally, they were sleepy enough to go to bed. Franny needed to be at the train station by nine o'clock in the morning.

# Chapter Forty

When her alarm went off at seven thirty, Annie hit the snooze button. She hit the snooze button ten minutes later, too. It was eight o'clock when she finally got out of bed.

"Oh crap!" she muttered. She ran into the bedroom where Erin was sleeping. "Erin, get up! It's eight already." Then Annie dashed into the room Franny used, but she wasn't in the bed. Annie ran downstairs and heard Grandpa talking in the kitchen.

Grandpa saw Annie. "Good morning, sleepyhead. I was just about to send Franny upstairs to get you out of bed. I can make some breakfast if you're hungry."

"Thanks, Grandpa, but I'm not hungry and we have to get going."

"I'm packed and ready, Annie. I woke up early and I've already eaten," Franny informed her.

"I'll hurry up and get dressed so we can go. You don't want to miss your train."

Annie and Erin got ready and fifteen minutes later the car was loaded with Franny's suitcases.

"Thank you so much for everything," Franny said goodbye to Grandpa Liam.

"It was my pleasure, Francine. I hope to see you again, real soon. You and Erin are always welcome to stay here if you need to."

"I just might be back when the second semester starts this year. I'll see how it goes." Franny gave Grandpa a hug.

"Come on, Franny. We've got to go!" Erin hollered from the car.

She and Annie were in the car and anxious to get going. Traffic was sometimes heavy at this time of day and the station was in the old downtown section of SoHam. Franny got in the back seat. Annie waved to Grandpa as she took off.

"Do you think you might graduate early, Franny?" Annie asked.

"Yes, I would like to. I guess it all depends on if I get accepted at North Park. If I don't get in here, I'll be stuck going to school in Kearney. I'll just die if that happens."

"It can't be that bad, Franny."

"Oh, yes it can! There's nothing to do and I just know I'll love going to school with you guys."

Franny kept talking all the way to the station. Annie found a parking spot close to the entrance. They got out and helped Franny with her luggage. In a few minutes they were through the station and waiting for the train.

"I'll miss you, Erin."

"You'll be back here soon. I just know it," Erin answered.

"We will both miss you, Franny. Are you sure you know what to do once you get to Chicago?" Annie asked.

"Absolutely! I'll find the best looking guy in the station and pretend to be a damsel in distress. Then he'll carry my bags and show me where to go." They laughed because that was most likely exactly what would happen.

The train arrived and the girls hugged Franny and she boarded.

"Bye! I'll call you when I get home, Erin," Franny hollered.

"Bye, Franny, be safe!"

Annie and Erin stayed until the train moved out of the station. They headed back to the car.

"What do you want to do today, Erin. Matty has to work until six and Mace will be watching Keyshon."

"Is there anything you want to do, Annie? I just want to kinda chill and be lazy."

"We can do that. We've only got three days left before we move back into Howe Hall. I still need to do some shopping. Maybe we can do that tomorrow. Let's go back to Grandpa's for now."

They spent the rest of Wednesday at the farm. Grandpa didn't have any chores for them, so he just let them chill out. They ate an early dinner, then Annie talked to Matt.

"Would it be all right if I just stay home tonight? I'm wiped and I've got to get some shopping done. I need some new clothes for school. Most of my shirts are worn out from wearing them to work."

"It's okay, Matty. We're just being lazy today," Annie said. "I think I will find a book and get ready for bed early. Erin and I are coming into town tomorrow to do some last minute shopping. I want to find some warm pajamas for the winter. Sometimes Howe Hall can be kinda chilly."

"Are you going to buy some pajamas with feet?" Matt asked.

"Why? Do I have cold feet?"

Matt laughed. "No, I saw a photo of you as a kid wearing pajamas with feet like a rabbit."

Annie giggled then said, "I'll see if I can find some like that."

"Would it be all right if I pick up Mace and we come out to the farm for dinner tomorrow evening?" Matt asked.

"Sure! Could you pick up a couple pizzas? We could have that for dinner. I could make a salad or something, but I don't want to cook."

"I can do that. I'll get Mace after work and we could be there around seven."

"Okay, I'll see you tomorrow. I love you, Matty."

"I love you, too, Annie Mercer."

"Even if I have cold feet and have to wear footy pajamas?"

"Even if you wear footy flannel pajamas," Matt said.

Annie told Erin about the plans for tomorrow night.

"That's fine with me. I wasn't going to see Mace tonight, anyway. Are we still going into town tomorrow?"

"Yes, I need to."

By ten o'clock the farmhouse was dark and quiet. Grandpa was downstairs in his room snoring. Annie had just turned out the light after finishing her book when she thought about Franny. *I wonder if you're home yet. I hope you may made your connection without getting lost. I'd hate to think you're wandering around the train station like the girl in that movie.* Annie clapped a hand to her mouth. *Oh no! The girl in that movie gets murdered.*

# Chapter Forty-One

Erin's cell phone rang early in the morning. She was still half-asleep, but managed to answer the call.

"I'm sorry to wake you up so early, Erin, but it was too late to call you when I got home last night."

"Where are you, Franny?" Erin asked.

"I'm home. I have to tell you about my trip. I met this guy on the train after we left SoHam."

Erin she sat up in bed. "Hold on! I'm barely awake. Slow down so I can understand you."

"I met a guy on the train. He was going to Cheyenne so I sat with him. We talked and I learned he goes to the University of Wyoming. He's got one year left, then he's moving to Chicago where his grandparents live. Oh, Erin! He was such a hunk!"

"Did you get his number, Franny?" Erin teased.

"Of course, and I gave him my number. He carried my bags for me and he was a perfect gentleman."

"You were on a train, Franny. What was he supposed to do?"

"I don't know, but he didn't have to be nice to me. He could have ignored me."

"Nobody ignores you, Franny. I'm happy you made it home and maybe you and... what was his name? You never told me."

"Adam Dougherty. He's lived in Cheyenne all his life but his parents are from Chicago. I'm sorry for calling so early, but I just had to tell you about him. You can go back to sleep now."

"I'll talk to you soon. Say hi to Mom and Dad for me."

"What about Eddie?" Franny asked. "You do remember our brother, right?"

"Tell him I said hello and he better pay me back the money he owes me."

Annie slept until nine, then dragged herself out of bed. By the time she and Erin were ready to face the day, it was eleven.

"Are we still going into town, Annie?"

"Yeah, I'm ready to go if you are."

"I'm ready," Erin said.

"Let's tell Grandpa we're leaving."

Grandpa was outside on the front porch swing.

"We're going shopping in town, Grandpa. We should be back this afternoon. Matt and Mace are bringing pizzas for dinner. Do you need anything?"

"If you are close to a store, could you pick up some stuff for breakfast. I need more eggs, milk and maybe bacon or sausage. If you girls want donuts or any of that kind of health food, you should grab it. I'll pay you when you get back."

"We'll do that. See you later, Grandpa. Love you."

"I love you, too, sweetie. Bye, Erin. See you later."

As Annie pulled out of the driveway, Erin said, "Franny called this morning. She made it home okay."

Annie turned onto the county road leading into SoHam. "She didn't get murdered after all?"

"What are you talking about?"

Annie explained.

"I saw that movie, too. I never thought about Franny being like that character, but now that you mention it, she can be a bit ditzy at times."

Annie and Erin spent four hours in town shopping for new clothes and other necessities. They stopped at a store and picked up supplies for Grandpa. They didn't get back to the farm until nearly five. Annie showed Grandpa what she bought for breakfast, then put the groceries away for him.

"Are you hungry now, Grandpa?" Annie asked. "Matt won't be here until seven. I could make something, if you want."

"I think there is some shepherd's pie left from last night."

"I'll warm it up for you, Grandpa."

"Thanks, Annie. That would be better for me than pizza. If I eat pizza too late at night, I pay for it. Guess I'm getting old."

"You're not that old, Grandpa!"

"Well, I'm not as old as Moses."

Matt and Mace arrived with the pizzas just after seven. Annie put a salad together. They ate in the family room and watched TV.

"Why isn't there ever anything good on TV?" Mace asked.

235

"This show sucks big time."

"We could watch baseball if you want to be bored to death," Annie said.

"Let's stick with this," Erin said. "It's almost over."

After they were through eating Annie suggested, "Let's go down to the lake. It's still hot out and we can cool off."

"Are you suggesting we go skinny dipping?" Mace teased.

"We can if you want. Unless you would be too embarrassed, Mace," Annie teased him back. "You're probably afraid I would laugh at you."

"Let's go, girl! I'm game."

Annie looked at Matt to see how he felt about going swimming. "What do you want to do, Matty?"

"It would feel good to cool off in the lake. As long as we don't stay out there all night. I need to get home sometime."

"Let's do it then. You better behave, Mace Franklin, and not be looking at Annie," Erin warned him.

Annie found Grandpa in the kitchen. "Grandpa, we're going to the lake. We're going skinny dipping so we can cool off."

"Be careful, Annie," Grandpa answered absentmindedly as Annie took off. Then he realized what Annie actually said. "Annie Mercer O'Dell, you come back here!"

Annie came back and smiled at Grandpa. "Yes, Grandpa. Did you need to tell me something?"

He looked at her, then realized she wasn't a little girl anymore. He waved a hand at her. "Oh, all right. I guess it doesn't matter. Just don't take any beer with you, okay?"

"We weren't going to, Grandpa. You know Matty has seen me naked and I don't care if Mace sees me."

"Go on and get out of here before I take a switch to your bottom." Grandpa reminisced about how Annie used to go swimming in the lake when she was just a little girl. She hated to wear anything in the water.

Annie grabbed some towels and handed then to Matt.

"Are we really going skinny dipping?" Matt asked.

Annie grinned then said, "We'll find out soon enough."

The kids ambled to the lake. Mace teased Annie and they

ended up chasing each other to the dock. Matt and Erin looked at each other and laughed.

"Do you think those two will ever grow up?" Erin asked.

"I doubt it. They will probably act the same way a hundred years from now."

Erin laughed. "Except they will be chasing each other in wheelchairs."

By the time Matt and Erin reached the dock, Annie and Mace were already in the water. Matt and Erin joined them and they stayed in the water for the next forty-five minutes. Erin got out of the water first. She toweled dry and sat on the edge of the dock with the towel around her. Annie and Mace were still horsing around so Matt got out. He dried off, sat next to Erin and they watched Annie and Mace.

"Are you going to stay in the water all night, Mace?" Erin asked.

Annie splashed him as he looked at Erin.

"I suppose not. I just need to dunk Annie under the water one more time, then I'll get out," Mace said.

Annie screamed and tried to get away from Mace, but wasn't quick enough. Mace dunked her under the water, then swam away. He got out of the water, dried off and sat on the dock next to Erin. Annie paddled around in the water as the others sat on the dock watching her.

"You should come out of the water now, Annie."

"I will. Are you all going to watch me get out?" Annie now seemed shy all of a sudden.

"It was your idea to go swimming in our underwear in the first place, Annie," Matt said.

"Fine! I guess it doesn't matter now." Annie swam over to the dock.

Matt offered his hand to help her out of the water. Mace handed her a towel. She dried off but didn't get dressed, yet.

"I feel so much better now. That was fun," Annie said.

They sat on the dock in their underwear and towels and talked with their bare feet in the water.

"Did I tell you about the man Franny met on the train?"

"No, what happened?" Annie asked.

Erin explained about Adam and how Franny seemed so excited. After they have been talking for a while, Erin started getting cold.

"I need to get dressed now." Erin looked at Matt.

He told her, "I won't watch, Erin. I'll keep my head turned."

Annie stood up and announced, "I don't care if Mace watches me. He's seen my underwear before."

Annie dropped her towel as the guys were watching. She stuck her tongue out at the guys, then got dressed.

"It's like watching a sister get dressed, Annie," Mace said. "You look good, but..."

"I get the picture, Mace." Annie smacked his arm. "Let's go back to the house. We can sit on the porch and have another beer."

They headed back to the farmhouse and sat on the porch as they continued talking about the coming school year.

"Have you decided what you're going to major in, Annie?"

"I think it will be something in education. I think I might want to become a teacher. How about you, Erin?"

"I'm not going to become a teacher. I know that for a fact. I have no idea what I want to do though," Erin said.

"I want to coach basketball after I graduate." Mace was positive about his future plans.

"What about pro basketball? Do you think you might be able to make it in the NBA?" Matt asked.

"We'll see how it goes, but I'm not counting on that."

Everyone looked at Matt. Annie knew what Matt wanted to do with his life, but he had never told anyone else.

"Matty, tell them," Annie encouraged him.

"All right. I want to be an accountant and have my own firm. I figure one of these days I will have Dad's businesses to run so I want to have a solid business background."

Annie leaned against him. "Tell them the rest."

Matt looked at Annie and said, "I want to have a farm in the country like this one. I want kids and I don't want them to live in the city."

"Sounds like a good plan, Matt," Mace said.

238

Soon the girls were ready to hit the sack. Erin told Mace good night and started to head inside to her room after a quick good night kiss. Annie hugged Matt and he kissed her cheek.

"I have something for you in the car, Annie. Let me grab it real quick."

"Okay," Annie said. *What did you buy for me I hope it's something pretty and sexy.* She looked at Erin who was waiting to see what Matt bought.

Matt went to the car and returned with two items. One a medium size square box and the other a bag just the right size for some clothes. Mace didn't know what Matt purchased so he was interested also. Matt set the box on the small table on the porch.

"What do you think?" Matt asked after opening the box. "I know you need some new ones."

Annie nodded her head noncommittally. Matt opened the bag and pulled out the item inside. Annie took one look at it, then looked at Matt, who was smiling. Tears formed in Annie's eyes as she looked at the item. Matt was expecting a hug and kiss, but Annie turned around and ran into the house.

"Annie! What's wrong?"

"Go away, Matthew Sullivan. I never want to see you again, ever!"

Matt looked at Mace, then at Erin. He looked as though he had just been hit with a sledgehammer.

"I'll talk to her, Matt," Erin offered. "I know she doesn't mean what she said."

Erin went inside and upstairs to Annie's room. She tried the door, but it was locked. "Annie, it's me. Can I come in?"

"No! I don't want to see or talk to anyone. Please make the guys go away."

"Is this because of us swimming?" Erin asked.

"No!" Annie yelled. "Please make them leave."

Erin went back outside and talked to Matt and Mace. The guys didn't understand, but decided it might be best to leave.

# Chapter Forty-Two

Erin knocked on Annie's door for the third time around ten the next morning. "Annie, will you please let me in? Matt called again. He is sorry for whatever he did and wants to talk to you."

Annie shuffled over to the door dragging her blanket. She opened the door to let Erin in, but then walked over to her bed and climbed under the covers. "I'm never talking to him again, Erin. There's nothing you can say to convince me otherwise."

Erin sat on the edge of the bed. "Did you get any sleep? You look terrible."

"Gee, thanks."

"I mean your eyes are all red. Are you hungry? Can I get you something to drink?"

Annie shook her head.

"Are you going to stay cooped up in here all day? Do you want to get dressed and do something?" Erin asked.

"I'll get dressed if you promise not to mention his name."

"All right. I won't mention either guy."

Annie got dressed and she and Erin ate some lunch. They walked to the lake, but Annie wouldn't talk about why she was so upset with Matt.

Late in the afternoon Annie decided to go home.

"Do you want me to come with you, Annie?" Erin asked.

"No, I'm just going to grab some clean clothes and come right back. If that man calls again, don't tell him where I am."

"I won't tell him," Erin promised.

Annie drove home and stormed into the house. She saw her father in the kitchen fixing dinner. She angrily set a box on the island countertop and dropped a bag on the floor.

"Dinner will be ready soon, sweetheart. I'm making your favorite. Meat loaf and cheesy potatoes. How are you today?" he asked while checking the oven.

"Daddy, I never want to see that man again. Not ever! Not as long as I live!" Annie waved her arms for emphasis. "I can't believe I've been so stupid."

Dad closed the oven with a bang, turned and stared at

Annie. "What's wrong, honey? Did you and Matthew have an argument?"

"Not really an argument. I'll show you why in a second."

Annie ran to her bedroom and returned in a flash. She was holding a picture of her and Matthew in her hand.

"I mentioned a couple things to Matty the other day. I told him the plastic glasses we have are all scratched up and sometimes I get cold in my dorm room."

Dad nodded.

"I never would have mentioned those things had I known he would react the way he did," Annie said as she placed the photograph face down on the island.

"And what did Matt do?" Dad asked.

"First he gave me this." Annie lifted two glasses out of the box and showed them to her father. "He bought me these!"

"How nice. New glasses."

"Exactly! Can you imagine?" Annie hollered as she shook her head in disgust. "That's not the worst thing he did. Look at this!" Annie opened the bag she had dropped on the floor, and pulled out a nightgown. "Look at this. This is horrible!"

Her father looked at the nightgown. "Oh my."

"Yes! Yes! Oh, the nerve of that man!!!" Annie yelled as she shook the nightgown as if trying to rip it apart.

"Oh my. Oh my." Her father looked at the nightgown again. *I have no clue what could possibly be wrong with it.*

"How could he think I would wear this?"

Dad looked at the nightgown for several seconds then said, "It looks like it would be very warm."

"Daddy! It looks like something only a nun would wear to bed." She set the nightgown on the island. "He will never want to sleep with me if he sees me wearing that thing."

"Yes, I see." *I still have no clue.*

"If he calls, I will not speak to him. If he comes over here, I will not see him!" she exclaimed. "Do you understand?"

"What should I tell him?"

"You don't have to tell him anything just show him this!" Annie picked up the nightgown and threw it toward the trashcan.

She stormed off to her room leaving her father in the kitchen still dumbfounded. He looked at the new glasses and couldn't see anything wrong with them. *They actually look very nice and are real glass. They're a lot better than the old plastic ones we use.* He set them down and picked up the nightgown. He held it up and looked at it. He felt the fabric. *This feels like it would be comfortable and warm.* He shook his head, looked up at the ceiling and muttered, "What should I do, Amy Catherine? I need your help."

He replaced the nightgown in the bag and moved the gifts to the living room. He went back to the kitchen and pulled the baked beans out of the oven. The meat loaf and potatoes were already on top of the stove. He walked out of the kitchen and down the hall. He knocked on Annie's door.

"Dinner is out of the oven, sweetie."

"I'm not hungry. I can't eat anything and you know meat loaf and cheesy potatoes are your favorites, not mine!"

"Can I come in?"

"The door's open."

Dad came in and sat on the edge of the bed next to Annie. She was holding one of her stuffed teddy bears to her chest.

"Are you okay? You look like you've been crying again."

Annie rubbed her eyes and wiped her nose with the back of her hand. "I'll be all right, Daddy. I'm glad I found out how he feels about me now and not later. Just think! I actually thought we might get married one day."

Dad put an arm around her shoulders and held her. He didn't know what to say. He remembered the scene from *Father of the Bride*, Annie's favorite movie. "At least it's not a blender."

"Oh, Daddy, how can you say that? It's not the same. This is much worse. Much, much worse."

"Maybe I should talk to Matty..."

"Don't you dare! Don't you meet him at the Hungry Lion and sit at the bar and have a drink like in that movie. I forbid you to talk to him. I absolutely forbid it!!!" She plopped onto her back still clutching the teddy bear.

"Okay, Annie. I won't have a drink with him. Why don't

242

you try to eat something. You're probably hungry."

Annie went to the kitchen with her father and sat at the island. Daddy fixed her a plate of food and she ate it all. She even fixed a second plate and ate all of that. Daddy remained silent as they ate because he couldn't think of just the right thing to say.

"That was very good, Daddy. I know we use Mommy's recipes to make this. Is it as good as she used to make? Can you remember how hers used to taste?"

Dad smiled and chuckled.

"What is so funny?"

"I remember the first time Amy Catherine tried to make meat loaf, baked beans and cheesy potatoes. First of all she put way too much salt in the meat loaf, two much ketchup in the baked beans and... I can't remember, but there was something wrong with the potatoes, too. To top it all off, the meat loaf was burnt and the potatoes not cooked enough. The beans were like soup."

"Did you eat it anyway?"

"I tried. I really tried. Your mother took a couple bites and just started crying. I told her it wasn't that bad and I would eat it all. She told me I didn't have to because she knew it was awful. She promised to learn how to cook better and she did. The next time she made meat loaf and stuff it was perfect. I ate everything. I don't think we had enough left to save for the next day."

"Oh, Daddy! I love you," she said as she wrapped her arms around him.

Just then the front door opened and Matthew Sullivan raced inside. "Annie, where are you?"

Annie heard him, ran out of the kitchen, into the hallway and jumped into his arms. She kissed his mouth, then kissed his eyes. Matt held her tightly and kissed her back.

Dad followed Annie and scratched his head. *I don't get it. Help me out here, Amy Catherine.*

"Oh, Matty! I love you so much. I'm sorry. Will you forgive me?"

"I'm sorry, too, Annie. I love you more than anything in the world! You didn't do anything wrong. It was all my fault," he said then squeezed her tighter.

243

Dad watched as they kept kissing. "Be careful! You're going to trip over the rug."

Matt and Annie didn't hear him because they kept kissing without stopping to breathe. Finally, they paused.

"Annie, I am so sorry," Matt said. "I'll never do anything like that again."

Dad spread out his hands. *What did you do that was so terrible?* He thought of the glasses and the nightgown again.

"I guess all couples have to have some burnt meat loaf for dinner at least once," Annie told Matt and then smothered him with kisses.

Matt had no clue what she was talking about and Dad just shook his head; still as bewildered and clueless as ever.

He looked up at the ceiling and whispered, "Thank you, Amy Catherine."

Check out these other titles by the author. Visit my website.
kennethleemcgee.com

## The Emmy's Story Series

1. We We're 'posed to Get Married
2. One Of The Guys
3. A New Friend
4. Did You Like the Ravioli Tonight?
5. Completely and Forever: A Wedding
6. It's Time To Go!
7. How Difficult Can It Be?
8. Forever... Isabella... Forever
9. The Forgettable Year
10. Turning Thirty
11. Hello, I'm James

## The Annie Mercer O'Dell Series

1. Roosevelt High
2. North Park College

## The Stand Alone Books

1. Growing Up In Kinmundy Junction
2. Grandpa, Lions and Kitty Cats: A Collection Of Short Stories For Children Of All Ages

www.ingramcontent.com/pod-product-compliance
Lightning Source LLC
Chambersburg PA
CBHW022003170626
46808CB00001B/270